BARRETT
FULLER'S
SECRET

BARRETT FULLER'S SECRET

a novel

SCOTT CARTER

DUNDURN
TORONTO

Editor: Allister Thompson
Design: Jennifer Scott
Printer: Webcom

Library and Archives Canada Cataloguing in Publication

Carter, Scott, 1975-
    Barrett Fuller's secret / Scott Carter.

Issued also in electronic formats.
ISBN 978-1-4597-0693-4

    I. Title.

PS8605.A7779B37 2013   C813'.6   C2013-900779-2

1 2 3 4 5   17 16 15 14 13

  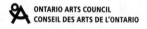

We acknowledge the support of the **Canada Council for the Arts** and the **Ontario Arts Council** for our publishing program. We also acknowledge the financial support of the **Government of Canada** through the **Canada Book Fund** and **Livres Canada Books**, and the **Government of Ontario** through the **Ontario Book Publishing Tax Credit** and the **Ontario Media Development Corporation**.

Care has been taken to trace the ownership of copyright material used in this book. The author and the publisher welcome any information enabling them to rectify any references or credits in subsequent editions.

J. Kirk Howard, President

The publisher is not responsible for websites or their content unless they are owned by the publisher.

Printed and bound in Canada.

Visit us at
Dundurn.com | @dundurnpress | Facebook.com/dundurnpress | Pinterest.com/dundurnpress

Dundurn
3 Church Street, Suite 500
Toronto, Ontario, Canada
M5E 1M2

Gazelle Book Services Limited
White Cross Mills
High Town, Lancaster, England
LA1 4XS

Dundurn
2250 Military Road
Tonawanda, NY
U.S.A. 14150

TO KERI, HARLOW, AND CLIVE

ONE

Let's be honest. For most people, the best part of secrets is telling them, not keeping them. The thrill of sharing other people's private information, the sense of importance that comes from letting someone else in on this precious information, the implication that in a world that wants to know tomorrow's news today, you are special enough, connected enough, and liked enough to be the conduit.

Barrett Fuller's mentality is the antithesis of these people. Barrett prefers to keep secrets. To remain a mystery, to be the sole keeper of truth, in control and completely free to create whatever past, present, or future a situation demands. Over the years, this mentality has served him well, proving to be not only convenient but also lucrative.

When Barrett was twelve, his English teacher asked him what he wanted to do with his life. She meant what did he want to do for a living and suggested computers, banking, firefighting. Barrett took the question literally, blew a bubble of Bazooka Joe, and said, "I want to be rich."

Twenty-five years later, he definitely is. Barrett should be at a library today, where his pseudonym, Russell Niles, is being honoured as man of the year for his charitable donations for the building of schools across eastern Africa. He should appreciate the room full of journalists and children that buzz about as if waiting for a rock star to appear. He should be there to hear the grey-haired host praise him not only for his impact on the minds of millions of kids as one of the world's leading children's authors, but also for his tireless commitment to literacy and disadvantaged communities. Instead, his agent is accepting the award on his behalf and telling the crowd he is in Ghana working with impoverished children while Barrett lies beside a brunette woman fifteen years younger than him in a bedroom the size of most peoples' apartments.

This is a man who basks in his wealth. Sixteen-foot high ceilings, glass doors leading to a balcony overlooking a ravine, heated floors guiding the way to a hot tub at the other end of the room. This is a life only multimillionaires can afford. This is the dream that actually came true.

Sweaty and winded, Barrett clasps his hands over his chest. He's not fat, but it's clear he doesn't work out. The brunette had too much red wine flowing through her yesterday evening when they'd met to care. And not just any red, of course, but the better part of two bottles of Petrus Pomerol, the merlot that Kennedy made popular during his White House years. Barrett unclasps his hands to light the cigarette dangling from his lips.

"What do they feed French women that makes them so amazing in bed?"

Another body stirs beside Barrett and removes a pillow from her face to reveal milky skin, large eyes, and a canopy of red hair.

"Arrogant, rich men," she says, not fully awake.

"Confident, rich men," Barrett says after a cloud of exhale. "Arrogant is just nasty."

The redhead pulls the pillow back over her face and rolls over.

Barrett turns to the brunette, who is now on her feet.

This is the first time he's got a sober look at her standing, and from this angle, he's even more impressed than the night before. Her body is lean, but not model skinny. Her shoulders are too strong for the runway. He finds himself wondering if she used to be a gymnast when her voice breaks the silence.

"Oh my god."

She stands in front of a bookshelf with a smile that seems to fill her face. Barrett pushes himself up on his elbows to a get a better look before cringing. She's looking at the second shelf, the space reserved for books he keeps because he has to.

"What?" he says, playing along.

A book is now in her hand, and everything about it looks out of place inside the grip of silver rings and manicured nails. "You have the Russell Niles books."

Barrett drops his weight back onto the bed, clearly unimpressed with her interest. "Some of them."

"I've read these books to my nephews ten times each."

"They were a gift."

She removes another so that there is now a book in each hand and steps closer to the bed. Barrett notices that her shadow on the ceiling looks like some sort of lobster-clawed monster.

"You don't have to be embarrassed," she says, holding up the books like he's never seen them. "These stories are the best. Every kid in the country's reading them."

Every kid in the world, he says to himself.

"They're brilliant."

The swell of his ego brings out a grin as he sits up again to put out his cigarette and taps the bedstand, where there's a thick envelope. "I left both of you an extra hundred this time."

The woman leans in to kiss him. "Thank you."

Somehow, after a night of boozing and a pack of cigarettes, she still tastes like cinnamon. As they kiss, he takes the book from her hand and drops it onto the floor.

"No, thank you."

The truth is, he picked a brunette because two nights before that it was a Korean woman named Cindy and three nights before that a blonde with streaks of pink named Shyla. The brunette is the first woman he has ever had sex with without knowing her name, and it adds too much of a rush of excitement to ask. He ordered his first escort one evening when he was watching porn and it occurred to him that it was pointless to watch other people have sex when he could buy the real thing. There's no shame for him in escorts. From his point of view, buying fantasies is something many people would do if they could, so he does his best to enjoy it for everyone.

This is how Barrett flows through life. Compulsion over reason, lust over responsibility. He is perpetually the kid in the toy store with no rules, boundaries, or financial limits, and yes, he is ethically suspect and full of moral cavities. A week ago, after far too many drinks and a few Vicodins, he had returned home and pushed his dining room table against the wall to fully open up the massive space. Hunched in front of a chair on either side of him, he wore only goalie pads, a jock, a catcher's glove, and blocker while a woman in a black lace thong took slap shots at him. That night he said he was an investment banker.

Two days later he got in a scuffle on the rooftop patio of one of the city's most prestigious art galleries. Barrett had invited a real estate tycoon's wife home, turned to get another drink, and received a fist in the face. There was nothing macho about this fight. This was awkward, drunken flailing at its most laughable. Barrett left with a split lip, an eighty thousand dollar painting of a woman's eye, and an Italian art dealer named Bridgette. That night he said he owns a company that manufactures sexual lubricant.

The next night involved proposition betting: five grand on the table, an apron that said "Look into my eyes" printed in the middle wrapped tightly around his body, and five minutes to eat three six-ounce ribeye steaks. That night he said he owned a chain of restaurants in Vancouver. That night he lost five thousand dollars.

And then there's the reason for his new, close-cut hair. A friend's thirty-eighth birthday, half a bottle of sixty proof scotch, an eight-ball, a third-floor patio, and six men and women in a turtle pool led to Barrett sitting on a stool while a woman with cornrows hovered over him with an electric razor. Two more shots of Scotch later, he let out a roar that would have made any frat superstar proud as the woman shaved beehive layers into his hair before peeling the sides of his head altogether. That night he said he owned a mining company.

Immature. Irresponsible. Inane. Don't think he doesn't notice those that judge him, he just doesn't care. And being worth millions of dollars, revered, and written about daily, it's not hard for him to feel as if he has earned a little levity.

Before all the money, Barrett assumed he would be married by twenty-five, thirty at the latest. It wasn't a plan, just something he figured was generally a given in life, like graduating high school or getting a driver's license. But marriage hadn't happened by thirty, partially because he never focused on more than the moment, mostly because he put his career before everything and entirely because he didn't care enough. When the big money started coming in, women did everything short of proposing to him, but by then his assumptions had changed. He knew why they were with him and he accepted that love was never going to flow under those circumstances. It became easier to have a good time than to care, more practical to choose his interests over romance.

A quick glance at the clock shows it is past noon. Time to get to work, time to generate some ideas. He has learned over the years that his best brainstorming happens at the beach. In the winter, the solitude helps to open up his mind, and in the summer it feels like he could be anywhere in the world. Sky blue water, sailboats, and a sun that gives everything new detail make him feel like anything is possible.

He takes a seat on his usual bench beside the boathouse and begins writing feverishly. The words flow fluently, if uninspired. This is the reward of surviving years in a genre. The outline is as clear as neon and all he has to do is fill it in with what the market desires. And the market craves the three A's: adventure, adversity, and achievement. At this point in his writing career, it's like counting sheep. Forget the story's impact, morality, or the genre's tradition, he does this for the money, and more specifically for the luxury, excess, and travel the money buys.

The sky is surprisingly bright for April and the waves hit the sand at a steady pace. He opens a bag of potato chips and stares out at the water until a boy of no more than nine approaches him holding an orange tennis ball with Velcro on one side.

"What are you eating?"

Barrett takes a moment to realize the boy is speaking to him. "I'm sorry?"

"What are you eating?"

"Potato chips."

"What kind are they?"

"Sea salt. You wouldn't like them."

The intrusion unnerves Barrett. This is his time to work and he doesn't need pointless distractions. He appraises the boy.

Wearing a blue hooded sweatshirt and oversized grey track pants that make his frail body look even smaller, he looks like a waif. Barrett doesn't see a cute, innocent kid filled with curiosity — he sees two food stains on the kid's sweater and holes in his pants exposing nasty-looking scabs on both knees. He glances past the boy to see a woman farther down the boardwalk playing with an even smaller child. No one else is around, so he assumes she's the mother.

"I've never tried that kind," the boy says, pointing to the chips.

"Yeah, well you're not going to."

"What's sea salt?"

Barrett looks at the boy for a moment, then past him to his mother, before looking back at the boy.

"Fuck off, kid, you're weirding me out. Go on back to your mom."

The kid's face contorts first into fear and then into sadness before he runs down the boardwalk. Barrett pops another chip in his mouth. This is not the tone you would expect from a man who makes his millions captivating kids, and this not the type of behaviour you would expect from a world famous children's author. Yet there he sits, munching on chips as if he just shooed away a seagull instead of traumatizing a boy.

TWO

Richard Conner has a secret too. And it's not the type of secret any eleven-year-old should be burdened with. In fact, it's the type of secret that few kids his age have ever had to bear. The type of secret that carves one's character.

Eleven months ago Richard left school with thoughts of playing video games and eating zesty corn chips. It was a Wednesday and he was supposed to go to badminton after school, but it was cancelled because of repairs to the gym floor. He broke into a full smile when he saw the sign on the gym doors, because no badminton meant more video games. Specifically, more video games before five o'clock. This was his favourite time of the day. The hour and a half before his mom or dad came home from work, when he had the place to himself. It was only ninety-minutes, ninety-five if he ran home, but they were his minutes and he basked in the freedom. He blasted music while he played his favourite war video games, drank straight from pop bottles, and ate his chips directly out of the bags. He made the rules — he was king.

When Richard thinks about that day now, he realizes a lot of things were off. The temperature was bizarrely warm for

February. At eighteen degrees, it was hot enough that some people actually walked outside in T-shirts. The traffic lights were out on the corner before his building, which caused a chaotic blur of honking, screeching, and yelling, and his cat limped by him into a bush beside the building with trickles of blood littering each step. The cat his parents had given him on his birthday three years after he begged for a puppy.

"Diamond," Richard called with concern, but the cat disappeared. He ran over to the bush, bent down, and did his best impersonation of his father.

"Come here, girl. Come on, Diamond." But she didn't. Her brown coat made her difficult to spot behind two rotting fir trees, so he went in after her. A branch scratched the side of his neck as he bent down but he pushed on. Scared, the cat hissed at him until he picked her up and she burrowed into his armpit, careful to leave the injured, bloody leg dangling.

Richard looked down at the leg and adrenaline shot through him. Blood matted the fur, and not the red blood he saw in movies but a thick, brownish red appropriate for pain. The wound was too perfect for a bite; from the length of the gash he guessed she was raked by a piece of the chain-link fence she climbed under regularly to get to the apartment's garbage bins. He ran into the building and down the hall to his apartment on the first floor, when music from inside stopped his momentum. A tingle of discomfort rippled up his spine. Neither his mother nor father would ever leave the apartment with the music on. He believed this with confidence due to how often both of them nagged him to turn off any light he left on before leaving a room. Images of two men wearing Halloween masks as they robbed the place flashed through his mind until the upbeat tone of the music forced his imagination back to reality. This was happy music, the type his parents played when they had parties.

After struggling to hold the cat while he fished the key from his pocket, he opened the door grateful to have help. "Mom? Dad?" But no one answered. The music blared but the room was empty. He charged down the hall into the bedroom, but it was also vacant. That left the bathroom. The shower wasn't running, so he approached the door slowly in an effort to hear something that could clarify the situation, but the music played so loud, it dominated. Blood dripped from the cat's leg onto the tile, so he wiped at it with a shoe, but it only smeared the blood into a streak.

He put an ear to the door and relaxed when he heard his father's deep voice. The bathroom door was already open a crack, so he pushed it all the way in and entered cat-first.

"Dad, Diamond's hurt. She's bleeding. I think she cut it on a ..."

Only his father wasn't on the toilet. Richard's head bobbed back as if he had come too close to fire, and his eyes focused on the floor where his father kissed another man. The image startled him so much that the details were hard to make out, but the bottom line was clear. His father lay on top of a man with blond hair, a beard, and a hairy chest, and they were kissing.

"Shut the door," his father said, with an index finger pointing in panic. But Richard was too shocked to move. The image jarred his reality and his thoughts slowed to a pace that made a verbal response impossible. "Shut the door," his father yelled again until he scrambled to his feet and slammed the door on Richard himself.

The look in the blond man's eyes still haunts Richard. The irreverence, the way his neck arched to get a good look at the disturbance, the way his face contorted in disappointment when they made eye contact. Richard thought the man should be as startled as he was, but that wasn't the case. The blond man wasn't flustered, he was bothered.

Richard remained in the hall for a minute as the moment washed over him. Kissing a man? He didn't fully understand what this meant, and he didn't need to in order to know how this would affect his mother. He knew that married people didn't kiss other people, at least not the way his father and the blond man kissed, and he knew that this put his idea of the family in danger.

The sound of his father approaching the door pulled Richard into the moment.

He didn't want to look at him, let alone talk with him, so he ran down the hall to his bedroom, pulled the door shut and held the cat tight. Fear surged through his body for the first time he could remember in that apartment. His father didn't have a bad temper and never yelled at him or hit him, yet there Richard sat on his bed with trembling hands and a heart beating out of control. He may only have been ten, but he was old enough to know that this was a life-changing event, and that realization made him cry like he hadn't cried in years.

His father eventually entered the room, took the cat from Richard's arms, said only that he was going to the vet and left. A week later his father moved out. No warning, no explanation, just a short letter saying he was sorry, but he couldn't live with the family anymore. Richard still hasn't told his mother what he saw that day. That is his secret. He watched his mother cry every night for the first month; he listened to her rant on the phone to anyone that would listen; and he never told her that he saw her husband kiss another man.

THREE

Barrett never planned on being a children's author. What he wanted to be was rich, so he enrolled in Economics at McGill University, finished his first year on the dean's list, and got a summer job with one of the largest investment companies in the country. Everything was on course, but Barrett has never taken pride in outworking people, so in an effort to do whatever necessary in order to have Fridays off his second year, he signed up for a Twentieth Century Literature class. And as stories from the likes of Morrison, Hemingway, and Albee washed over him, something happened, something that went against every one of his instincts. He fell in love with words. Until then he had never been a big reader. He read what he had to in high school and a couple of autobiographies about entrepreneurs, but he was far from avid. By the end of the Twentieth Century class he was obsessed with books, and by the end of his second year of university he was writing drafts of short stories.

Even after he graduated with a double major in Economics and English, the plan was to get an MBA, but with every passing year at the investment firm that give him his first job, he did more writing and less advising clients until he found himself unemployed, in a coffee shop and down to his last thousand dollars. It was then, while flipping through a trade publishing paper in search of proofreading jobs that his eyes settled on an ad for a contest: a two thousand dollar first prize for the best submission of a children's book manuscript. A thousand dollars for second place and five hundred for third. Barrett scoffed enough to spit some of his coffee.

The journal where he had published his second short story paid him twenty-five dollars, and this contest was offering the potential of two grand for entertaining kids?

He grabbed a napkin from the counter, borrowed a pen from the teen with heavily pocked cheeks manning the cash register and started writing. Ideas had never flowed so smooth. Simply by knowing that his audience read simple sentences, he felt like a god of storytelling, like the creator of the English language, so far above his audience that he understood what they wanted to know, who they wanted to hear about, and what combination of words would keep them wanting more. He wasn't sure what audience a children's book meant, but while he wrote he envisioned grade school kids more than kindergarten, so he rolled with his instincts. Six weeks later he won the two thousand dollar first prize.

Book launches are different for Barrett than for most authors. Instead of spending weeks thinking of something clever to say, debating what part of the book to read, and enunciating in the mirror, Barrett simply finds an out-of-the-way spot and watches a guest reader read the book for him. This is one of the many advantages of writing under a pseudonym. There is no reputation to uphold other than mystique, and the more mystique the more intrigue. It's bizarre, but he knows he sells far more books by never promoting himself and being the mysterious recluse than he ever would representing himself and his work in public.

Tonight, he leans on a metal railing while Sidney stands beside him on a balcony far above a stage crowded by so many people that it looks like a celebrity should appear.

"Who's reading this time?"

"Are you ready?"

Barrett nods, his eyes still locked on the stage.

"The minister of education."

This pries a smile from Barrett. "You're a sick pup."

"I've got to admit, you pushed it on this one. Lineage, legacy, and growing up without a father? If I hadn't known you so long, I'd think you've had a hard life."

Barrett raises his middle finger without making eye contact. He's too busy watching the minister of education approach the microphone.

"Good afternoon, everyone. It's my pleasure to read from Russell Niles' latest book, *Mil Bennett and the Journey of Acceptance.*"

The crowd claps until the minister raises a hand.

"A story of loss and perseverance, this may be Mr. Niles' most important book yet." The minister looks into a TV camera with his best political smile. "Now I know how you feel about public appearances, but I speak on behalf of all of your fans when I say, if you're out there watching, thank you Mr. Niles, for giving us another one of your wonderful books to read."

An eruption of applause excites Sidney and he turns to Barrett. "What inspired this one exactly?"

Barrett shrugs a shrug Sidney's seen since they were teenagers. "Where does any of it come from?"

The next stop is Sidney's office. Barrett met Sidney Taylor back in the tenth grade, and being that Sidney was already a lawyer when the book offers first came in, it wasn't hard to lure him into the agent game.

Despite making more than his share of money, Sidney's life isn't easy. He has to be best friend, guard dog, and financial advisor every day, which is why despite being only thirty-seven, he pops antacid pills like they're breath mints.

This afternoon, Sidney's challenge is to get Barrett to be nice to the head of a toy division that hawks the Russell Niles dolls.

Sidney is the type of handsome that makes other men feel inferior, and he uses it regularly to get his way in the business world. And when Sidney gets his way, Barrett is happy, which means fewer antacids.

Today, Sidney is introducing Barrett as one of Russell Niles' advisors. Barrett shakes Mark Drake's hand with a scowl. He hates go-getters like Mark, especially one that is still in his twenties. Mark is fit and well groomed, but Barrett can see that it stings the guy to see the power suit Barrett is wearing is worth twice as much as his.

Sidney slides a folder open to a contract towards Mark. "Here's our standard confidentiality agreement that we use whenever discussing Russell Niles products. Not many people get to meet with one of Russell's personal advisors."

"No problem."

Mark hovers over the document without reading anything very closely and picks up a pen when Sidney holds up a finger.

"Ah-ah-ah. Eyes on me for a minute before you sign anything."

Mark knows enough to take the demand seriously and looks up with his full attention.

"Understand that by signing this, any information we give you will be used only to sell Russell Niles products. In terms of your personal life, you need to forget any details about this project or Mr. Niles' advisor as soon as you walk out of that room.

"If you ever mention anything about these projects to anyone in your personal life or heaven forbid, a competitor, your children's children will be paying off a lawsuit the size of some country's gross national product."

"Understood."

Sidney taps the table. "Good man."

The business of using the pseudonym Russell Niles was the publisher's demand. Within twenty-four hours of winning the children's book manuscript contest, Barrett received three publishing offers. At the time, he looked at the opportunity as a stepping stone. A chance to get a publishing credit, meet some people in the industry, and earn a little money.

The first publisher he met was Don Harris, a former sales rep who decided he would rather make the books that are read to children at nap time than sell them to the stores. He started the company on government grants, and twelve years and eight bestsellers later, he reigned as one of the most powerful publishers in the country. With a strong jaw, thick shoulders, a heavily wrinkled brow, and warm eyes, he looked more like someone you would find in a fire truck than a publisher, but everything about his tone proved he was all about business.

"We love your idea, we're expanding our print runs, and we're ready to make you an offer to write the manuscript, but there are a few things we need to discuss."

Barrett rubbed at his eyes. He'd smoked a joint for a little levity an hour before the meeting, and the look on Don's face suggested he knew Barrett wasn't suffering from allergies.

"This industry is so tight now that we need to invest in more than a good product. With the importance of print,

TV, and radio interviews, we're investing in you as much as your manuscript."

Barrett blinked twice, scolding himself for not using Visine.

"And because of this there are some things we need to get very clear."

Both the tone and the term "things" reminded him of his father. Neither ever meant good news.

"Forgive me for being so direct," Don said with eyes that made Barrett feel like he was back in a grade school principal's office. "But considering the audience for your story, this is the most important question."

He let the anticipation linger the way cheap cigar smoke wafts through a room before shifting his weight towards Barrett. "Have you ever been arrested?"

Barrett blinked another sticky blink. Had he been arrested? There was the possession of marijuana charge his freshman year of university. He'd broken up with Cheryl Lang the day after the first time they had sex, and before dinner the police received a tip that Barrett's apartment housed a dozen plants. Fortunately, a mind bent on revenge tends to lean on hyperbole, so when three officers showed up at Barrett's door all they found were two plants that supplied his personal use.

Then there was the illegal gambling charge. In comparison to working at a bookstore or coffee shop, raking the pot of a weekly poker game was a breeze. Seven to eight hundred dollars a week, status and more than a few women along the way. The run lasted most of his second year at university until he left one too many phone messages promoting the game and the police showed up.

He escaped year three of university without any drama, but after the homecoming game his senior year he was charged with public indecency. More specifically, he, Shawna Williams, and Katy Green were charged with public indecency.

After all the teen movies he watched growing up, how was he to know it's actually illegal to slide around the bleachers naked?

He looked at Don the way he'd looked at each of the officers that arrested him. Eyes straight ahead without a single blink. The type of eyes that wanted contact, the type of eyes people believe.

"No, I've never been arrested."

Don smiled politely and moved on with the meeting. Later that afternoon, he called Barrett and invited him to an organic juice bar. Don sipped on a smoothie while Barrett drank a cup of coffee from a place down the street, wishing he could get rid of the smell of orange rinds wafting through the air.

"I know you lied about not being arrested," Don said, looking pleased with himself. "I had a police friend run a unified search."

A part of Barrett wanted to toss the smoothie in his face and tell him that all the juice in the world wouldn't change that dried prune of a forehead, but that required more energy than he was willing to expend.

"Then I guess we're done here."

"Not even close. Your story is testing so well with our people that we've decided we still want to work with you."

"Really?"

"On the condition that you write under a pseudonym and put as much distance between your lifestyle and the product as possible."

Barrett nodded, and the need for a pseudonym was born.

And here he is years later pretending to be one of Russell Niles' advisors while a toy company rep signs a confidentiality agreement. After the document is signed, Sidney leads them into the conference room, where Barrett takes a seat at the head of a horseshoe table.

Barrett grimaces while Mark removes a laptop from his briefcase. The man begins his pitch while he's setting up.

"Our goal is to increase sales by thirty percent. Which is doable considering our overseas numbers. The figures outsell the books in most places over there."

"And that's a good thing?"

"It's a reality. And in order to maximize our profits, one that we need to pay attention to." He spins the computer towards Barrett. "Here are the five colours we've narrowed down this year for our hero, Mil Bennett. We'd like you to choose what you think would be his favourite three."

Before Barrett can focus on the screen's images, Mark pulls two action figures from his briefcase. These are the last things Barrett wants to see. His face flushes and his forearms pulsate as if it's possible he might tip his section of the desk over.

"As you can see," Mark says, pausing to adjust an action figure's neck, "this year's figures are the most life-like yet."

"Life-like?"

Mark nods. This is the Super Bowl of pitches, and Barrett knows from the look on the man's face that he promised himself when he woke up that if he didn't close the deal it wouldn't be from a lack of effort.

"The hands grip and every muscle is represented. The design was made with motion-sensor techniques, which means that they twist and turn the way a human does.

"And look at this." He steps closer to Barrett to give him a better look at the figure. "It's a widow's peak. It's a small detail, but it's a priority for us to do justice to his characters."

"No, it's not."

"I'm sorry?"

Barrett's tone is usually reserved for telemarketers that call during dinner or salespeople that buzz his gates. "You don't care about doing justice to his characters, you care about selling dolls, and so do I. Then you get your bonus cheque, he gets his percentage points, and we all get paid. So why don't you save all of our time, stop bullshitting, and pick whatever colour you think is going to sell the most."

Thirty minutes later, Barrett lies on a chaise lounge on the deck of his one-hundred-and-twenty-foot luxury yacht. Sidney approaches with a blender in one hand and plastic cups in the other. Barrett gestures to Sidney's feet.

"Hey. Back it up, superagent. Even supermodels take their shoes off on my baby."

Sidney smiles, steps back, and removes his shoes on a mat that Barrett changes once a week. Barrett points his cup at him.

"I don't care how long we've known each other, if you make me sit through another meeting about dolls, you're fired."

Sidney opens a laptop. "People bought as many of those figures as your books the past three years."

"I fucking hate dolls."

Sidney's eyes are now locked on his, not staring, but engaging the way only an agent's can. "How do you feel about the money they bring in?"

White sand, Italian wine, and Brazilian woman streak past Barrett's mind until his lips form a smug smile that compels him to raise his cup.

Sidney taps the laptop and extends his own cup until Barrett pours him a new drink from the blender. "You're not going to stiff Don on his party, are you?"

"I'll be there."

"He is your publisher."

"I'll be there."

"And we are negotiating a new contract, a contract we've been waiting years to have this leverage on."

Barrett swats at a wasp. "Spoken like a true agent."

Sidney gestures to the laptop. "Speaking of which, you agreed to three print interviews a year."

"Get an intern to do it."

Sidney reads off a list of questions. "What celebrity will Mil grow up to look like?"

"Are you kidding me?"

"Your publisher's holding me responsible for this."

"Sucks to be you."

"I'll take you to Vegas for the long weekend."

"Monte Carlo."

"Done." Another glance at the questions. "Why do you think *Mil Bennett and the Journey of Acceptance* is on pace to be your best seller yet?"

"Because parents are brainwashed into buying anything that's synonymous with being a good parent, and my publisher has successfully associated my books with coaxing predominantly seven- to ten-year-olds to read."

Sidney's on his feet now. "Keep it up, and you'll be lucky if I take you to Atlantic City."

"Okay...." Barrett lights a cigarette, takes a thoughtful drag, and sits up. "There are a lot of single-parent families, so even if a kid's not from one, they can relate to the idea of a father leaving a family through friends."

The words get Sidney to stop pacing. "So there is a method to the vodka." He scribbles for a moment. "Almost done. What was the inspiration for the latest book?"

"Other than the house in St. Tropez?"

"I love the house in St. Tropez."

"I know a kid whose dad abandoned his family."

"Yeah?"

Barrett nods as he looks into the sky.

"Method, huh? I knew there was something to this one. Who was the kid?"

"There were a few. I wanted to get a taste for what it's like for these kids. But nobody specific."

Sidney tosses the notebook onto the table. "Done. They want you to make up the last question, but that I can get an intern to do."

"No, no, no. That's the fun part."

Sidney raises his eyebrows and Barrett gestures to the notepad with his cup. "Who would win in a death match between Mil Bennett and Harry Potter?"

FOUR

Richard steps into the first floor washroom at school and stares at graffiti as he urinates. GERALD JONES IS GAY. Written in gold permanent marker, the colour pops on the faded white tiles, and as he re-reads the words, he wonders if his father qualifies as gay.

Back at home, he removes a pad of paper from under a box of old books in his closet and takes it with him to the computer station in the living room. The computer is positioned there so his mother can monitor his computer time, and while she is still at work and leaves him with a few private hours every day, he understands that she still checks the Internet history, so he has to delete the search history every time he conducts research. Her persistence means he has to write down the sites he visits to keep her from asking questions she doesn't want the answers to.

The day after his father left he started searching for any information he could find about gays and lesbians, and eleven months later he has one hundred and seventy gay-related sites in his notepad. Once he worked through the porn sites, he found titles with more depth including: Being Gay or Lesbian; Living

With Two Moms; and How to Tell Your Family. The content usually surpasses his understanding and he rarely reads more than a paragraph or two, but the search always proves satisfying enough to continue. And his research transcends the Internet. He has taken out every book that his two neighbourhood libraries have on the topic, he watches any TV show or movie he can with gay characters, and three months ago he added a modest but graphic gay sex magazine collection when he found a discarded box full of them in the park across from his school.

This research is often confusing and overwhelming, but the pursuit is soothing, and the more he learns, the more he wants to learn.

Every time he reads a chapter about gay bashing or watches a show starring a gay character or looks at pictures of two men kissing in a magazine, he hopes to feel closer to understanding why his father left. To discover a clue or a possible reason for the motivation. But that never happens. All he knows for certain after all this net surfing, reading, and looking at pictures, is that he feels more distant from his father's motivation than ever.

Even pinning down a definition for gay is complex. What he knows is this: kids at school, like the one that wrote the graffiti in the washroom, make fun of gay people by using lisps or holding their wrists limp, and many TV shows he watched before implied that gay people were weak and weird, but it isn't that simple. His soccer coach told everyone he was gay, and he is as muscular as a body builder and talks with the deepest voice Richard has ever heard. This is not a man who is weak or weird. Maybe Richard's father is bisexual. He saw a movie one night a month ago about a man that had both a boyfriend and a girlfriend. The man referred to himself as bisexual, and as far as Richard can tell, his father enjoyed kissing his mother as much as he enjoyed kissing the blond man in the bathroom.

The "what if" thoughts started the week after his father left. Before that he couldn't remember the details of any trip home from school — it was just something he did to get to where he was going. But that changed, and the details became magnified to the point where they took over. Like sewer grates. He must have walked past and over thousands in his young life, but the week after his father left, one in the middle of the sidewalk, a block from his apartment caught his attention in an obsessive way. He looked at the ten slits on each side of the twelve slits in the centre and asked what if he stepped on it and the metal collapsed?

What if he fell through, into the sewer, scraped his arms on the dirty walls as he ricocheted from one side to the other before cracking his head on a cement ridge and drowning face first in brown water at the bottom, so that his bloated body left his face unrecognizable when finally discovered? He doesn't walk near sewer grates after those thoughts.

He clicks on a site titled: 20 GAY STEREOTYPES AND WHY THEY ARE BULLSHIT and scans through the list. Gays throw like girls; gays are egocentric; gays like shopping; gays hate sports; gays are good dancers; gays don't smell; gays are sensitive; gays like pop music; gays don't like their fathers. He closes the site, erases the search history, and decides to tell his mother what he saw that day in the bathroom. Suddenly it feels like he should have told her long ago. And as he sits in a daze, he notices every particle floating in the beam of sunlight shining through the living room window. Little flecks of dust that appear to float randomly, but in this light, he knows they move with purpose. He is ready to tell her, ready to share his secret without fearing what she might say or how she'll look at him. He just isn't sure how to tell her.

Rehearsing anything important has always brought him comfort, so as he clicks on a driving video game and begins dodging his futuristic car through traffic, he runs through a number of scenarios, but none of them feels right. If he tells her, he has something to tell her as soon as she walks in the apartment. The drama will stress her, and if he randomly brings up his dad at an unexpected time like when she's doing a crossword, that will be weird and stress her, and if he blurts out that he saw his dad kiss a man on floor of the bathroom during dinner, she'll probably faint.

When his last futuristic car crashes, he sits on the couch and waits for his mother to get home from work. With his stomach swirling more nervously with every passing second, he is desperate for a distraction, so he picks up a photo album from under the coffee table.

The photos look different now with his dad gone, and he can't help but look for clues that the man didn't love his mother, that he was unhappy with the family or that he was attracted to men. But there aren't any clues. Smiles centre most photos. Some jovial, others forced, but they are no different than any other family album. Pictures of birthdays, special events, and parties, they chronicle the best of times. The tradition with photos is to leave the dark clouds out of these painted horizons.

He pulls out a picture of his father standing beside his mother in a park. They both look young enough that it could have been before marriage, and with big smiles and their hands entwined, they certainly appear in love. Everything about his dad looks cool. His tan is deep, his shirt is off, and a cigarette hangs from the corner of his mouth. Richard hopes to be that confident one day.

The apartment door opens and Richard feels the muscles in his throat tighten. The sight of his mother makes telling her about his father real, and his mind begins to scramble for reasons not to reveal the secret. He doesn't want to make her life worse than it is, and he doesn't want to admit he has been keeping the truth from her.

She hangs up her coat and turns towards him with eyes clearly red from crying. Tears offer an excuse. If she is already upset, then this isn't the right time. Part of him wants to excuse himself to his room, but a bigger part of him wants to get the secret off his conscience. He takes another breath and decides to start with something light to buy some time, something to cheer her up.

"Do you want to play cards?"

She looks at him with eyes that burn. "What I want to do is talk with you. Wait here."

She disappears into her bedroom and reappears with two large plastic bags. Richard doesn't know what to make of her aggression. She gets upset a lot, but he can't remember the last time she was angry. Anger just isn't her temperament.

"Can you explain this?"

She tips the bags upside down, and all of the gay magazines and photocopies of articles from underneath his bed spill onto the coffee table. Some drop to the floor and others drop open to pictures of men kissing. Richard wants to run into his bedroom and pull the covers over his head but she blocks the path.

"Is there something you want to tell me?"

He considers telling her the secret just to deflect the attention, but she is so angry he hesitates long enough for her to seize control.

"Did someone give you these? Is someone touching you?"

Touching him? The questions confuse him. Confuse and worry him. What she found is research, but she just gave it an evil quality that makes him feel uncomfortable. The muscles in his throat tighten again, forcing him to swallow back another gag.

She sits beside him now with both hands wiping at her eyes until she leans into him. "Do you like boys? Is that what this is about?"

33

A pressure in his head makes him feel dizzy. The way she emphasized "boys" makes him wince. He wants to scream: *It's dad that likes guys. How could you be with him all that time and not notice? This isn't about me, it's about him.* But he can't even look at her.

She takes a deep breath through her nose, and he watches as the muscles beneath her eyes twitch. "Because if you like boys, that's okay. It's normal for some people to like the same sex, but you're pretty young for magazines like this. I can, uh, I can buy you books that will help you sort out your feelings, if you've decided that you like boys."

The tone and repetition of "boys" makes him cringe. He looks at her in disbelief. He wants to faint, but he knows the only way to stop this debacle is to speak.

"They're not mine."

"Don't lie, Richard. I found them under your bed."

"They're a friend's from school. His dad's gay and he wanted to find out more about it, but he didn't want his dad to find the magazines and stuff, so he asked me to hold onto it all for him."

"And you expect me to believe that?"

Of course, he thinks. She wants to believe anything other than that he is sexually curious, so all he has to do is give her a way out.

"It's the truth. It's not his fault his dad's gay. He's just trying to make sense of his situation."

His mother's face contorts into a look equal parts ashamed and relieved. "I want you to give these back to your friend. You're too young for stuff like this. Way too young. Do you understand me?"

Richard nods and waits until it is okay to slip off to his room. For a moment, he thought the day might end with a diary entry about telling his mother the secret, but instead he writes: 1) *Find a better hiding place.*

FIVE

Barrett discovered just how little children's books have to do with reading two weeks after his first book went on sale. He figured the pseudonym gave him the distance to deliver the manuscript, collect some money, and never be heard from in the kid's industry again. But when his book debuted at number three on the bestseller list, everything changed. Sitting with the third highest selling children's book in the country didn't humble him and it didn't make him grateful, it made him want to find out everything he could about who wrote numbers one and two. He scribbled down the names: Sheryl Orange #1; Horace Night #2. An hour later he returned from the bookstore with over two hundred dollars on his credit card. Each of them had ten books in print, and all of them wore stamps championing their award-winning status. The Golden Kite award, presented by the Society of Children's Writers, the American Library Association medal for children's literature, the Newberry Medal, the Boston-Globe-Horn award, and a slew of lesser known stamps from governing bodies around the world.

Horace Night has a series called *Traveling with Timmy*. Barrett cracked open the first of the series, and by page six he tossed it on the floor in amazement. This was the second best-selling children's book in the country? A blandly written, on-the-nose tour of New York and all its wonderful cultures led by Timmy the turtle and his multicultural friends. He couldn't bear to read another page, so he decided to try the Orange books. *Adventures with Amy* is aimed at older kids and stars a curious girl with full cheeks and big eyes, and while he hated to admit the writing had punch, it soothed him to find the allegories were spoon-fed to the lowest common denominator.

The importance of manners; respecting differences; being kind to elders. Suddenly it made sense that most people he met had the creativity and flare of a white wall.

They have been raised on books like this, which make life appear to have clearly defined boundaries with rules as easy to follow as tic, tac, toe. He needed to know more, he needed to meet these authors, so he searched the Internet for their next public readings and counted down the days for the next two weeks.

Horace Night's reading was first, and while Barrett knew the man's books were popular, he wasn't prepared for the event's scale. A red carpet greeted guests outside the bookstore, some-one dressed as Timmy handed out candy, three hundred kids were crazed with excitement in the reading area, and at least a dozen tables sold Timmy books, candy, bed sheets, pencils, T-shirts, pajamas, and wallpaper.

Two things stood out to Barrett despite the chaos. First, the crowd around the booth selling the Timmy books consisted entirely of adults. Second, all of the kids were standing around two wall-mounted TVs that played the Timmy cartoon. A man wearing the bright yellow uniform of the bookstore approached the microphone on a stage two feet high. He was a large man, well over two hundred pounds, but he spoke with one of the highest voices Barrett had ever heard.

"Welcome, people. Come get your seats and get ready for one of the most exciting events ever to come to our store."

Parents pried their kids away from the TVs and ushered them to the front rows. The seats filled up quickly, and the buzz increased in volume until the large announcer stepped in front of the microphone again.

"It's my pleasure to introduce one of the world's best-selling children's authors, Horace Night."

Barrett expected the loud cheers kids make when they are encouraged to be noisy, but the applause that erupted would have made movie stars envious. And Night didn't disappoint. Dressed in a Superman sweater and beige slacks, he skipped on stage strumming a guitar that hung from a strap on his neck. The kids clapped and the parents nodded along as he worked his way through a series of Timmy songs, each of them available on the official *Traveling with Timmy* CD.

When it came time to read, the room was silent, eerily so in Barrett's opinion. It was like a classical conditioning experiment where the very sight of a book prompted quiet. Having read the latest *Traveling with Timmy*, he knew what to expect, but listening to the audience laugh on cue created a brand new sting of jealousy. If he was going to write children's books, this was how he wanted kids to respond. Suddenly being number three on the bestseller list felt like three hundred thousand.

When the reading ended, Barrett followed Horace down a corridor. No one asked him why he was in a private area, so he kept following until Horace disappeared behind a door with his name on a cartoon-style star. Barrett looked down the hall to see who was watching. Two suits chatted on cell phones, but neither of them were paying attention to anything else. Barrett opened the dressing room door and froze for a moment. There was no celebrating, no gaudy tray of food or drinks. Instead Horace sat on a couch with tears running down his face. And these weren't tears of joy; these were tears that flowed from eyes burning red with anguish. Barrett stepped forward for a closer look when two hands pressed against his chest.

"What are you doing here?"

"I work here. I was told to ..."

"It's not a good time."

The man steered Barrett's shoulders so he had to turn around and ushered him out the door. Crying? Crying after a performance like that? The sight of an acclaimed children's author with tears streaming down his cheeks made him wonder. Burnout? Divorce? A personal tragedy? His imagination had just begun to warm up when a bald man with close-set eyes stepped in front of him.

"Would you like to purchase the *Traveling with Timmy* video game? It's testing off the charts with the kids, and it won't be in stores for another month." He held the video game box up for inspection. "Your kid will think you're the coolest."

Barrett wondered if the man knew Timmy's creator was bawling his eyes out just two doors down the hall.

Two days later, he arrived at Sheryl Orange's reading an hour early. He didn't need to see another performance — what he wanted was some time with the author. Not long, just a moment to look in her eyes and ask a few questions.

There was already a lineup for signings when he arrived. He looked at the row of at least a hundred and worried that he might not reach the signing desk in time, but within minutes it was clear this was an efficient operation. The line moved quick enough that he wasn't done his crossword before he was next in line behind an Indian boy with cheese popcorn flavouring smeared around his lips. When the boy was done, Barrett folded his newspaper and stepped forward.

Sheryl looked better than he expected. He knew she was forty-eight, but the pictures he saw of her made her look more weathered. In person, she was a lively forty-eight. Fresh skin, sparkling eyes, and always smiling. He wondered what he'd look like at forty-eight, hoped to still have nose cartilage and a liver and extended a hand.

"It's a pleasure to meet you."

Sheryl Orange nodded with a smile. Her marker hovered just above the book's cover. "And who should I make this out to?"

"My son, Eric," he said without hesitation.

She looked at him for a moment, like she knew he was full of shit, before signing anyway.

"You've done a great job with promotion," he said, picking up the freshly signed book. "I'm in marketing, and I've got to say, this is quite a campaign."

Her eyes lit up. This wasn't the usual chatter she'd grown to expect at her signings. "I have a degree in marketing myself."

"Really?"

"And an MBA. I know the value of details."

Barrett nodded slowly and raised his book in goodbye. He noticed her watch, her necklace and her wedding ring. Clearly, she knew the value of diamonds too.

Sitting in the back of a gun-metal grey stretched Mercedes, Barrett looks at a crystal decanter of cognac and wonders what Sheryl Orange thinks of his sales as the car pulls up in front of the winding cement steps of his publisher's mansion.

He promised Sidney he would attend Don's disco-themed party, and with his shirt unbuttoned to his chest and his hair slicked back, he has kept his word. He steps out of the car, walks up the steps past two greeters dressed as go-go dancers and into the party.

Not two steps inside, Don approaches. He's dressed in a satin shirt with disco balls, grey bell bottoms and three-inch heels, and Barrett can tell from the pride in Don's eyes that the man isn't just satirizing an era. "I'm glad you made it." Don brings Barrett in for a hug.

"You think I'd miss this?"

"Come on, there's someone I want you to meet."

Barrett moves through a living room set up as a lounge where many guests are already dancing and into the kitchen in time to see Don put his arm around a man with his back to them.

"Barrett, I'd like to you to meet literary genius Martin Brouge."

Martin turns around, and Barrett stops on the spot. Shock tingles through him as he looks at the man like he is the last person on the planet he wants to see. With thick hair, a natural smile, and a face that looks like he drinks more water than alcohol, Martin looks like he hasn't worried a moment in his life. Even in a baby-blue suit jacket with an oversized white collar jutting out and a number of fake gold chains around his neck, he looks good.

"It's been a long time," Barrett says.

"It certainly has."

Don is surprised. "You two know each other?"

"We started out working the slush piles together." Martin punctuates the information by flashing Barrett a smirk.

Barrett knows Don gets a rush from introducing people, and he knows that Barrett's history with Martin will make him defensive. .

"Well, he's a long way from that now." Don taps Barrett's elbow. "Aren't you?"

Barrett feigns a smile.

"How do you two know each other?" Martin asks.

"Barrett's my, uh, my broker. And nobody makes me more money than him."

Barrett raises his drink.

Martin removes a postcard from his breast pocket and passes it to Barrett. "I have a launch for my latest book next week at the Vatic. I'd love you to come."

Barrett flexes his nostrils. "I promised myself I'd never go to another launch."

"I see."

This is more than Barrett wants to bear, so he pulls out his cigarettes and raises the pack. "Nicotine calls."

"Maybe you can give me some stock advice before you leave?"

They share a look of mutual loathing before Barrett exits. He walks through the party, past two men dressed as Rick James and steps out sliding doors to a patio, where he startles Layla. She has been married to Don for nineteen years. She is forty-six, but in her large blonde afro wig, knee-high white boots, and a fitting dress, she is the most stunning woman at the party.

"Hey," she says with an exhale of smoke. "You scared me." She holds up her thin cigarette to eye level. "Don't tell Don. He thinks I quit."

"I do a good job of keeping your secrets." He leans into her lighter to light his cigarette, and she smiles seductively.

"I hate throwing parties for self-absorbed publishing people."

"I hate writers."

Layla steps closer. "I think it's that time."

"I love that time, but here?"

Her fingers wrap around his hand and she leads him down an unlit path to the pool-shed. They kiss, and he isn't surprised that despite having just finished a cigarette, she tastes like vanilla.

She pushes an inflatable dragon off a table, raises her skirt, and pulls at Barrett's pants. This is how it has been since they first had sex a few months ago. All passion and impulse.

Fifteen minutes later, Barrett steps out of the pool-shed and is walking back toward the mansion when he sees Martin standing just outside the sliding doors with a glass of wine in hand. Barrett is about to turn, but it's too late. They lock eyes for a moment before Martin pivots and returns inside.

Dishevelled, Barrett re-enters the party but doesn't make it to the bar before Don passes him a Scotch. "Thank you again for coming. I know theme parties aren't your thing."

"You'd be surprised." Barrett holds up his drink and they touch glasses.

SIX

At school, Richard isn't that different from a piece of furniture. He sits in the same place every day, never speaks, and looks just enough like everyone else that he doesn't stand out. His grades are good enough that he doesn't need extra help, but they are also average enough that he never receives any recognition. None of his teachers would ever admit it, but not one of them knows his full name. Some of them know him as Richard, some as Conner, but none of them know more than they have to for grading and attendance purposes. This is a fact best illustrated by the time he went home in the middle of the day to watch cartoons and nobody noticed. It was one of those days where he couldn't stand another minute of school, so he just left. Neither of his afternoon teachers mentioned it the next day and nobody from the school called home. They simply didn't notice he wasn't in the room.

Today, he waits in front of the computer lab for the lunch supervisor to open the door for free computer time. He checks the doorknob to make sure it's not open when three boys hustle through the side doors. Terrance Hershelle, Derrick Walker, and Wendell James. Immediately, it is clear that only two of the three want to be there. Richard and Wendell met in the third grade. He is a nice enough kid, but the type that is always arguing with somebody, the type that always has to be right. Richard doesn't know exactly what Wendell said to be pinned up against the wall by two sixth graders, but he is positive that whatever it was, Wendell would happily admit he was wrong for once to get out of the situation.

"You know how we're going to fix this?" Terrance says, fueled by Derrick's nod of approval. "You're going to kiss our feet. You do that, you bend down and kiss our feet and we'll let this go. Won't we, Derrick?"

Derrick and Terrance slap hands as if the power of touch can confirm that they are as cool as they hope.

Wendell doesn't move. Tears fill his eyes, but not a single one falls. Paralyzed by fear, his eyes don't blink enough to cry.

"Did you hear me?" Terrance steps closer to him. "Kiss our feet and I won't beat you."

Wendell still doesn't blink, but he does turn his head to look at Richard. Terrance follows the look and steps away from the wall. They have been so focused, so high on themselves that neither Terrance nor Derrick noticed Richard until now. They share a look of confirmation that being seen wasn't good before Terrance beelines towards Richard, stopping just an inch from his face. He stands so close that Richard can smell the remnants of the cigarette he puffed before locking in on Wendell. Up close, everything on Terrance's face becomes clear. The sprigs of hair on his lip, the red pimples on his cheeks, and the beads of sweat gathering on his forehead. This isn't a handsome boy.

"Do I have to worry about you saying anything about this?" Terrance does his best to make this sound intimidating, but a slight lisp makes this the wrong word choice.

The delivery doesn't matter, though. Richard didn't hear a word anyway. He is too focused on the look of fear in Wendell's eyes and the weakness in his posture. But it is more than fear. Wendell looks at Terrance with admiration. He fears these boys, but he wants to be them. This is a kid that will be doing the same thing to a fourth grader by the end of the week.

Terrance bounces on the balls of his feet now that he is so full of adrenaline, and the words don't just leave his lips, he speaks with conviction.

"Did you hear me, homo? I said …"

And those are the last words Terrance says. Before he completes the thought, Richard's forehead smashes into the bridge of his nose with surprising force. Tears fill his eyes before they roll back in his head as he stumbles backwards until his legs buckle and he falls to the floor. Richard waits for him to respond, to get up and retaliate, but as he watches the kid's face twitch like a dreaming dog, it's clear he is unconscious.

Instinctually, Richard touches his forehead with two fingers. A bump throbs where he struck Terrance, leaving him stunned. He looks at Derrick, and as soon as they make eye contact, Derrick runs down the hall. Wendell is already long gone. Richard rubs his eyes and looks down at Terrance's nose to see the blood turning his T-shirt red. He never thought of head butts before, let alone practiced one, so it surprises him that he lashed out, but that is the power of rage. The right trigger at the wrong time and blood usually follows.

Richard walks to the closest washroom and cups some water onto his forehead. The bump looks smaller in the mirror than it feels, but it is swollen enough to make him turn from the reflection. Unease replaces the rush of adrenaline, and without warning he starts to cry uncontrollably. Not because being called homo reminded him that his father was gay but because being called homo reminded him that his father abandoned the family and the pain that accompanies this sadness makes him capable of anything.

By the first period after lunch, rumours circulate that Richard hit Terrance with a hammer. One kid's version has Richard biting off a piece of Terrance's ear. Another claims he has rabies.

"But he's so scrawny," one kid says, pointing to where Richard now sits at the back of the room.

"You don't have to be strong if you're crazy. He beat him with a baseball bat."

Everyone is too busy whispering about Richard to listen to Mr. Davis's history lesson, but Richard doesn't care. The welt on his forehead hurts too much, and with the adrenaline rush gone, he starts to worry about Terrance's revenge. Terrance is meaner, older, and stronger than him, and now the kid's reputation is at stake. Richard lifts two fingers to the welt to see how much the bump has grown since he last checked when an East Indian woman steps into the classroom doorway. None of the kids know this woman's name, but they all knew who she is. This is the woman who checks their hair for lice twice a year. Only she already checked the class a month ago, so her presence causes a buzz of unrest.

The woman speaks close to Mr. Davis so that nobody can hear her. Mr. Davis pivots, locks eyes with Richard and gestures "come here" with an index finger. Richard knows this has nothing to do with lice. Everyone watches in admiration as he walks up the isle and out into the hallway. He is not just Richard anymore to his classmates, he is the kid that beat up the school bully. He is a grade five legend.

"Follow me," the East Indian woman says.

Richard doesn't remember hearing the woman speak when she checked the class for lice, so it surprises him to hear such a warm tone. All the other authority figures in the school speak like they want people to fear them.

The woman leads Richard to a side room at the end of the hall that smells like a mixture of floor polish and perfume.

Besides a small cactus on a file cabinet, everything is bland. Fading white walls, grey furniture, and speckled tiles make Richard think of hospitals. The woman sits behind a desk covered in stacks of paper and Richard settles into a chair in front of her.

She is more beautiful up close than he remembered. With large eyes, full lips, and close-cropped hair that accentuates her features, he thinks she looks more like a model than someone who works at a school. He wants to take a candy from a large dish on the desk, but the look on her face warns him not to.

The woman leans forward, and from this angle Richard notices a sizable scar the shape of a lightning bolt just over her left eyebrow. Thick and bevelled, this is the type of scar that makes people wonder about its origin. A car accident? A sports injury? Or something more basic like a fall?

"I'll give you one guess," she says, gesturing to the scar.

Richard feels embarrassed for staring but curiosity drives him. "A coffee table."

The woman smiles. "A hockey stick. Ninth grade. But ..." she tilts her head back to reveal a bulging scar beneath her chin, "this was from a coffee table."

Richard smiles. It feels good to be right. Almost good enough to forget about his throbbing head.

The woman digs into the candy dish and tosses Richard a wrapped mint. "You recognize me from my classroom visits, yeah?"

Richard nods.

"Well you should know that I don't just check for lice. As a health worker I'm also a counsellor, which is why you're visiting me before the principal."

A poster on the wall of a giant thumbs up seems to taunt Richard so he drops his eyes to the floor.

"What you did has a mandatory two-day suspension, but Mr. Haskins wanted you to meet with me before he sends you home."

The increasing stress makes his welt feel the size of a grapefruit.

"Why did you hit Terrance?"

Richard doesn't flinch.

"Is everything at home all right?"

He offers a blank stare.

"Because there's no record of you being in trouble before, and Mr. Davis says this incident is out of character. Is there something specific that made you angry?"

The questions began to anger Richard. He knows the woman suspects things aren't going well at home, and all of this counsellor-speak only guarantees she isn't going to get an answer.

"I understand why you're not in the mood to speak right now." She turns to a mini-fridge beside the desk, opens the door, and removes an ice pack. "So I'm going to end our meeting for now, but I'll be monitoring you after the suspension, and if you need to talk just come and see me." She slides the ice pack across the desk, and Richard immediately picks it up and holds it against his welt. "Okay?" the woman asks, just above a whisper.

Richard nods. This is only the beginning of questions about his family, if he starts to get in trouble, and he knows it, so he makes himself a promise on his way home. He promises himself not to get anyone's attention anymore.

Whether good or bad, it doesn't matter; what he now knows for certain is that any attention will lead to questions about his family, and that those questions will in turn lead to talk about his father.

SEVEN

Mornings are never easy for Barrett. His rhythms are off, the air smells funny, and his thoughts bargain for more sleep. This is why he is sitting in the trendiest breakfast spot in the city. If he has to be up, then he is going to do it with some style. The pompous décor makes him think of movies, and despite the early hour every seat in the place is filled with people happy to pay thirty dollars for breakfast.

Barrett sits by himself looking exactly like a man who has been out drinking all night should. His shirt is wrinkled, his eyes are puffy, and his consciousness is devoid of regret. He is about to cut a blueberry crepe when a bell rings. This is the type of bell that short-order cooks have been palming for decades, the type of bell that makes his hangover feel like a tumour.

He forks the crepe into his mouth, and the warm sweetness is beginning to sooth him when the bell rings again. And again. Three short dings in total, each more obnoxious, until he finds himself white-knuckling his napkin. Stretching his neck, he turns to see a small boy hitting the bell with increasing frequency. Of course. He looks at his food and decides he's done.

With the quick tap of an index finger, he shakes two Aspirin out of a lipstick-style tube and chases them with his coffee. He begins to check his messages from his iPhone until the bell's ding compels him to stand up and walk over to the boy. With his fingers spread wide, he covers the bell with a hand.

"Enough."

The boy is stunned. His face contorts in fear, but he doesn't cry. A woman in her thirties steps towards Barrett with a baby in a sack on her chest. Her hair is cut short and her outfit is three price ranges down from anyone else in the place.

"Excuse me?" she says. Her tone is ready for confrontation.

"Are you his mother?"

"I am."

"Do you really think he should be running around here like it's a playground?"

"He's three."

"He's annoying."

The woman's face runs flush. "And you aren't?"

"This is a five-star restaurant. There are more than enough fast food places within walking distance that are waiting to please a soccer mom and her brood."

The woman scoffs in disgust and leads her kid away from him by the hand.

Barrett returns to his seat and a man with grey hair a table over raises his juice glass in a toast of appreciation.

The next stop is a children's literature lecture. He walks into a crowded lecture hall with a white mocha and sits beside a young woman who looks more ready for a club than a classroom. Knee-high leather boots, a skirt, and a fuzzy black sweater make Barrett wish he was an undergrad again.

Professor Gibson steps in front of the podium with a large bottle of water. In his early forties, this is a man who lives for his chats with admiring students in the front row. This is not just an academic platform for Gibson — this is a stage. After reading Gibson's two dozen published articles about Russell Niles and listening to the man promote himself as the eminent academic expert on the Niles books on talk radio, Barrett decided it was time to see the man for himself.

Barrett leans into the young woman beside him and gestures at Gibson with his coffee. "How is he?"

"Douchebag," she says, mimicking squawking with her hand.

"Well, you know what they say. Those who can't write, lecture, and those who can't lecture, lecture about children's lit."

Gibson clicks a few buttons on a laptop, and the name Russell Niles appears on a screen behind him, quickly followed by the cover of *Mil Bennett and the Journey of Acceptance*, a dramatically colourful piece with Mil in a yellow sweater, holding his head in his hands against the backdrop of a blue ocean.

Barrett cringes. If he'd ever attended a cover meeting, he would never have let that happen.

Gibson sets his water down on the lecture podium. "Today we will explore Russell Niles and the connection between his work and Aesop's fables."

Barrett leans back into the young woman. "I call bullshit." She offers a smile of approval that would normally inspire him to continue, but he can't focus on anything except what Gibson's saying.

"The inspiration for Niles' latest book can be traced back to 'The Man and the Serpent' from Aesop's *Life and Fables*." He points a remote at the screen, and a picture of The Man and the Serpent appears.

Compulsion leads Barrett to hold up his coffee as a raised hand but Gibson's too into the moment to notice yet.

"Now this may be a piece of work written over five hundred years ago …"

But Barrett's waving coffee cup is too much to ignore so Gibson steps towards the audience and gestures at him. "Yes?"

With the room's collective attention shifting to him, Barrett takes a moment to make sure everyone is listening. "Maybe Aesop's isn't children's lit?"

"Really?"

"Is there really anything child-centred about exploring the origins of the universe or nature or the evolution of communication?"

Up for the challenge, Gibson steps into the aisle. "It's children who still flock to these stories hundreds of years later."

"Only because they're the only ones with enough imagination left to see the connection between the fantastic and what happens in front of their faces every day."

"Clearly Niles understands the appeal of the fable."

"Or maybe he understands that all stories are didactic on some level, and that kids will listen to anything they like, whether it's catered to them or not. Or maybe it's not that complex. Maybe he just knew a kid who lived through his father leaving the family and based the book on how he dealt with it."

Gibson looks at Barrett for a moment before breaking into a smug smirk. "Mr. Niles doesn't have to be here for me to know he'd be insulted by that suggestion."

Barrett wants to reply with something witty, but the words trouble him, so he waits for the lecture to continue and exits the hall.

On the drive home he thinks about putting in a day of writing. This isn't guilt, this is greed. He loves this lifestyle and he's well aware what pays for the luxuries.

Being rich isn't about appearances for him, it's about fun. Maybe it is a trait he inherited from a great-grandparent he never met, or maybe it's a reaction to being raised by parents who were conservative and cautious with money, but once the riches started coming in, Barrett embraced the lure of compulsion. Instinct over analysis, lust over love, and a persistent and insatiable desire for more of everything. This is a man who still keeps his play money crumpled in his pocket.

What he needs to do is write, but as soon as he gets home he stretches out on the couch with a cucumber mask pressed tight against his face. Bed is never an option after a night of partying. Being so far off the ground feels wrong, so he always spends the afternoons after these nights on the couch with a football or soccer game on the big-screen and a carton of organic lemonade beside him on the floor. He's finally managed to get to sleep when the front gate buzzer sounds. The pitch cuts through his haze but not enough to make him move until it sounds twice more. He pulls off the mask with a huff, gets to his feet, and stumbles to the video-intercom, where he sees a kid with a hat and a hood pulled tight on his head so that his face is a shadow.

"Hello?"

The kid's voice is strong but young. "Delivery."

"Hold on."

He slips on a black terrycloth robe, steps out of the mansion, and walks with slow steps down the half-moon shaped driveway past the rose bushes, the Italian marble fountain, the magnolia trees, the ground sprinklers on timers and over the imported interlocking brick and the forty feet of heat panels below them that ensure nobody will ever have to shovel snow in the winter, until he sees that the boy is East Asian and no older than twelve.

As Barrett approaches the gates, the boy extends a swollen manila envelope through the bars. The boy's face is stoic, and as soon as Barrett takes the package, the kid runs down the street.

"Wait …"

Barrett cranes his neck, but the boy is gone. He looks around to see if anyone is watching before examining the package to see TO BARRETT FULLER computer-printed on the label. He looks around one more time before walking back to the mansion.

Standing in his kitchen, he places the package on a granite island and takes a butter knife from a cutlery drawer. He slits the envelope from corner to corner and removes a typed letter. The first impressions are generic: Times New Roman font, black ink, and stock paper. He reads as quickly as possible.

Dear Barrett Fuller,

I know who you are. I know that despite the fact that you make millions of dollars entertaining children with stories about making the right choices, you are actually a pig of a man.

Flashes of Barrett's favourite strip club take over his thoughts. A private booth, a bottle of vodka, and his favourite dancer, Jill, sitting beside him half-naked while a redhead with a tattoo of the sun around her belly button dances on the table.

I have proof that Russell Niles is your pseudonym and I have documented truths about your life that will ruin your career if I release them to the media.

Suddenly he thinks of a night when he had a nurse hook the two of them up to IVs so that they could drink copious amounts of alcohol while remaining hydrated.

In a Herculean twenty-one hour session, they drank enough to kill frat boys while she told him everything she knew about the weird shit she'd found in peoples' blood and did her best to convince him that he could live a happy life without his arms and legs.

I am giving you two weeks to complete six tasks that will help you live up to the morals you currently prostitute.

The words remind him of a night when he fought a man at the local pub. In truth, fought is too romantic a word for such awkward movement. Scuffled is more accurate. The man, at least three inches taller than Barrett, took offense to an acerbic quip about his hair plugs, and a moment later the two of them were wrestling on the floor. For the next month, Barrett told anyone who would listen that he won a bar fight.

> *If you fail to complete these tasks or ignore my demands I will expose your lifestyle to the media, ruin your credibility and end your career. In order to avoid humiliation and save the money train you call Russell Niles, you will prove that you have embraced each opportunity by creating a website titled Once Upon a Hypocrite and entering the required proof upon completing each demand.*

The letter should provoke a response. Fear, anger, or at the very least acknowledgement that it's creepy. But all Barrett can think about is a night three months back when he got so drunk, he let a husband and wife shave his testicles at a penthouse party on the lakeshore. The sun was rising with a beautiful glow of possibility, and there he sat on a deck chair with pubic hair in his lap and a double D bra as a bib.

You are likely questioning my legitimacy, so I've sent your agent a package addressed to you that will provide evidence of my seriousness.

Seeing the words "agent" and "package" conjures up memories of last Christmas when he and Sidney delivered a truck full of gifts to a homeless shelter.

Feeling good about themselves, like they'd bought a little time with karma, they celebrated by drinking a twenty-two-hundred-dollar bottle of Coley Porter Bell Scotch in Sidney's office. They'd talked about how corrupt they thought pharmaceutical companies were and about politics and ordering Russian escorts. Barrett spent the night on the floor holding a copy of the *Charter of Rights and Freedoms* the way children hold stuffed animals.

As Barrett leaves the kitchen and walks down a hallway decorated by a wall-sized tank of miniature sharks, the letter's anger sets in. He stops moving for the first time since picking up the package and reads it on the spot.

Demand number one is in that package. You have twenty-four hours to complete it and upload the proof or the world will know that Russell Niles is actually a low-life alcoholic, a drug addict, a womanizer, and a money-hungry liar.

Barrett places the letter on the kitchen island, picks up his cell phone, and calls Sidney.

Each ring drags on until Sidney finally answers with a distracted hello. Barrett steps through sliding doors onto a back deck that overlooks his pool. "Did a package come today in my name?"

"I'm your agent, Barrett. Packages come here every day in your name."

"Not for Russell Niles, for me."

"I don't know, I left earlier for a few hours. Let me see what Molly has."

Barrett picks up the extortion letter, leaves his house, and heads for the Audi. With his earpiece in, his mouth struggles to keep up with his thoughts. "We need to meet right now. I'm on my way over."

"I have a meeting in ten minutes."

"Then cancel the meeting. This is serious." Barrett swerves through traffic like a skilled cab driver.

"Okay," Sidney says. "I'm with you, just breathe."

"Just be in your office."

Barrett flicks off the phone and honks at the mini-van in front of him.

On the elevator up to Sidney's office, he looks at the three people riding with him like any of them could have sent the extortion letter. A middle-aged black man, an up-and-coming suit with a brush cut, and a woman on the verge of retirement. The faces don't make any of them more or less guilty. All of them work in the building, which makes all of them suspects. He steps off the elevator and walks with purpose. He walks by an open door and turns into Sidney's office as fast as possible. The office is larger than some one-bedroom apartments, and with two leather couches, a wall-mounted flat-screen TV and an espresso machine, it's more comfortable than most cafes.

Barrett locks the door and turns toward Sidney, who sits behind his desk with a smoke burning in an ashtray filled with butts.

"How did you get the letter?" Sidney asks.

"An Oriental kid dropped it off through the gates."

"A kid?"

"I know. He had to be delivering it for someone; he wasn't more than ten or eleven."

Sidney looks like he's holding back the urge to vomit and points to the flat-screen with a controller. "You need to see this."

"Okay."

Sidney presses play and footage of a factory appears on the screen. A female voice speaks over the footage with all the showmanship and dogma of an award-winning newscaster. "This Indonesian factory where the American company, Blast, manufactures its energy drink is currently under investigation for child labour use." The woman's voice fades and an amateur header appears on the screen. BARRETT FULLER OWNS 20% OF BLAST INC. BARRETT FULLER ALSO WRITES THE MIL BENNETT BOOKS UNDER THE PSEUDONYM RUSSELL NILES. HIS IDENTITY CAN BE IDENTIFIED AT THE LIBRARY OF CONGRESS WHERE THE COPYRIGHT FOR THE RUSSELL NILES BOOKS IS UNDER SANFORD CORBETT, WHICH IS A COMBINATION OF HIS FATHER'S FIRST NAME AND HIS MOTHER'S MAIDEN NAME. Sidney pauses the image on the screen. "And you need to read this." He passes Barrett a letter.

Barrett unfolds the paper and looks at the title, which is centred on the page. OPPORTUNITY #1: SACRIFICE. "*And Mil learned that day that things are just things and that no possession is more important than people.*"

Barrett holds up the paper. "This is from my first book."

"Keep reading."

Barrett's eyes return to the letter.

> *My connection between you and the copyright will give the press enough fodder to expose you completely, and if you are revealed as being connected to a company that is under investigation for child labour, your career will be destroyed.*
>
> *So, to avoid the end of your career, you will donate the equivalent you have invested in Blast to the Child Labour Project and the local Big Brothers centre equally, tomorrow, from your yacht, dressed as Sindu the starfish from Mil Bennett's imaginary world or I will release all my information to the press. You will also invite children from youth centres around the city to your yacht, where you will announce that you are donating the yacht for sale with the proceeds to be divided evenly amongst youth centres across the city.*

He reads the letter twice more, and the words make him wish for five minutes with the extortionist, five minutes to hit him until he didn't feel like a threat anymore.

"What can this really do to me?"

Sidney's not used to seeing concern on Barrett's face. The expression prompts a painful exhale.

"What can it do to us? Well, we could claim the link between you and the name Sanford Corbett is a coincidence, but it's not, and the press could care less either way, because it's enough of a story to be red hot, so they'll push until they expose more and more links. Eventually the connection will be undeniable. And then we'll be tainted. Parents buy books for their kids, and they want anyone associated with their kids to be good people. A kid's tutor may very well be an alcoholic, but if the parents find out, he's fired. A kid's soccer coach may very well cheat on his wife, but if the parents find out, they don't want the kid on his team. If this extortionist exposed your investment in a company associated with child labour, then your reputation as a humanitarian would be ruined, which means in addition to stopping any future books, the backlist would be worth next to nothing. And there's no way the toy companies will be associated with someone tied to child labour, so you can say goodbye to the bedsheets, video games, action figures, and every other spinoff we have."

And there was the truth. A reflex response to the question, but one that illuminated Barrett's real fear. This wasn't about protecting an image or a career, this was about protecting his income. Barrett's never heard Sidney so stern. Images flash through his mind of headlines calling him a monster, parents throwing out his books, whispers about him being a train wreck and aspiring writers laughing when they hear his name.

"I wouldn't be writing under a pseudonym if I was a role model, but I don't want millions of people looking down on me."

"I won't let that happen, but you're going to have play along until we catch this asshole. How much do you have invested in Blast?"

"Two million."

"Can you cover that?"

"Yeah, but I'll have to sell off some property to build that cash flow back up." Barrett lights a cigarette, and a deep drag calms him enough to continue. He points at Sidney with his smoking hand. "Who would want to punish me like this?"

"Who wouldn't?"

"What do you mean who wouldn't?"

Sidney leans his weight on the windowsill. "The paparazzi, any woman you've dated that feels used...."

"Or Evan." Barrett waves a finger in the air like he's closed the case. "That fuck could have caught wind that I'm going with another artist on the next book."

Thoughts of the artist's smug smile leave his face flushed, but Sidney doesn't allow time for contemplation.

"Any number of interns that you've treated like shit, a rival publisher...."

"Or it could be Sheryl Orange," Barrett interrupts with the dogma of a self-help guru. "That bitch has been trying to catch my sales since my second book."

"A former cleaning lady, any one of the journalists you refuse to grant an interview. But that isn't the right question. The question isn't who would do this. The question is who found out that you're Russell Niles?"

"So what do we do?"

Sidney runs a hand over his face. This is what he does every time he needs a moment. The agent game taught him early that saying the wrong thing isn't an option, so he developed a few physical crutches to buy time in crucial situations.

"I don't know entirely. Get me your security tapes and we'll see if we can find the delivery kid. For now, we start with getting someone from IT to set up this website on the sly, and we go to your fan club to see if any wackos have been making noise in the last few weeks." He hits the speaker phone with a middle finger. "Molly, I need you to call Rebecca at the Russell Niles fan club and let her know I'm coming to see her."

Barrett isn't listening. He's too busy examining a framed group photo on Sidney's desk like the extortionist could be any of them. The seventy-something man with sun spots where brown hair once flowed, the Chinese man with a goatee, and an aging man with capped teeth that give him a smile like a donkey. Any of these guys could be responsible. If they have access to Sidney, then they have access to him.

Sidney lights another cigarette just a beat after putting out his last one. "I'll tell you this much," he says before a deep inhale. "This is definitely personal."

"Why do you say that?"

Sidney holds the extortion letter to eye level.

"Because you have millions of dollars and millions more in property, and there's not one mention of wanting money in this letter."

EIGHT

Richard hasn't been on a subway since his father left. The lack of light, the confined space, and the incessant rumble of grinding metal in an underground vehicle all unnerve him. The last time he rode the subway he thought he was going to faint. The car was packed with riders squeezed shoulder to shoulder, and when a sound like the car might come off the tracks prefaced a jerk that made people scramble to hold anything to keep them on their feet, an intense dizziness made him want to leave the train. That day, he got off a stop early and vowed never to ride a subway again.

His mother still gives him fare but he puts it in an empty pickle jar every morning instead. Not taking the subway means he has to cut through the nature trail to be on time for school, and despite his disinterest in the building, being on time is very important to him. So important that just the thought of being late makes him anxious, because lateness means attention and questions about his home life that he doesn't want to answer.

His mother told him explicitly that she didn't want him in the nature trail. A few kids have been robbed there in years past and a dog was found decapitated, and the press those incidents received was enough for her to deem the heavily wooded area off limits. He doesn't like disobeying his mother, but he doesn't want to go on the subway or be late, so every morning and afternoon he cuts through the nature trail.

Sometimes on the way home he just sits and enjoys being outside. His favourite spot is on the side of a hill beside a large tree that was split in half by lightning a few years back. From the tree's girth, he figures it would take five people holding hands to circle its circumference, and yet lightning destroyed it in seconds.

Everything about the broken tree and splintered wood is violent, and the image makes him wonder what happens when lightning strikes a person.

Today, he sits on the hillside with a can of Coke. As he lets a mouthful fizz against the roof of his mouth a man walking on the path below catches his attention. People walk, jog, and ride by him regularly, but something about this guy forces him to take a closer look.

Both the physique and stride trigger something in his memory, something familiar. Richard stands up to get a better view, and shock tingles through him as he gets a glimpse of the man's side profile and realizes it's his father. The muscles in his forearms twitch. His father. A part of him wants to charge down the hill and wrap his arms around the man, but another part is too afraid to make contact, so he pushes his way through the brush and follows his father from above. The terrain is overgrown off the path and branches scratch at his hands, but the need to watch his father keeps him focused. Despite his racing heart, despite the blur of trees, he notices a lot about his father's appearance. His hair is cropped short just like Richard remembers, he wears the same style of blue jeans and black jacket that were his staples for years, and his stubble is at least a few days old. Richard assumed he would look different since leaving the family. Maybe a brighter coloured jacket, maybe a ponytail, or maybe a shaved head. But he looks the same, and if he looks the same as before, if he didn't want to be different, then why did he abandon his family?

Richard plows forward with his eyes locked downhill on the path until he stumbles on what feels like a mattress. He shuffles to the side as if he just stepped on hot coals and looks down to see he stepped on a homeless man. With wild eyes and a dirty beard creeping far too high on his face, the man makes Richard think of a caveman. A guttural yell spills out of the man's mouth, quickly followed by flailing arms that fill Richard with fear.

He wants to scream, but he knows it will draw attention, so he regains his balance and runs forward to keep pace. When he gets parallel with his father again, the man stops walking. Richard watches his father remove a cell phone from his jacket, thumb a number, and bring it to an ear. The lull is an opportunity to get closer, so he creeps down the hill to a large maple tree twice his width. A cigarette now dangles from his father's mouth as he talks on the phone, and the smell of smoke in the air makes Richard stare in disbelief. This is the smell of home, what home smelled like when they were still a family. He looks around at the trees surrounding him and the dirt at his feet and admits it is weird to realize that the odour of smoke makes outside feel more like home than his apartment has felt since his father left.

His father paces while he talks on the cell, so Richard shifts his weight to get a better look. A branch snaps beneath his feet, sending a small log rolling down the hill. The noise draws his father's attention, so Richard tries to dart behind the maple tree, but it is too late. Their eyes lock, and for a moment, while they explore each other, Richard feels a connection again, but then he blinks and before he has a second to enjoy the moment, his father turns and heads down the path.

A type of anger Richard has never felt before shoots through him, and he decides watching isn't enough. He needs to confront his father, and if the man is going to turn his back on him again, then he is going to chase.

By the time Richard reaches the path his father has twenty yards on him. The man never looks back, but Richard knows from the brisk pace that his father knows he is being followed. Richard's thoughts race to keep up with the chase. Should he beg his father to come back home? Get a phone number to call him? An address to visit?

As he closes the gap, what really drives him begins to crystallize. If he never sees his father again, he wants the chance to ask one question: How could you leave us without ever talking to us again? And it is that simple. All his research into gays and lesbians, every time he looks at his mother's sad eyes, and every step he takes now in chase, leads him to the need for that answer.

"Dad?" he yells as loud as possible. But the man doesn't turn around. His father exits the park and Richard bursts into a full sprint to close the gap. Running isn't fluent for Richard and he fights his stride, but there is no way he'll stop moving. He surfaces onto the street in time to see his father heading down the subway steps. A cab honks at Richard as he jogs across the street, but he doesn't care. The idea of going down into the subway station makes his stomach turn.

From his perspective, there appears to be hundreds of steps, and each one looks steeper than the one before the last. Instinct tells him to turn around and go home, to head for comfort, but the need to see his father burns stronger. Dozens of people move up and down the staircase, and he knows the chances of catching up with his father are fading with every passing second, so with a hand on the railing, he hustles down the steps as quickly as possible.

The ticket line is backed up ten deep at both booths. Richard looks at the westbound line up and sees his father walking through the turnstile. With no money in his pockets and two huge lineups, his options are clear. Two deep breaths fill his lungs before he charges the middle turnstile, uses his wrists for purchase and hops over the pay booth. He takes a few strides towards his father on the westbound platform, but two large hands grab him by the shoulders.

"What the hell do you think you're doing?"

Richard turns to see the face of a security guard. The man's eyes are angry. He smells of cough drops and a thick layer of fat under his chin shakes with every move he makes.

"You're too young to be doing this nonsense."

Richard strains his neck to look for his father but the platform is lined with people. "You don't understand."

"Oh, I understand."

"No sir, you don't. My mother's in the hospital. They just called my school; she got hit by a car."

"Why isn't your father taking you?"

"I've never met my father."

The security guard examines Richard's eyes for a beat then releases his grip on the boy's shoulders.

"Go on."

Richard nods thank you and beelines for the westbound platform. The rumble of a train draws people closer to the edge of the platform, but he still can't spot his father. He can hear the train approaching, so he moves faster down the platform, but there are so many people that it is difficult to focus.

He arches on his toes to get a better look but everyone blurs into indistinct masses, each jockeying for positions closest to where they anticipate the doors will stop. Richard moves toward a bench to climb and get a better look when his father steps out from behind a pillar and hugs him tight.

The lights flicker as the subway roars into the station, but Richard's face is pressed too close to his father's chest to notice. The hug feels good, so good that he doesn't want to let go, but his father's hands guide him in front so that they stand face to face. There is so much Richard wants to say, but the warmth in his father's eyes compels him to stare until the man releases him and steps onto the train. Richard wants to get on with him, but his legs won't move, and within seconds the doors close and the subway accelerates out of the station, leaving him standing alone on the platform. He wants to believe his father's stare was a look of regret, but the only thing he believes with any certainty is that he will never see the man again.

NINE

When thinking of the Russell Niles fan club, don't think comic book cult following or boy bands. Think Beatlemania or the Mouseketeers. The operation runs out of the ground floor of an old downtown house, but this is every bit a large-scale venture. To put this in perspective, the *New York Times* website receives over nineteen million hits every month. For the past two years, the Russell Niles fan club site has averaged over twenty million hits a month. That's forty grand a year in bandwidth costs alone.

In the last three years the fan club has sold over nine million books, eight hundred thousand T-shirts, and half a million dolls. This isn't just a fan club, it's a marketing empire. Most of the hard labour is contracted out to a customer service company that handles all the online orders and the suburban warehouses that hold all the products. As far as the actual fan club, there are only three full-time employees: the receptionist, Margaret, a forty-year-old with a lisp; a graphic designer, Joel, who reeks of pot and works from home three days a week; and Rebecca, the office manager and liaison between the publisher and the fan club. The irony is, Barrett's never seen any of these people.

"You've never been to the fan club, have you?" Sidney asks as he negotiates downtown traffic.

Barrett shakes his head. He wants Sidney to drive faster and continuously shifts his weight in his seat.

Sidney lights a cigarette without lowering a window. "You know, thirty-two percent of your fans are adults."

"That's sad."

"No, that's power. Kids aren't the ones paying for your books."

This is a fact that makes Barrett want to scream. What he hopes is that adults will one day read his writing because they want to, not because they have to. All stories are about being alive in his mind, and kid's stories are no more just for kids than Bugs Bunny or *The Simpsons* are for kids because they are cartoons. And while he knows there are millions of people who respect great children's writers like Roald Dahl, he also knows there are millions of people who think that true genius lies only in the adult-oriented works of Shakespeare and the rest of the award-winning literary canon that is glazed with drool from the masses. These people consider him the boy band of the literary world. The necessary introduction to reading and something that will be fondly remembered as adults, but not the same as real writers.

Barrett follows Sidney into fan club headquarters. Immediately, the Russell Niles paraphernalia overwhelms him. Blown-up book covers decorate the walls, signed copies are propped up on shelves to show off the signatures, and six-foot cardboard representations of characters fill each corner. It always surprises Barrett to see his characters in any form. Trading cards, action figures, stickers, and cartoons all freak him out. Every time he sees one of his characters it blows his mind that it's based on something he imagined. People spend their lives dreaming of making millions, and here he is a millionaire many times over and counting for imagining the right thing. People have thought of more complex things a billion times over, but few of those thoughts have the emotional purity and universal appeal of a lonely, impish child with shaggy hair.

Despite the millions, the artist in Barrett resents all of these items. They have nothing to do with writing in his mind, and it's certainly not how he wants to be remembered. He's uncomfortable, and his eyes burn with a look like he might break everything he sees.

An attractive woman in her early thirties hovers over a middle-aged woman typing at a computer until she notices Sidney.

"Hi, Molly said you were coming over."

She walks around the desk, and Sidney greets her with a handshake. "Rebecca, this is uh, Mr. Fuller. He's new in marketing."

"Welcome."

The first thing Barrett notices is how soft her hand is. The skin is dry and smooth, the type of soft that feels like it's never been touched. The second thing he notices is that she's abnormally beautiful. Not Barbie-assembled but pure. Every feature on her face works together to create a beauty that makes Barrett feel ugly. Specifically, he can't stop looking at her eyes. They are so green, with so much going on that he can care less if she thinks he's staring.

"You run the fan club?" he says.

She nods.

"I pictured someone in a muumuu with a double chin."

"Come back in twenty years."

"I'd bet my house your mother's still beautiful."

"Do you want her number?"

"Tempting, but I'd prefer yours." He turns to Sidney. "The marketing department is looking to work closer with the fan club, isn't it?"

"They are, but that's not why we came, is it?"

Rebecca picks up a stack of folders. "Why don't we talk in my office?"

Sidney nods, and they follow her down a corridor to a room without windows. This is not the type of office befitting the manager of a fan club responsible for millions in sales. It's large, but it looks more like a storage room than a working space. Rows of cardboard boxes piled four high fill the far corner of the room, books and bubble wrap take up all the seating on a black leather couch, and four old computers sit at the base of a metal file cabinet.

Rebecca sits behind a desk and Barrett and Sidney sit in front of her. Barrett immediately notices that his framed book covers fill the wall behind her, and he wonders what Rebecca would say if she knew he was the reason for this fan club.

"So how can I help you?" Rebecca asks, looking more at Sidney than Barrett would prefer.

"We've been getting some disturbing letters at the office regarding the Russell Niles books."

"How disturbing?"

"Not violent, but annoying and persistent. Have you been getting anything from particularly eager fanatics lately?"

"Every day."

And just like that she has Barrett's full attention.

"We get book ideas, people claiming the series was their idea, marriage proposals, death threats."

"Death threats?" Barrett was still processing fanatics.

His reaction makes Rebecca smile. "That's not something the marketing department wants to hear, is it?"

Barrett is thinking of being shot on the street after leaving his favourite pub when Sidney's voice snaps him into the moment.

"Do any of these letters come with return addresses?"

"Almost all of them."

"Good, I need copies of any letter that's bitter in tone, makes a threat, or is resentful."

"Of course."

Barrett leans forward. "So how many of these death threats do you get?"

"Hundreds."

"Hundreds?"

"At least two a week."

"Who wants to kill a children's author?"

"The same type of people that threaten schools, churches, hospitals. Anger's nothing without a target."

"I just never thought about death threats."

"Well, luckily you don't need to. All you to worry about is selling the books."

Sidney looks at Barrett to see how he'll respond to the irony, but Barrett is staring at the wall. Death threats? The fact that strangers want him dead leaves him puzzled. Puzzled and unnerved. Death threats are for politicians and social activists, not children's authors. For the first time, he wonders if the extortionist wants to kill him. Humiliate him, shame him, and then end his life.

Barrett doesn't say anything while Sidney drives him home, until the car stops in front of his mansion. Sidney takes a deep drag and points at Barrett with his cigarette.

"You know how you win in this situation?"

Barrett looks at him like winning is impossible.

"You keep writing."

"Spoken like a true agent."

"You stop writing, you get distracted, and this asshole wins."

This is where years of friendship have sway. If any of the country's other agents used this tone they'd risk getting fired, but two decades of friendship supersedes tone.

Sidney taps the steering wheel with an index finger. "When are you taking care of this first demand?"

"First thing tomorrow."

"Do you want to talk about it?"

"Talking about it won't stop it from happening."

TEN

Richard doesn't talk much with his mother. She spends most of her time on the phone in her bedroom and chooses to acknowledge him more with hugs than words. Their time together consists mostly of occupying the same room while watching television. Game shows, reality shows, murder mysteries, old black and white movies, anything that makes noise, anything that makes it seem like there is something else to do other than think about being abandoned. Their place is small, but it's on the ground floor of a three-storey building, so they have a patio large enough for a table and chairs and a few potted flowers in the spring and summer. When his father was around, there was talk of moving to a house, but now that they are living only on his mother's pay as a graphic designer running a small business, that talk disappeared. A reality show about people losing weight is playing when Richard decides to add a live voice.

"Did Dad ever talk about when he was a kid?"

"Why?"

"I'd like to know some stories."

"I don't think we should talk about that now."

"Why?"

"Because I don't have anything nice to say about your father."

"I don't have to hear nice things."

She gets up from the couch and heads for the kitchen. This isn't what Richard wants. The idea is to talk about his father, to get a better understanding of the man that co-created him and to bond with his mother, not to upset her or push away the only blood family he has left.

Richard walks to the hall closet and grabs a white moving box from the second shelf. This is the box he wasn't allowed to touch for years; these are his father's possessions, but the man did leave without them, so Richard figures they are fair game.

He takes the box into his room so his mother won't react and removes the first item, a bone pipe the length of his forearm. A scoop of the pipe's dish reveals it was used often, and as he rubs the residue between his index finger and thumb, he imagines the pipe in his father's mouth.

The next thing he removes is a silver watch with a brown leather band. He straps the worn leather to his wrist and winds the second hand a few times, but it still doesn't move. He wonders how long his father wore the watch. A dark blue silk scarf at the side of the box draws his eyes. The fabric still smells of cologne, and as he holds it to his nose, he thinks of his father in the black suit he wore for special occasions, like the time they went to the circus for his mother's birthday.

A wooden bowl catches his attention next. The hand-made grain looks new and without shellac it still smells of pine. Three rubber bands sit in the bowl's centre. He hooks one with a finger and slips it over his wrist. After pushing aside a hammer and a wrench, he exposes a pair of silver cuff links that look so old, he wonders if they belonged to his grandfather; wonders if

75

they are something meant to be passed on from one generation to another.

A business card is stuck to the bowl's bottom. Parts of it stick to the bowl as Richard pulls it off so he can inspect the maroon card with gold trim. MIDNIGHT LOUNGE. The card smells of his dad's cologne, and a phone number written in black pen is beveled.

The number immediately sparks an idea, and Richard hustles down the hall, looks to see if his mom is in the living room, and grabs the phone. Three deep breaths give him the composure to punch in the number. Every ring seems like minutes, and with each one his heart flutters until he feels a wave of dizziness that almost makes him hang up when a man answers.

"Hello?"

The voice is rich and confident, like someone used to being in charge.

For a moment, Richard freezes. He knows what he wants to say, but he can't will his tongue to move.

"Hello?" the man tries again.

And then finally the words come out. "Can I speak to Malcolm, please?"

"Malcolm?"

"Yes."

The question is met with a dial tone, and Richard almost drops the phone. Either his father is there or the man knows him, and either way he has to call back. He hits redial and within seconds the phone rings again, only this time no one answers, and no voice mail ever picks up. He lets it ring twenty times until it's clear that no one will answer.

Richard hangs up determined to go to Midnight. He searches for an address online, but the only midnight is a nightclub in Amsterdam, so it takes the phone book to get details. After finding a Midnight paintball range and Midnight massage parlour,

Richard finds the Midnight lounge, writes down the address, and heads for the top drawer of his desk where he keeps his money in a Ziploc bag. The last time he checked, there was twenty dollars and seventy-five cents.

This mission requires precision, so just to be sure he takes it out and counts it again. Three fives, eighteen quarters, twelve dimes, and a nickel. The smell of metal makes him wince but this is no time to be fragile.

A light rain greets him as he steps outside. He tries to hail a cab, but the first two just drive past him. They ignore him because of his age, so he walks closer to a man with a briefcase in one hand and a cell phone in the other. This is the consummate businessman. With a dark suit under a trench coat, freshly cut thick hair and a clean-shaven face, this is the type of man cabs look for. Sure enough, the next one stops, and when Richard slides into the back seat, the heavy-set driver with only tuffs of hair left on his head turns to him with a scowl.

"Just you?"

Richard holds up the money for credibility and passes him Midnight's address.

"Here, please."

The driver examines him for a moment, seems impressed that he maintains eye contact, then hits the meter. The cab smells like tuna, so Richard opens the window a little. The driver looks at him in the rear-view mirror with a smile that reveals two missing bottom teeth.

"You're a little young to be going to a bar, aren't you?"

"I'm meeting my dad."

The man nods, pops a cigarette between his lips, and turns onto the road. Midnight is only ten minutes away by car, but ten minutes into the city's core, where neighbourhoods and par-kettes give way to buildings and traffic.

They drive past the homeless begging and smoking other peoples' cast-away butts, squeegee teens splashing dirty water on the windshields of unhappy drivers, and a seemingly never-ending flow of people walking down, up, and across the streets. The driver honks at a jaywalker in a mini-skirt and stops in front of Midnight. Richard looks at the meter: eleven-fifty. He keeps a dollar fifty for bus fare and passes the driver eighteen and a quarter.

"Thanks kid," the driver says, genuinely impressed. Richard steps out of the car to see a woman sitting in front of Midnight on a wooden stool with many chips in its brown paint. Her head wobbles on her neck, and she smokes a cigarette as if the nicotine is oxygen. Scabs cover the pale skin of both forearms and a burn disfigures the top of her right hand, leaving what should be a network of veins and tendons a thick mass that resembles window caulking. Richard looks up and admires the black font against a grey backdrop that looks three-dimensional on Midnight's hanging sign.

The woman on the stool erupts into a coughing fit as he walks past her. He's approaching the door when a teenager with pale skin, a shaved head, and a jacket with a fur hood stops him.

"Where are you going, little man?"

Everything about this guy makes Richard nervous. The anger in his tone, his vacant eyes, and the aggression in his body language.

"To see my dad."

"In there?"

Richard nods and the teen laughs.

"You know what goes on in there?"

Richard nods again.

"Don't lie. You're lost, aren't you?"

As confused as Richard feels, instinct tells him to stay quiet.

"Are you giving me attitude, you little shit?"

The increased aggression is confusing, so Richard takes a step back. The woman on the stool stares into traffic as if they don't exist.

The teen gestures to Richard's wrist. "I like your watch." Everything about the teen's tone suggests this isn't a compliment. "Do you like it?"

A verbal response feels necessary so he manages, "Yeah."

The teen removes a metal baton the width of a soup spoon from his pocket and flicks it so that it extends in length. "Enough to get cracked on the head for it? Because that's what's going to happen if you don't take it off and put it in my pocket in the next minute."

Fear shoots through Richard and suddenly he feels like he might throw up, cry, and faint all at once. The teen steps closer to him. Midnight's door opens and a slight man with blond hair and a white dress shirt points at the teen with a baseball bat.

"What did I tell you about coming around here?"

The teen hustles off down the street and Richard hears a trail of "Fuck you fag...." before turning to the blond man, who now faces the woman on the stool.

"Let's go, honey. There's better places for you to hang than in front of this bar." The woman wobbles off on cue and the man turns to Richard. Looking at the man's face, Richard realizes this isn't just a man, it's the man he saw kissing his father on the bathroom floor. The man speaks, but all Richard can do is look on in shock.

"The asshole that approached you has been robbing kids all year around here. You're better to just run when you see trash like that coming," he says.

Richard hears the man, but he isn't listening anymore, because this isn't just a bar owner, it's the man partly responsible for his father leaving.

The man exhales in frustration and lowers the baseball bat. "You recognize me, right?"

Richard nods.

"I know why you're here, but you need to go home, kid."

Richard doesn't move, partly because he has too many questions to ask but mostly because he is overwhelmed.

"You're not going to leave, are you?"

Richard shakes his head.

"Okay." The man sits on the bar's stoop, sets the bat down, and removes a pack of cigarettes from his breast pocket. "Look, I don't know what to say to you, but you've made your way here, so if you have questions, ask them."

He lights a cigarette and Richard watches him for a moment. The man looks younger than the image in his memory, and his eyes are warmer.

"What's your name?" Richard asks.

"Kellen."

"Is this your bar?"

"Hell, no. I'm a bartender. I've been working here the past five years."

"Does my dad come here?"

"He used to. All the time for a while, but I don't see him as much anymore."

"You're not together?"

"Together?" Kellen lights his cigarette, draws deep, and exhales a steady stream of smoke. "No, we were never together."

"Do you know where he lives?"

"Now? Somewhere in Brazil, I guess."

"Where's that?"

"South America."

The words sting. He's not sure where South America is, but he knows it's another part of the world. "When did he go there?"

"A couple days ago, I heard."

"Why?"

"I have no idea. It's not like he told me. I heard it from somebody else." Kellen looks at the consternation building in Richard's eyes. "I imagine you hate me."

"I don't hate you," Richard says. "I hate that he left."

Kellen grabs the front door's handle. "I've got to get back inside. How are you getting home?"

Home. Richard can care less about home at this moment. "The bus, I guess."

Kellen reaches into his pocket and pulls out a bunched-up twenty dollar bill. "Take a cab."

"It's okay."

"I insist. You deserve it for coming here."

Richard takes the money and Kellen disappears inside. Brazil. A part of Richard wants to earn the money and go there, but another part of him knows better. That part knows that this is only another chapter in a longing that will last a lifetime.

ELEVEN

Barrett puts on the starfish's pointy headpiece and looks at his reflection through the costume's basketball-sized opening for his face. Monkeys in miniature sports uniforms don't look this ridiculous. With white tights to his knees, a white kilt, and Styrofoam points covering his arms and legs, he looks like he should be greeting guests for some seafood franchise or leading a crowd through cheers as a team mascot.

He drops himself onto a leather recliner in the yacht's master bedroom and acknowledges that most people don't have bedrooms this large in their main residence. A picturesque sun draws his attention through the side window until the reflection of his giant, pointy headpiece sparks a series of memories. Three of the best nights of his life happened on this yacht. Coming in third is the night he had sex with two Parisian supermodels after the yacht provided the background for a photo shoot. That night he lived for every young man that was ever hypnotized by a swimsuit issue. Number two on the list brings a smile to his face every time he thinks about the evening. After hosting yet another night of debauchery, he found himself lying on the deck staring up at the stars when a man with a thick Russian slur asked him for a cigarette. Only this wasn't just a man, it was renowned math genius Sergey Tsakoev. That was his first night in the country, and he held a bottle of Scotch in his large hand like he planned on dying with it. Barrett gave him half a pack of cigarettes, and as they smoked and drank, Sergey explained that Russians only received surnames in the population census of 1897 and that the last names were based on the father's first names. For example, if the father's name was Ivan, than the last name would be Ivanov, which was the appropriate answer to the question, "Whose are you?"

After their fifth drink, Sergey convinced Barrett that numbers are not just the universal language but the spark of modern civilization. They calculated the odds of existing and then Barrett passed out. When the sun woke him up the next morning, Sergey was gone, but there was an empty bottle of Scotch beside Barrett's head. Cigarette butts half-filled the bottle and the symbol for pi was written on the glass in black marker. The bottle now sits in Barrett's home office, and he enjoys looking at it as much as anything else in the home.

But his favourite night on the yacht stands alone. That was the time he met emerging porn star Jenn Kutz, aka Amber Breeze, the night before her mainstream debut in a horror movie. With shocked blonde hair, a lean body, and a beach tan that east coasters can't pay enough to replicate, she was a fusion of all his most satisfying fantasies. And they hit it off immediately. Her laugh inspired him to be charming. Somewhere between throaty and mischievous, her voice made him want to keep her talking. Their rhythms flowed, and then she offered him an 80 mg Oxycontin. Thirty minutes and three tequila shots later, they sat cross-legged in their underwear with a Scrabble board between them. Deep in the muck of their high this felt appropriate, and he has never enjoyed words as much. Stripped of pretense, etiquette, and norms, they laughed with the purity of children. One turn he spelled "apple" while thinking of an "orange" and another he stared at his tiles with a grin for fifteen minutes before she poked him in the stomach, and in the end he spent one of the greatest nights of his life with a porn star and didn't have sex.

Barrett lights a cigarette, peers through the cabin window at a crowd of kids entering the deck, and hates the extortionist with an anger that makes him want to throw a tantrum. To yell and whine and tell anyone that will listen that it isn't fair, until someone tells him he can keep the yacht.

Barrett never intended the Sindu character to be so popular. As part of Mil's imaginary world, Sindu represents the years when stuffed animals soothed him, and while he has little interest in the character, Sindu has developed a huge following with kids. He is cute, loyal, and relatable, and as a result, in three of the last five years, Sindu dolls have sold almost as much as Mil Bennett, so as Barrett looks at the pointy head of his reflection and exhales a cloud of smoke, he wonders what those fans would think of Sindu now.

The youth centres accepted Barrett's invitation and brought kids from their programs. These are not well-manicured, well dressed kids. These are kids that wear faded T-shirts. Their bodies are either skinny from a lack of food or flabby from cheap food. Kraft dinner, canned ravioli, grilled processed cheese, and two-for-one pizza slices contribute to the jowls belying their youth. They sit cross-legged on the floor and fill the deck. Some poke others in the ribs, others wait patiently, and all of them are excited. Small, dirty footprints smudge the white floor that is usually walked on by high heels and manicured feet. Barrett winces from his spot in the doorway where he can see them without being seen. To him, they look as out of place on the deck as a toy stethoscope in an operating room. He takes a final drag, butts it out in a crystal ashtray the shape of a hexagon, and walks slowly onto the deck. The kids cheer wildly and he absorbs their enthusiasm for a moment before nodding at Sidney, who begins recording the event with a video camera in the far corner.

Barrett should start speaking, but he can't take his eyes off the chocolate staining the corners of the mouth of a fat kid to his left. He wants to toss the kid a wet-nap, but he knows he is running out of time, so he clears his throat and steps to the microphone.

"It's my pleasure to, uh, to be with you today to announce that I am donating one million dollars each to The Child Labor Project and the Big Brothers Program. And, that ..."

For a moment, he imagines tossing himself over the side and into the water. "And that the proceeds from the sale of this yacht will be divided among your centres evenly."

Everyone screams and the kids begin to chant. "Sindu song! Sindu song!"

Barrett begins to turn from the microphone, but Sidney offers a quick shake of his head to keep him on track. Barrett curses the marketing people for creating the jingle, but there is no escaping the tune. Between toy commercials and the cartoon, the Sindu song has successfully burrowed into his subconscious like a bad pizza jingle.

He thinks about the beach house in the Canary Islands and the way the azure water looks like glass at dawn. He thinks about the banana chocolate chip crepes he eats at a one-hundred-year-old-picnic table at his place in Paris. He thinks about the adult award show after party that he hosts every year at his Vegas compound. He thinks about all of these luxuries, and the words spill out of his mouth.

"S.I.N.D.U. Sindu's about love and ..." With the microphone extended towards the crowd, the kids take over. Their collective voice is more a movement than a sound.

"We are too!"

Barrett pivots and leaves the deck as fast as possible. Back at the mansion, he stands in his massive backyard and passes Sidney a photo of him dressed in the Starfish suit for the Once Upon a Hypocrite website.

"I never claimed to be a role model. All this just happened."

"I know."

Barrett knows this isn't Sidney's favourite part of being an agent, but he also knows his friend understands how important it is to be a soundboard, a source of reinforcement.

And as Barrett carries the Starfish costume's mid-section to a metal drum beside them and drops it inside, he knows he has never needed Sidney more.

"I loved that yacht."

"I know," Sidney says calmly.

Barrett hustles back to the patio and picks up the Starfish costume head, tights, and boots so that his arms are full as he heads back to the drum.

"I drank Scotch with Sergey Tsakoev on that yacht."

"I know."

"Not vodka, Scotch. With Sergey Tsakoev."

"I know."

Barrett stuffs any overflowing material into the drum, picks up a can of fuel from the ground, and dowses the costume. He attempts to spark a lighter and grows increasingly frustrated with every failed strike, until Sidney extends a match.

"Thank you."

The flame only promises a small measure of revenge, but he'll take it. He drops the match and the drum bursts into orange, leaving the two of them to watch in silence as the Starfish costume burns.

Thirty minutes later, Sidney tries to focus Barrett with a few pints at one of his favourite pubs. As an agent, his job is to think ahead, and he knows they need his foresight more than ever. People have been trying to find out who Russell Niles is since the publication of his first book.

A few angry journalists bent on revenge after being snubbed for interviews even tried to claim that Russell Niles was actually a famous athlete that hides behind a pseudonym because no one would take the writing seriously otherwise, but as the copies pushed into bestseller numbers, the rumours faded under the power of success. For a while, it was common to read tabloid articles about Russell Niles sightings around the world. One picture of a beer-bellied man with a sunburn and a panama hat covering most of his eyes had the caption: RUSSELL NILES SPOTTED ON TOBAGO BEACH. Another photo of a dashing young man at a London pub had the caption: FAMOUS AUTHOR REVEALS HE'S JUST AN UNDERGRAD. But Barrett's personal favourite is a picture of an elderly East Indian man with a caption that claims that he uses the pseudonym Russell Niles so that his ideas will be accepted by North Americans.

Sidney used to encourage Barrett to sue until the publisher realized that the more attention these rumours received, the more copies of the Mil Bennett books they sold.

The Russell Niles intrigue has such a mystique that an aspiring young journalist, Brittany Holmes, started *www. whoisrussellniles?.com* and created a cult following of her own. Unlike many editors who filter their sources in search of the rare grains of truth with true market value, Brittany encourages the extremists, whack jobs, and fanatics. If you have a theory about who Russell Niles is, she'll add it to the blog, and if you have a picture she'll happily post it without any questions. This is about quantity, traffic, and one rumour fueling the next. This is a way of doing business that gets her three hundred thousand hits a week and guest spots on talk radio shows as the Russell Niles aficionado.

"You really think it's her?" Barrett asks across a basket of chicken wings.

"Who has more to gain than that gossip whore?"

"You're right, she's worth a visit."

And Sidney doesn't even stop eating to set up the meeting — he simply texts his personal assistant, who tracks down Brittany Holmes' personal email and then sends Brittany an email saying that he would like to meet to see if she has any book ideas. And before they finish their food, Brittany agrees to meet that evening at a raw food restaurant in the west end.

The drive to the raw food restaurant is quiet until Barrett taps the dashboard.

"Don't introduce me from marketing this time."

"What do you care?"

"I hate marketing."

"So, this time you'll be an editor."

"I don't like editors either."

"Have some fun with it. We're talking about her book ideas anyway."

Barrett thinks about it for a second then nods his approval while lighting a cigarette.

The raw food restaurant makes Barrett think of rehab centres. Sterile, paranoid, bland places driven by dogma and guilt. He long ago promised himself he would never go to rehab or become a vegetarian, and if there wasn't so much at stake, he would rather have his arm hairs plucked out one at a time than enter a raw food restaurant.

They meet Brittany Holmes at a booth adjacent to the juice bar, and Barrett is immediately shocked by her appearance. When he heard journalist, he stamped her as a strong-jawed, stoic woman with her hair in a bun, but Brittany looks more like a model.

Long brown hair styled with seventies drop curls, mink eyelashes that accentuate hazel eyes, and a collared black dress that reveals a five-times a week at the gym body frame her as a stock character from any one of Barrett's fantasies. This is a woman destined to take over the Hollywood gossip scene.

A waiter with receding red hair and a T-shirt with the slogan THINK GREEN approaches. "Good evening, Ms. Holmes, what can I get you?"

"A pot of chai tea, please."

"And for you sir?" he asks Sidney.

"What are our options in terms of liquor?"

"We have an organic microbrewery on tap."

"How about vodka?" Barrett adds.

"I'm sorry, sir, we don't serve hard liquor here."

"Two pints will be fine, thank you."

"They come in half pints."

"Then we'll have four," Barrett adds, doing his best to kill the waiter with a glare.

It's time for Sidney to do what he does best. Focus the conversation, disarm, flatter. He addresses Brittany. "Thank you for meeting us on such short notice."

"My pleasure."

Barrett can't take his eyes off her lips. Forget lipstick, they look like they were born red.

"I was surprised you'd want to meet with me, considering you represent Russell Niles."

"Well, I'm in the business of making money and you get

three hundred thousand hits a week, which could translate into a lot of money."

She smiles in agreement. "You know I'll be writing about our meeting on the website."

"I wouldn't have it any other way."

The arrogance sparks Barrett. "What do you think of the Russell Niles books?"

She looks straight into his eyes. "I think they are some of the most inane, immature works ever published."

It's hard to tell whether she's toying with him or being honest, but he knows to find out he has to keep his composure. "I couldn't agree more. In fact, I'll take it a step further. I think it's a sad reflection of our society that his books sell so many copies."

She smiles mischievously and Sidney raises a finger. "Easy. I am the man's agent, and I don't care why the books sell, I just care that they do."

Brittany pats the top of Sidney's hand. "Which is why I agreed to this meeting." Her gold phone vibrates on the table, prompting her to stand up and excuse herself.

She isn't fully out of sight when Barrett leans into Sidney. "So what do you think?"

"I think she's hot. And innocent."

"I don't know. It feels like she's fucking with me."

"I disagree."

"Excuse yourself."

"What?"

"Use the washroom or something."

She walks back to the table, and it's clear that in heels she's at least six feet. "Sorry, we just had a call from a woman who claims she's pregnant with Russell Niles' baby."

Even as a figment of someone's demented mind, the words unnerve Barrett.

Sidney rises from the table and gestures to the back of the restaurant. "That way to the washroom?"

"Straight to the back on your left," she says while thumbing a text message into her cell.

Barrett waits until she's finished. "Now that he's gone, you've got to tell me. With all your expertise, who do you think Russell Niles is?"

"Do you promise you won't repeat this?"

"Of course."

"Swear on your testicles."

"This better be good."

"Do it."

"I swear on my testicles I won't repeat what you're about to say."

"You better hope you don't."

The look on her face is convincing, but Barrett knows he needs to move this along before Sidney returns.

"So? Who do you think he is?"

"I'm not sure yet, but I know who he isn't."

"Really? And who isn't he?"

"He's not the man this last attention seeker claims impregnated her."

"Why's that?"

"Because Russell Niles isn't a man."

"And how do you know that?"

"Because it's obvious a lesbian writes these stories. The villainizing of materialism, the heroism of mothers and female role models, the bashing of traditional male roles and expectations. When you look at the Mil Bennett books as a collection, it's clear they're more than allegorical, they're ideological."

Relief comes to him in the form of a smug smile. "You really think Russell Niles is a lesbian?"

"I know she is, and soon enough, I'll prove it."

"Amazing."

"What's amazing?" Sidney asks, returning to the table.

"I'm going out for a cigarette, but you need to hear this," Barrett says with a gesture to Brittany.

Once the cigarette touches his lips, the humour dissipates into a stark reality. All Brittany's innocence proves is that he's no closer to discovering the extortionist and that there is a website about him devoted to nurturing the most extreme rumours in circulation. And none of that information will bring his yacht back.

TWELVE

Richard is surprised to see a supply teacher when he arrives at school. He can't remember Mr. Davis missing a day, and while he can care less about adverbs or hot writing, the eager look on the supply's face unnerves him.

The supply looks at the clock and then over to Richard. He leans into the desk enough that Richard gets a full blast of his coffee breath. "And what's your name?"

The attention makes Richard shift his weight in his seat. "Richard."

The supply examines him for a moment with an intense look of concentration. "You're cutting it close today."

The man's presence makes him so uncomfortable that it takes him a moment to realize that he is referring to almost being late. Richard nods, hoping that will get rid of him, and the supply rises and backs up to address the class.

"Good morning, all. My name is Mr. Phelps and I'll be your teacher for the next month." The class groans and Phelps raises an index finger. "Mr. Davis had a fall." The class now stirs with concern. "He's okay, but he's hurt his hip, and he'll need some time to recover. Which means that I'll be with you for the next twenty days."

Richard looks at Phelps. Short, with little left of his blond hair, his belly hangs over his pants despite perfect posture, and his heavily wrinkled brow droops unusually low over his eyes. This is not a man who projects happiness. He paces from one end of the class to the other, and with each step he snaps the toes of his shoe forward to heighten the click.

"To begin, we are going to read a poem about family. Please take out your texts and turn to page forty-eight."

Richard flips to the page and looks at the title. THE WEB OF LIFE. A flash of his mother's face the day his father left fills his mind, and while he stares at the poem all he sees is a blank page. He hears Mr. Phelps ask a kid in the front row to read the first stanza, but all he can think about is the afternoon he heard his parents fight over money. The argument happened a good six months before his father left, but he had never heard them so angry with each other, and he wonders if that fight was the start of their ending.

"Excellent," Phelps says with spittle spraying from his lips. "Please read the second stanza," he says, gesturing to a boy at the back of the class with a shaved head and a cut in the middle of his lip. The kid begins to read, and Richard guesses that this is Mr. Phelps' favourite poem. He looks at his fancy watch, replays the way he pronounces words, and knows he comes from a great family. He is sure that these lines about holiday dinners, tobogganing, with siblings and summer trips to the cottage aren't just lines for him, they are memories. "Excellent," Phelps says again. He pivots toward Richard.

"Richard? Can you read stanza three, please?"

Richard glances at the first line. The love between ... He would rather chew glass than read the third stanza. "Pass," he says.

Phelps stops pacing. "Pass?"

They stare at each other long enough for Richard to notice all the shades of purple in the bags beneath Phelps' eyes. Richard nods to confirm his position.

"Okay. Then I'll do the honour. The love between them filled the room and they communicated more in that moment of silence than people do in a day's worth of conversation." He continues to read, but Richard is too busy wondering if the man has a son to listen. And if he has a son, is he as bad a father as he is a teacher?

Or is he as passionate about fatherhood as he is about the lines he's reading? Richard listens to the toes of Phelps' shoes click on the tile and decides that if the man has a family, he is willing to abandon them.

"Next, we are going to free-write."

Richard waits for a ripple of grumbles or Jayson with ADD to make a farting noise, but Phelps is new and aggressive enough that everyone plays along.

"I want you to take yourself back to the greatest day of your life, and for the next five minutes you are going to write down every detail you can remember."

Richard feels his throat tighten. He clears it twice until the girl next to him looks at him like he's weird.

The greatest day of his life. He thinks of his ninth birthday party, when his mother arranged for a dunk tank and a trampoline, the time he stayed up twenty-four hours playing video games, and the night his dad took him to a bar to watch a boxing fight on the big screen in a room full of men that swore, yelled, and treated him like he was just another guy. But none of those memories are the greatest days of his life. That designation goes to the day his mom and dad took sick days to take him to a water park north of the city. His mother convinced him to go on the thirty-foot free-fall slide by going first, and his dad joined him in the wave pool, even though he can't swim. He felt different about life that day, and the feeling lasted for a few weeks. They were supposed to go to the park again the next summer, but then his dad left. He hasn't mentioned the water park to his mother since.

"Okay," Phelps said with a smack of his lips. "Let's hear some samples. Richard, start us off, please."

"Pass."

"You just passed. And my guess is with that attitude, you pass every day."

Richard locks eyes with him. "Pass."

The class now oohs and the buzz causes Phelps' face to flush. "Look," he says, putting a hand on Richard's desk, just above the paper. "If you're going to be a member of this class then you have to contribute. Now, read us what's on the page."

Richard stares through him in defiance.

Phelps taps the desk with an index finger. "You must have written something, and I'd like to hear it."

Richard grabs his paper and raises it slowly to reveal FUCK YOU written in block capitals. Phelps breaks into a weird smile.

"That seems about right. You're out of here. Straight to the principal."

Defeat leaves Richard too weak to do anything but rise from his desk in compliance. He wants to shove the free-write paper down Phelp's throat. He wants to hit the man with a book and erase that awkward smile. He wants to punch him in the balls and remind him that he's not God, but he doesn't do anything.

At home, Richard sits on a couch in the living room and waits for his mother to get off the phone. He knows what the principal is saying, he knows how bad it sounds, and worst of all, he knows his mother will never understand how he felt when he told Mr. Phelps to fuck off. She hangs, pivots toward him, and he palms the armrest to brace himself.

"What were you thinking?"

"He was picking on me."

"Asking you to participate in class is picking on you?"

"It was how he was doing it."

"That's lame. You swore at a teacher and you know that's wrong. And not long ago you hit a kid. And you knew that was wrong. I'm making an appointment with a therapist. And ..."

"But ..." Before he can get out the next word her volume silences him.

"And I know you don't want to go, but I love you and I won't let this self-destructive behaviour continue, and I'll do anything I have to that gets you to a positive place. That's what you do when you love someone, and when you grow up I know you'll be willing to do the same for your family."

He drops his head until she leaves the room and thinks about her words. He knows she wants the words to help him reflect and mature, but all they do is reinforce his fear that wherever he is, his father doesn't love him anymore.

The next day he sits beside his mother in Dr. Burns' office. The layout is different than he expected. Both he and his mother sit in leather armchairs instead of a couch, and the doctor is perched on a long-legged wooden stool. Richard looks at Dr. Burns and thinks the man seems pleased with himself. He is tall and angular with large white teeth and a smile that is too big to be natural. With thick brown hair just long enough to run his hands through and thin-rimmed glasses, he is handsome.

Dr. Burns leans forward to make it clear his attention is on Richard. "You should know before we begin that your mother selected me because of my reputation for innovative techniques, so I won't be asking you about your feelings and quietly taking notes while you pour your heart out. This will be intensely interactive."

Richard's face shows he can care less.

"Your mother said you've been having some problems at school. Do you want to talk about them?"

Richard stares past him to the eggshell-coloured wall and wonders what outer space would look like if it was white.

"It's been eleven months since your father left, correct?"

"Twelve in a week," his mother adds.

Burns' eyes are still locked on Richard. "Feeling sad and stressed is expected when there is a change in the family structure. Sometimes those feelings take a while to surface, and sometimes those feelings come out in our behaviour. Are you sure you don't want to talk about what happened at school?"

Richard's mind is still on a white outer space with black stars, so his mother taps his knee.

"Go ahead. Dr. Burns is here to help us."

"No need to rush," the doctor says. He passes Richard an empty journal with a generic yellow happy face on the cover. "I want you to start writing down your feelings. The simple act of putting your stress on paper helps release the anxiety that's upsetting you."

Richard looks at the happy face, and for a moment he's sure it winked at him.

Burns turns to Richard's mother. "I'm going to start him on Ritalin to help with the anxious energy."

"Okay." Her tone is positive, but she can't hide the concern in her eyes.

The doctor opens a folder, removes a brochure, and passes it to her. She looks at the picture of a Chinese boy sitting with an overweight redheaded kid at a round table.

They appear to be looking at a textbook and both faces are full of purpose. The title reads: A PARENT'S GUIDE TO MEDICAL THERAPY.

"Ritalin has a high rate of success, but you should be aware of the side effects."

"What's a side effect?" Richard asks.

"Nothing to worry about," his mother says.

Burns looks at Richard until he has the kid's attention. "Side effects are things that can happen to your body when you take a certain medication. They shouldn't be hidden from you because of your age. You have the right to know."

The image of blood running from his ears flashes in Richard's mind. "Like what?"

"It's all laid out in the brochure for your mother to be aware of, but you don't need to think about it."

"But it's going to happen to me."

"Chances are nothing will happen."

"It's just precautionary," his mother intervenes. "In case people need to know."

"Like what?" he says again.

Burns scribbles something in a folder. "Do you often feel like this when you don't get what you want?"

"I just want to know what the side effects are."

"I have prescribed this medication to hundreds of people, and I assure you that the benefits to your life far outweigh the potential hiccups."

"Can I die from taking these pills?"

"Of course not." His mother can't hide her concern or her need to touch him, so she rubs the top of his hand.

Burns nods at Richard's mother and gestures to the pamphlet, which prompts her to open it to the side effects page and hand it to the boy. The list fills the page, and he doesn't recognize most of the words, and the ones that he does don't offer any comfort. Diarrhea, dry mouth, headache, joint pain, skin rash, stomach pain. His throat tightens and he restrains a gag. This is what passes for help? He may be sitting in evil Phelps' class next week with a red rash on each arm and shit in his pants, but as long as he does it quietly everyone will be happy. He imagines the happy face on the journal sticking out his tongue and wishes he could rip the paper into a thousand pieces.

THIRTEEN

Barrett can't say he values money. He understands the power and he enjoys its luxury, but he has never been precious about a dollar. Whether it was the first royalty cheque he received for two hundred thousand dollars or the day his bank account hit five million, he has always spent what he has. And as long as there is more coming in, he never worries about waste or saving for the future. But with the first extortion demand leaving two million dollars and a million-dollar yacht gone in a day, each one of those dollars takes on new importance. Two million dollars equals selling eight hundred thousand copies. That's years of branding, that's hundreds of thousands in marketing, that's one for every person in San Francisco.

During the past decade, his spending account has never been this low, and he feels an urgency to get back to his comfort zone. He considers his properties. There's no way he is selling the condo in Vegas. He's had so many amazing nights there that he would be buried in the place if he could. He thinks of the back-yard in the south of France, the outdoor pool table at the farm in Italy, and the view of the ocean from the beach house in the

Canary Islands. He loves all of these places, he'll feel incomplete without any of them, and while he'll be able to buy more in the future if he plays along with the extortionist, the properties are his and the thought of selling any of them makes him sick. He picks up a dart, storms over to where the extortion letter is taped above his computer, and stabs the centre of the demand.

He hits speakerphone and punches in Gerry's number. Gerry has been his accountant since the beginning of his writing career, and his spending philosophy is Barrett's antithesis. Gerry's been an accountant for thirty-one years, he's seen markets boom and bust twice over, and he swears by investments over purchases.

"How are you doing, kid?" Gerry's voice is cigarette-roasted and he punctuates the question with a cough.

"I've been better."

"I've known you ten years and I haven't heard this tone in your voice once. Don't tell me you started gambling. Because your personality and gambling ..."

"I'm not gambling."

"Thank god." Gerry coughs and makes a noise that emphasizes it's a painful one.

"I want you to put the farm in Italy up for sale."

"Swear to me you're not gambling."

"I'm not gambling."

"You love Italy."

"I do. And it kills me to make this call, but it is what it is at the moment, and if I can ask you not to ask any questions right now, that would help."

There is a beat of silence before Gerry begins to cough again but quickly stifles the eruption. "Anything you want, kid. You know me."

"Thank you, Gerry."

"Just let me know if I can do anything else."

Barrett should try to use these feelings to write, but all he can think about is going out anywhere that might get his mind off the extortion.

The playground of choice is his favourite strip club, and nothing about this is generic. This is for millionaires only. Booths are a grand an hour and completely over the top. He leans his back into the booth's leather and can feel his blood pressure settling with every passing minute.

The eighties music pumping out from the speakers, the soothing overhead lighting, and welcome burn of his Scotch all contribute to distract him. This is what he knows as comfortable, this is his perpetual daydream.

This glassed-in booth is the most private one in the place. He could have an orgy in the room if he wanted to, but this visit isn't about sex, it's about forgetting. To his right is a blonde with legs that would make Hugh Hefner jealous. She runs her neatly manicured fingers over his forearm before examining his eyes.

"Rough day, baby?"

The daydream now eclipses his yacht and the place in Italy.

"It's getting better."

The woman laughs and lights a cigarette. Then another woman enters the booth. Her red hair is brushed into a tight fountain ponytail, and her dress shirt and pants define her as working at the coat check. She passes Barrett a manila envelope, which is heavier than it looks.

"Some kid just dropped this off for you."

"What kid?"

"Some Spanish kid, too young to be a courier. Maybe like twelve."

"Did he mention my name?"

"No, he just handed me the package with your name on it and asked if you were here. He was real polite."

Barrett nods a thank-you before looking at the envelope. No address, no stamps, no other markings of any kind. Just a fat bulge in the middle. He turns to the blonde.

"Can we pick this up in a few minutes?"

"Of course, baby." She rubs his leg playfully, but he doesn't feel anything. He's too busy imagining what is in the package. She points to the stage. "They're playing my song anyway."

Barrett doesn't give her the goodbye she wants, so she exits the booth and heads for another booth packed with suits at the far end of the room.

Now that he's alone, he takes a deep breath and opens the envelope by tearing the top corner and slitting the rest with an index finger. He removes a letter first. The paper is heavy stock with twelve-point font and a quote in the centre. A quick scan of the second sentence places it from his third book. A shiver runs up his forearms, but he reads anyway: OPPORTUNITY #2: NOTHING IS MORE IMPORTANT THAN FAMILY. *"After all his family gave him that summer, Mil was able to give something back, and nothing he had accomplished felt as satisfying."*

He steps outside the booth to see if anyone is watching, but all eyes are on a statuesque black woman moving as if she was trained at Juilliard. Just reading the word "family" makes him uncomfortable. He senses the rest of the letter is about his own family and considers crumpling it up, but fear of what the extortionist has planned stops him. He steps back into the booth and turns his back on the door. This way, if someone is watching, at least they won't get the satisfaction of seeing the look on his face. He lights a cigarette and takes a deep drag before reading.

> *You have a sister raising a child on her own and you do nothing to help her. This is a pathetic reality for someone that makes millions writing*

allegories about family values. You have one day
to spend some time with her kid, record some of
your activities, and download the proof or the
world will see just what a con artist their precious
Russell Niles is and your career will be over.

He thinks of Susanna, a Polish cleaning lady he fired a month after having sex with her. No reason, no warning, just two grand and a note telling her not to come back.

She has reason to send him a letter like this. Reason, access to his personal life, and motivation to snoop long enough to uncover his secret. She has all the fuel in the world, but he knows it's not Susanna. With her limited English, she couldn't write a letter like this if a billion dollars were at stake. And what bothers him most is that he knows Susanna would never do something like this because she's too good a person, and right now that makes him feel even worse than the letter does.

He folds the paper and exits the booth just as the manager approaches. Heavy bags under his eyes fit his high-strung tone.

"Would you like me to freshen up the entertainment, Mr. Fuller?"

For a moment it makes sense that this is the extortionist. But that is what eats at Barrett — anyone could be sending these letters, and in the right light and at the right moment, everyone seems suspicious. He offers the manager what he can form of a smile.

"I'm afraid I have to get going."

"I hope it's not anything we've done."

"Not at all. Something uh, something just came up."

"Say no more, I'll put today on your account."

Barrett nods a thank-you. He's not used to having people look at him like this. He takes pride in projecting a good time, and the manager's concern only adds to his stress. The urge to go home has never been stronger. To draw the drapes and take a moment to think about everything that's happened.

His sister. Dragging family into this makes him angry. Before the mention of her, he was nervous, scared that the money train would stop, but now he's livid. His relationship with his sister is precious to him. It's theirs, and having someone pass judgment on it makes him wish for five minutes alone with the extortionist to beat the audacity out of the threats.

As soon as he gets home, he sits with his legs crossed on the pool table and stares at the letter. His perch highlights both the size of the room and how empty it feels with just him in it. Barrett's mansion is more of a compound than a home. In the fifties it belonged to an ambassador, and the irony was enough for him to make an offer two minutes after seeing the property. The first thing Barrett did with the mansion was convert it to a Smarthome. Having all the electronics in his home programmed to his preferences appeals to his desire to have environments precisely how he likes them without having to devote any headspace to the process. The temperature in the bathrooms increase three degrees when he is in them, and his bedroom drops five degrees for a crisp, fresh sleep as soon as the sensors detect him in the bed. If the temperature outside is fourteen degrees or higher at night, the bedroom windows rise three inches to allow fresh air. Every light in the house also works in conjunction with his rhythms. The lights over the toilets brighten when he's on them so he can read, but the lights above showers turn a soft red every time he enters a stall. The house also does all domestic thinking for him. The Smarthome turns off the stove if he leaves it on, flushes a toilet if he doesn't, waters his outdoor flowers, and mists his indoor plants. But the feature he enjoys the most is the panels on his bedroom windows. As soon as the sun rises they tint and angle as it moves throughout the day to ensure that none of the rays interfere with his sleep.

The thought of losing his home because of the extortionist makes his chest feel tight. A cigarette hangs from his lips, and with his free hand he strikes a lighter.

He holds the lighter for a moment like he might bring it to the letter before raising it to the cigarette. He picks up a phone and heads up a flight of stairs to the back balcony. If he's going to do this, he needs fresh air.

The last time he spoke with his sister was at Christmas, and that was to tell her he couldn't make it for dinner. A part of him knows this is pathetic, but another part of him focuses on the cheque he sent her Christmas morning for a year's worth of rent. She thinks he runs a lucrative marketing company and he uses that façade as the reason for always being busy and out of the city. It's not that he doesn't want to see his sister. He's always enjoyed their time together, but lately the months have just passed, and while he's meant to call her, there is always another drink, pill, line of blow, flight, or woman that makes tomorrow seem like a better time. He punches in Carol's number and tightens his stomach muscles in an effort to control the fluttering, but after five rings, no one has answered.

He imagines her washing dishes. Pale, gaunt, and tired like the last few times he has seen her. Guilt washes through him for not doing more to prevent that look as she finally picks up.

"Hello?"

"Hey Carol, it's Barrett. How's my little sister?"

"Are you drunk?"

Her tone prompts Barrett to pace the balcony while he responds. "No. No, I'm not. I just finished up a big project so I've got some time on my hands."

"So you're bored?"

"Not bored, interested. I've been thinking of you, I have some free time, and I was wondering if you'd like me to have Richard over at my place for a night?"

"Overnight?"

Barrett looks down at the extortion letter for inspiration. "Yeah, I figure that way you can do something different. Maybe see some friends or a movie."

"So you are drunk."

She hangs up and Barrett pauses for a moment before the dial tone makes itself clear. He lights a cigarette and immediately redials her number. Ten rings in, she hasn't answered, but that's okay, it's a moment more to think about how to persuade her, time for one more drag. Finally, on the twelfth ring, she picks up.

"Don't hang up. I want to explain this to you."

Her sigh fills his ears with her disappointment. "It's been a long time since you've seen Richard, Barrett."

"That's why I'm calling. I've got some free time and I want to use it properly."

Even he has to cringe at the fluff flowing from his mouth, but this about self-preservation, and that means doing anything he has to for her to agree.

"In the last six months I've heard from you on my birthday and at Christmas, and both were voicemails."

"I've been really busy." As soon as the words leave his mouth, he knows it's a pitiful response, but it's all he can manage.

"And I've been raising a son that's devastated because he doesn't have a father."

She hangs up again, and this time he knows better than to call back. He lays the latest extortion demand in front of him. *You have a sister raising a child on her own and you do nothing to help her. You have twenty-four hours to spend some time with the kid.*

He looks at the clock to see he has twenty-two hours to meet the demand, lies back on his bed, and imagines what his sister wants for her son. This isn't the way most people imagine, with neat images from their point of view — this is the gift of a creator, the ability to feel what she might. He sits up and lights a cigarette with a grin he hasn't formed since the first extortion letter arrived.

By dinner, he stands in front of Carol's apartment building. He scans the directory for her name and presses the buzzer.

"Hello?" The surprise in her tone suggests she doesn't get many visitors.

"Hey Carol, it's Barrett."

"What are you doing here?" There's the tone he's accustomed too.

"Just come out, I have a surprise."

He walks over to a delivery truck and pulls open the side doors to reveal a Steinway grand piano with a maple inner rim. Pleased with himself, he positions himself for maximum effect and waits for Carol to come down.

Dressed in a white zip-up and khaki pants, she freezes as soon as she steps outside.

"I hope Richard's still taking lessons."

She points at the piano. "That's half the size of my living room."

"It can double as a coffee table."

"You're bribing me?"

"Proving my commitment. One night. I just want to hang out with the kid."

Richard stands behind his mother now. "Tonight?"

"Hey buddy," Barrett says, seizing the momentum. "That's what I'm hoping."

Richard looks up at his mother. "Can I go?"

She absorbs her son's enthusiasm and gestures inside. "Both of you, inside."

Inside it's smaller than Barrett remembers, about one-twentieth of the size of his ground floor. This observation leaves him disappointed both in himself and his sister, but he quickly focuses on the fact that he still needs to close the deal.

"I want to talk to you before you guys go," she says.

Barrett nods. Her tone makes him happy. This is his sister and he admires her spunk, but he holds back a smile knowing she'll interpret it as condescending. He moves a folded quilt and sits on the couch. Carol stands in front of him and Richard sits off to the side doing his best not to make eye contact. His jeans and white T-shirt are both well worn. Barrett quickly categorizes him as at the stage of life when appearance means little, but he notes that it's clear it won't be long before people consider him handsome.

"You should know that I have a lot of rules for Richard," Carol says.

A hug would be better, but Barrett understands. He knows this is time to play along.

"Okay."

"Now, I know how you feel about rules, so I want you to repeat each one so I know you understand how serious I am about these."

"Shoot."

"Not more than an hour of TV at night."

Barrett looks at Richard staring at the floor and thinks that TV is probably more educational than the carpet, but he nods again. "One hour of TV"

"No violent movies."

"No *Scarface*."

"No violent video games."

"I only have pinball."

"No refined sugar, and I mean none."

"Easy enough."

The no sugar comment grabs Richard's attention, and Barrett throws him a wink, which provokes a smile. The type of smile people get when they're happy to be in on something.

Carol's index finger points in Barrett's face before he can enjoy the connection. "I saw that. He's got to be in bed by ten. He's cranky if he doesn't get enough sleep."

"Got it, no fun."

"I'm serious."

"I'm joking. He's in good hands, don't worry."

"I don't mean to be overbearing, it's just that I can't remember the last time he didn't sleep under this roof."

Her passion cuts through the mirth, officially blowing his high. Instead, an empty feeling washes over him, like instead of being in on the joke, he is the punch line. It's time to play along like he means it, so he offers her a nod of agreement.

"I understand."

"What do you have planned for tonight?"

Barrett looks at Richard. This is an opportunity to give the answer she wants, to score some points with karma, but the look in Richard's eyes suggest there's an even greater opportunity here.

"I was thinking a Big Dog burger and some kung fu movies."

"You're kidding me?"

Richard holds back a smile while Barrett leans into the couch.

"Why?" Barrett asks.

"I just told you he doesn't watch violent movies."

"Kung fu's not about violence, it's about good vs. evil."

"Chopping people is violent, and I don't want him going around school chopping the evil kids." Her voice transcends passion now. Somewhere, preachers are jealous of her conviction. "I can't believe you're going to show him a kung fu movie after I told you no violence."

Barrett points at her and breaks into a smile that only a brother or sister can flash a sibling when they're tormenting them. "Gotcha."

Carol closes her eyes so she can calm down enough not to charge him and club him unconscious. "Hilarious."

He kisses her on the cheek. "Breathe. It's going to be fine, and it'll be violence- and sugar-free."

"Thank you."

Barrett looks at Richard and holds up his car keys. "You ready?"

Richard nods. He's been ready to leave this apartment since the day his father left. Ready to form new memories, free of the residue of sadness; ready to experience something that will create some space between him and the day he found his father kissing a man on the bathroom floor.

Outside, Barrett opens the passenger door of a Mercedes, and Richard gets in. This is the only time he's been in a car this luxurious, and it's exciting.

The TV screen on the passenger dashboard is better quality than the one in his apartment, and the seat is so comfortable he imagines sleeping in it.

Barrett watches him for a moment before pulling onto the road. "You want to ask me something, don't you?"

The attention embarrasses Richard.

"I can tell from your eyes. Just ask."

"Why do you have a TV in your car?"

"TVs, actually. There's one on each of the back seats."

"Then why do you have TVs in your car? Wouldn't you rather to talk to someone while you're driving?"

"It depends who's with me. But the answer to your question is I didn't think about it. The dealership asks me if I want it fully loaded, I say sure, and this is how it comes."

The answer leaves Richard confused. As someone who hasn't been in anything other than a taxi for two years, he dreams of driving his own car one day, so the idea of being wealthy enough to afford a luxury car only to leave the details up to a dealer blows his mind.

Barrett lights a cigarette and takes a deep drag, both of which catch Richard's attention. Richard pulls his shirt over his mouth.

"You shouldn't smoke."

Barrett takes another drag, the exhale streaming from his mouth as he speaks. "And you should mind your business, but we all do things we shouldn't, you follow me?"

This effectively silences Richard. He's simply not equipped or experienced enough in the art of repartee to respond, so he just sits in silence and scrunches his nose at the smoke.

Barrett smiles. He lowers the window a pinch and takes another drag like he just did the kid a favour.

Inside Barrett's living room, Richard looks around in amazement. The space is considerably larger than his entire apartment, and the architecture is something he's never experienced. High ceilings, floor-to-ceiling windows, wooden pillars, marble countertops. There is so much he wants to say, but all the comes out is, "You have a big house."

"Thank you."

Barrett fiddles with a laptop now.

"Has Mom ever been here?"

"Sure."

"When?"

"She's been here."

"So what are we going to do?"

"We're going to watch some TV"

The TV is wall-mounted with cutting-edge screen clarity. Richard takes a step towards the screen.

"This is the biggest TV I've ever seen."

"Me too."

Barrett begins to scan forty-one new emails and taps a high-back chair that resembles a throne. "Grab a seat. This is my favourite chair, and I'm giving you command tonight. You've got two converters and a thousand channels, go nuts."

He opens an email from an actress he dated a few times in France, then Richard's channel flipping grabs his attention.

"Go easy, you don't have to watch them all right away."

The channels flip faster. A car commercial, a country music video, a basketball game, a cereal commercial, a cartoon, the news, another cartoon.

"I said easy, you've got all night to go through them."

But the flipping continues. Acne cream, a talk show, a heavy metal video, reality TV, a monkey petting a dog.

"Seriously, can you choose a channel? You're killing my eyes with that flipping."

They now blur they flip so fast. Amazement washes over Barrett's face. "Stop flipping, are you retarded?"

The channels finally stop and Richard turns to look at Barrett. "No, but my best friend's sister is."

This is sobering news. Barrett wants to put the kid in his place, but he doesn't want to break his spirit. "Look, I'm sorry. I didn't mean it like that."

Richard breaks into a smile that would make a con-man jealous. "Gotcha."

A ripple of relief flows through Barrett, followed by a moment of admiration for the kid. More clever than he seems.

"A sense of humour, huh? You must have got that from your father."

Mention of his father makes Richard cringe, but he is having too much fun with Barrett to let it get in the way. He sets the television converters on the coffee table.

"I'm not allowed to watch much TV, so I don't really know what channel to pick. Can I watch a movie?"

"Sure. I've got my own rental store here."

Barrett heads to a case full of DVDs. The first one he selects at random is a porno about foot fetishes, so he slides it back and pulls out *Full Metal Jacket*. He considers it for a moment before deciding against exposing the kid to guns and suicide, but the third one he removes is a how-to film on tantric sex, so he slides it back in its place and pivots toward Richard.

"Why don't we rent one from TV? That way you're not limited to what I have."

"Okay."

There is no need for an explanation.

Richard is used to having his mother make the decisions and would have happily complied without questions, but Barrett prides himself on his resources and can't keep himself from wanting to impress everyone that sets foot in his home. He picks up the biggest converter and sets up the movie selection channel.

"There you go. Just press 'okay' to pick the movie you want. The code is four sevens."

Feeling good about himself, he retreats to the kitchen to check on his iPhone and enjoy a cigarette. Then he feels Richard staring at him. A quick glance across the kitchen and back into the living room reveals the kid looking over the couch's back.

"Do you have any popcorn?"

"I don't. Are you hungry?"

Richard nods.

"Okay, I'll get you something."

A deep drag gives him the patience to deal with this. *So the kid wants food? It's not a big thing*, he reassures himself. *Just throw a snack on a plate.* Another drag gets him to the fridge.

He opens it and after a quick scan raises his eyebrows at what is mostly drink mix, lemons, and limes. Another drag. A five-thousand-dollar, double door, stainless steel fridge, with four levels and six drawers, and there's almost nothing to eat. He removes a can of pâté, turns to the closest counter cabinet, moves three containers of margarita glass-rimmer to the side and takes out a bag of pistachios. He drops his cigarette in an ashtray, walks over to Richard and sets the food down on the table in front of him.

"There you go."

Richard points to the pâté. "What's that?"

"It's pâté. Lots of protein."

"For a snack?"

"There are people who would kill to have this while they're watching a movie."

"No, thank you."

A huff fires through Barrett's nostrils. "So have some pista-chios; they're like peanuts."

"I'm allergic to peanuts."

Barrett snatches the pistachios off the table and quickly wipes where the bag was sitting. "What do you say we order pizza?"

This is a dance Barrett wasn't prepared for, and he is exhausted. What he wants to do is call up a few of his female companions and go out for a steak and drink bottles of wine until Richard's visit becomes a hazy memory, but that won't pre-serve these surroundings, so he picks up the phone and calls for a pizza.

FOURTEEN

With Richard asleep in a bedroom the size of his classroom, Barrett is stretching out on the couch when there is a buzz from his front gates. He looks on the monitor to see Jill in a long cream coat. The timing is terrible, but this is Jill, so he buzzes her in and hustles to the door to make sure it is open to reduce the noise when she enters.

"What are you doing here?" he whispers.

"I have a surprise."

"It's not a good night."

"Really?"

Jill lets her coat slip off her shoulders to reveal a Wonder Woman costume with knee-high boots, gold bracelets, and a crown. This is why Jill is his favourite, and this is why he pays her whatever she wants. She leads him by hand up the stairs, and when they pass the kid's room Barrett holds a finger to his lips while Jill suppresses a giggle.

In his bedroom, Jill slips a blindfold over Barrett's eyes and leans him back onto the bed.

"Don't do that; I love looking at you."

"You'll like what comes next more," she purrs and has started tying his hands with a yellow silk sash when Richard opens the door. He watches them for a moment, fascinated by her outfit, before stepping into the room.

"Cool costume."

Barrett pulls at this blindfold awkwardly, slides off the bed bum first, and lands on the floor with a painful thud. Jill turns to the kid and then looks down at Barrett.

"You have a son?"

"No, no. He's my nephew."

"He's cute."

Barrett gets to his feet. "He's going back to bed. Aren't you, buddy?"

"I can't sleep."

"I'll give you one of my sleeping pills."

"Barrett ..." Jill interjects.

"Just a halfer."

Jill steps toward Richard and her boots click loudly. "What do you do at home when you can't sleep?"

"Read."

"Yeah, what?"

"The Mil Bennett books."

Barrett looks at the kid and wonders for a minute if this is actually a nightmare.

"They're my favourite too," Jill says, moving toward the bookshelf. "And your uncle has a bunch of them. Come over here and I'll read one with you."

"Okay."

Richard sits on the bed, Jill removes a book, and clicks back over to join him.

Barrett exhales a cloud of smoke and gestures to the door. "I'll ah, I'll be downstairs."

ॐ

The click of Jill's boots wake Barrett in the morning. He shifts his weight on the plush couch and rubs at his eyes.

"Morning, Mother Goose, how's the little one?"

"Sleeping."

Barrett sits up and notices she's wearing her jacket over her costume. "I'm thinking a literary theme next time. Maybe an Alice in Wonderland outfit."

"There's not going to be a next time."

"What? Why?"

"I have a son I don't see, and hanging out with your nephew last night really fucked with me."

"So we'll make sure the kid's not here when you come over."

"Sorry, baby. But our time is done."

She kisses him on the forehead, and her eyes tell him that no amount of pleading or money will change her mind. He listens to the last click of her heels as she leaves the house and arches his neck in disbelief.

An hour later, Barrett plays cards with Richard and sips at a jumbo cup of coffee. There are twenty-two messages on his iPhone, but he's too stressed to care about business.

He sets the phone to video record and tilts the device so that Richard is framed perfectly.

"Why are we taping this?" Richard asks, looking into the lens.

"So you don't cheat."

"I don't cheat."

"How do I know that?"

"Because I don't."

"Well, maybe I do. And this way, you won't have to worry." Barrett tosses some poker chips into the middle of the table. "Are you good with computers?"

"Pretty good." Richard matches the bet.

"Do you know how to upload things?"

Richard nods.

"Good. Because I want to put some pictures of us online so I can show people at work."

"It's easy to put pictures on your site."

Barrett puts his cards down and focuses on the kid. "What site?"

"The site you want to put pictures on."

"I didn't say anything about a site."

"You have to put them somewhere. Don't you have Facebook?"

"No, ah, but it's like Facebook."

"Myspace?"

"It might be called that."

He lays down two pairs with a smile until Richard puts down three kings. Swear words bang against Barrett's gritted teeth, but he holds them back while Richard takes in the pot and collects the cards. Barrett watches as the kid clears his throat and touches a rash on the inside of his forearm like he just lost.

"What do you look so down for? You just won."

"I'm fine."

"You don't look fine."

"I'm fine. I just hate my therapist."

Barrett gets up and refills his coffee. "Woman or man?"

"Man."

"How old?"

"I don't know, old."

"My age old?"

"Older."

"Um, hmm. Does he ask you about school?"

"Yeah."

"And your family?"

"Yeah."

"So he's old and he invades your privacy. Doesn't sound like there's much to like. I'm assuming it's not your choice to see this guy."

"Mom makes me."

Barrett extinguishes his cigarette in a large black ashtray with a roulette wheel painted in the middle. "Well, this guy may be a stiff, but don't be angry with your mother. She loves you and she means well."

"I still hate him."

"You know what I do when I'm angry?"

"What?"

"I drive fast." Barrett pulls a set of keys from his pocket and lets them dangle so that they jingle together. "Do you want to drive?"

"I'm too young."

"For your license. But not to drive."

Barrett leads the way out of the house and down the porch to a fleet of cars in the driveway. He walks past a black Porsche, a gun-metal grey Town Car, and a red Aston Martin before stopping at a white Lamborghini.

"Cool."

"Cooler than cool. This car used to belong to Frank Sinatra."

"Who's that?"

"He's a singer from a long time ago, but he's a legend. Saying you don't know him is like me saying I don't know what a video game is."

"Really?"

"Really."

Barrett pulls out of the mansion and honks at a mini-van crawling in front of him until it pulls over and lets him pass.

"I'm too short to drive," Richard says.

"You'll sit in my lap. You'll steer and shift gears and I'll work the gas and brakes."

Richard clears his throat incessantly during the drive, but he's too nervous to notice. The offer to drive is exciting, but he doesn't want to screw up.

Barrett turns the car onto a street behind a series of abandoned factories and stops at the side of the road. "No one comes down here anymore. It's like our personal road."

Richard looks into the distance, and the road appears to go on forever.

"Let's do it," Barrett says, tapping his knee. He pushes the seat back to create the maximum amount of room while Richard walks around to the driver's side. As soon as Richard touches the steering wheel, his fingers tingle. The leather is unbelievably soft and the sun's glare on the windshield looks beautiful, like everything should if it could be as illuminated. "Working the gears is simple. I'll call out a number and you shift to it. The wheel is the real challenge. The faster we go, the more it'll fight you. Your job is to keep it steady."

Richard wipes the sweat from his hands on his pants and grips the steering wheel again. The heat waves coming off the road's asphalt in the distance make Richard think of a crash. He imagines the Lamborghini flipping, the gas tank leaking, and flames engulfing the car until the paint peels and their body's burn.

"Ready?" Barrett asks.

His voice pulls Richard back to the moment. The kid nods. Barrett starts the car, and Richard turns the wheel toward the road until the vehicle crosses the yellow line before straightening out.

"Easy," Barrett says.

"Sorry."

"Don't be sorry. Be steady. Are you ready on the stick?"

"Yeah." Richard's throat is so dry, he croaks the word more than speaks it.

The car accelerates and Barrett smiles. "Second."

Richard pulls the gear, but it's stiffer than he anticipates, and it sticks for a moment, which causes the car to rock.

"Let's go."

Richard is sure he is going to push it into fifth instead of second, but he jerks it toward the slot anyway and it slides into place. The car accelerates and Barrett taps the boy's hip.

"There you go."

The road's white centre lines blur faster now. He's been on a highway at fast speeds many times, but he's used to cars that rattle and a hum from the tires. This car is different. The Lamborghini feels like it floats and the interior is soundproof so that the senses can adjust and appreciate the speed.

"Third," Barrett says. This time Richard slides the gear in a smooth motion.

The wheel jerks, but he steadies it easily enough, and before his eyes acclimatize, Barrett yells, "Fourth."

Richard changes gears again, and this time the car's burst pushes him back into Barrett's chest. The steering wheel jumps and he moves his hand from the gear, but the torque stops him from getting a firm grip, and the car drifts onto the side of the road, where the tires crackle in the gravel.

"Turn straight," Barrett says.

But Richard is lost in the image of the car flipping over and into the ditch, so Barrett turns the wheel himself. The front of the car heads back to the centre of the lane, but the back end skids on the gravel, and when Barrett pumps the brakes, the car spins sideways before stopping. A cloud of dust rises from the car and Barrett laughs until the look of terror on Richard's face turns to an adrenaline-fueled smile.

"I told you it's hard to keep it steady."

The rush leaves Richard so high, all he can do is smile and nod.

"You did great," Barrett says. "It was my fault for picking up speed too fast."

Richard looks at Barrett and believes the praise. He is about to say thank you when the sound of police sirens makes him turn around. Richard imagines juvenile hall, a cell that smells like eggs and only seeing his mother every other weekend.

"We're going to jail."

"Relax."

"We're going to jail."

"We're going to be fine."

Barrett helps Richard move to the passenger seat and removes his license from his wallet and the registration from the glove box in time to see the officer standing beside the car. He rolls down the window and extends the paperwork. The officer is middle-aged and burly with a harelip.

"You were driving one-twenty in a sixty. That's a four-hundred dollar ticket and four points. I could impound the car. The kid in your lap could be reckless driving, at least, it's endangerment and another five-hundred dollar ticket."

Barrett makes sure not to look at the harelip.

The officer leans in the window to get a good look at Richard. "You look a lot like the kid on the cover of those books. What's his name? Mil something."

"Mil Bennett," Richard says.

"Yeah. You're older, but you look like him."

Barrett smiles. "Are you a fan of those books?"

"Never read them, but my son can't get enough of them. We keep trying to get him the latest one, but we've been to three stores and they're all sold out. It's all the kid talks about right now."

The anonymity makes Barrett feel like a god. "I've got a boxful in the trunk. I own a marketing company and we're working on the campaign. You can have them if you want. I just give them away to other people anyway."

"You're serious?"

Barrett nods.

"You know this won't change the tickets?"

"Of course not."

"You were five kilometres over the speed limit and the kid was sitting in the passenger seat without a seat belt. That's two tickets."

Barrett grins in relief. "I understand."

Barrett pops the trunk and taps Richard's hand until the kid smiles.

Back on the road, with the cop gone, Richard finally speaks. "Do you really help sell the Russell Niles books?"

"I really do."

"How come Mom never told me?"

"I don't know. She knows I run a marketing company, but I don't talk a lot about it much."

"Can you introduce me to Russell Niles?"

"I've never met him. We just help sell the books. But nobody meets him."

"Why?"

"He just likes it that way, I guess. It's not about him, it's about the writing. I think he's been in Ghana the past year doing charity work."

"Where's that?"

"Africa."

Barrett stops the car in front of Richard's building, which draws considerable attention. A couple of kids throwing a football look at the car like it might house a celebrity and an elderly couple smoking on a bench start to whisper. The attention sends a ripple of excitement through Richard. He steps out of the car and his mother exits the building foyer to greet them, effectively ruining his chance to look cool. His eyes roll as she wraps her arms around him.

"There he is. Did you have fun?"

The collective stare of everybody on the street enhances his embarrassment, but he feels too good to let anything get to him, so he smiles and nods.

Carol notices that Barrett looks proud of himself. His lips form that same smug smile they did when he wanted praise as a kid. He lights a cigarette and blows out to the side.

"We need to do this more often."

"How about next weekend?" Richard asks.

The request shocks Barrett for a moment. Somehow he didn't expect the kid to answer, but now that he has there's only one response.

"Why not?"

Carol looks at Barrett and then Richard. This is a look Barrett knows all too well, a look that makes him emphasize his words with a nod to his nephew. Carol taps her son on the shoulder and extends a key.

"Why don't you take your bag up?"

A jolt of anxiety rushes through Richard's body. This is the last thing he expects after so much ease, but he understands that's the point. His father taught him that endings can be devastating, and as he prepares to say goodbye to Barrett, a part of him fears he will never see his uncle again. He looks at Barrett for a moment like he wants to hug him before raising a hand.

"Bye."

"See you, buddy."

The tone is honest enough that Richard believes him. It's something to hang on to anyway, enough to put the irrational thoughts of abandonment aside for now.

Carol watches Richard until he enters the building before pivoting towards Barrett. She examines him for a moment.

"Are you in rehab?"

He tries to dismiss the jab with a smile before finally shaking his head when she doesn't back down.

"A born-again group?"

"I'm fine."

"Whatever it is, thank you. He doesn't smile like that very much anymore."

There's the praise Barrett craves. One happy nephew, one happy sister. If he wasn't being forced to do this, he might actually feel proud.

FIFTEEN

Richard sits in front of Dr. Burns and exhales a small burst of air somewhere between a grunt and clearing his throat. His mother shifts her weight on the couch next to him. Her anxiety only intensifies his, so he turns to a painting with a swirl of primary colours in the form of spittle to distract himself, but he sees the reflection of his dry lips in the frame's shiny glass, and they remind him how much he hates the doctor and his medication.

"Has he been taking the meds?" Burns looks at Carol from his perch on the stool with his fingers hovering over a laptop that sits on his knees.

Richard wants to scream, "Look at my fucking cracked lips and tell me if you think I'm taking my meds." But he knows better, so he palms the couch's arm and squeezes until his knuckles stretch their skin.

"Oh yeah," Carol says. "He's off to a good start."

Dr. Burns clicks away at the keyboard, and Richard thinks this sounds too much like business for a place that's supposed to be about helping people.

"Okay," Burns says with enthusiasm. He sets the laptop on the adjacent table and stands with perfect posture. "Anger is a destructive force. Happiness brings us together, fear keeps us safe, and sadness makes us appreciative. But anger, anger destroys. The body is constantly in motion. The brain always suspends one emotion to embrace another. Now I don't expect you to understand all the words, but you can understand the concept. No two emotions can exist in our brains at the same time. Which means, if we are full of anger than we are literally incapable of happiness. So, our job is to get rid of the anger." Burns gestures to the journal. "Have you been writing in your journal?"

Richard notices the black dots of stubble on Burn's face and the thick hair sprouting up from his chest, but he doesn't say a word.

"Not yet," Carol answers. "But I'm reminding him every day, so he'll start soon."

"I'd prefer if you answer," Burns says. His eyes lock on Richard with judgment.

Richard shakes his head.

"Well, you will. But perhaps today talking will work better than writing. Today, we are going to talk our feelings out, which means we will use third person. Do you know what that means?"

Richard nods. Of course he knows first person. Every Russell Niles book is written in third person, and he's read each of them more than once.

"I'll start us off," Burns says, rising from his stool. "Dr. Burns' back is stiff from playing tennis this morning." He gestures to the boy. "Try it."

Richard offers him a blank look.

"Help us out, Mom." Burns gestures to Carol in a manner that makes her feel like she has to comply.

"Okay. Carol is hoping that Richard will start writing in his journal."

"Excellent example."

Richard turns again to the painting, is reminded of his cotton-mouth, and stares at the floor.

Burns stands, unfazed by the boy's disinterest. "Today I want to work on a self-soothing technique that you can use in any situation when you feel anger taking over. To begin, I want you to close your eyes and move both of them in a circle at the same time.

"Now at first, this will be uncomfortable, but your mind will slip into a trance quicker than you think if you stick with it." He demonstrates the movement, and Richard notes that the man's nose is larger than he first thought.

Richard decides to play along to limit his mother's backlash once they get home, and within seconds, he agrees with the doctor. Moving his eyes in a circle is uncomfortable and annoying, but the more he moves his eyes, the more the doctor's voice turns into one inaudible sound until a reoccurring nightmare fills his thoughts.

This nightmare has plagued him since his father left and he has never mentioned a word to anyone. It starts with him as a police officer, which is odd, because he has never thought of becoming a cop. It is hard to say how far into the future it is, but he is tall just like his father and it feels like he has been a police officer forever. He arrives at the scene of a car crash on a highway where a green mini-van is flipped upside down against the guardrail. The visible side of the van is crushed in the middle, and shattered glass litters the pavement. He steps out of his squad car and walks past skid marks and fuel stains toward the vehicle. About ten feet away, he sees a baby seat sitting on its side. The plastic and padded headrest are intact, but the straps have snapped. He hustles to the van to see a woman's broken body on the other side of the vehicle. Her face is bloody and her neck is clearly broken, but all he can think about is that there is no sign of the baby. He opens the passenger door but the vehicle is empty. The inside is clean, and despite being upside down, it is easy to scan. There is no baby. He moves to the sliding door, which has broken off and lies fifteen feet away interior up. Glass chunks crumble beneath his boots, and he prays that the baby is not under the door. He lifts the door and struggles with the weight, but the need to find the baby pushes him to move the metal upright.

Relief fills him seeing that the baby isn't there, but the sight of an orange pacifier beside a screw the length of a finger makes him feel faint with worry. He picks up the pacifier and imagines a baby's wail. The cry is panicked and incessant. He scrambles around the crash site, checks the vehicle again, and looks both ways down the road as far as he can see, but still no baby. Instinct tells him to look over the guardrail and down at the passing cars below, but there is no sign of tragedy. Cars drive as they always do and the road is clear. The baby must be somewhere. He repeats the sentence with each beat of his heart, and this is when he wakes up with an overwhelming sense of dread that makes him never want to close his eyes again.

The sound of the doctor's voice snaps him back to the moment.

"Excellent. Excellent. That is the healing power of silence. When we get our minds to a sensitized state, we are best prepared to face the challenges that tempt us to give in to anger." Burns turns to Carol, who looks too stoic to face anything. "Carol, what were you thinking about during the silence?"

"Nothing specific."

"Really? Because you look deep in thought."

"I'd rather keep that to myself."

"Okay. But remember, we are here to share, and by initiating the sharing you might inspire Richard to see how healing it can be."

The guilt works. The only thing she wants more than keeping what she was thinking about to herself is for Richard to be happy. "I was thinking about my brother and how he helped me through one of the most difficult periods in my life."

The mention of his uncle grabs Richard's attention.

"You are lucky to have such a caring person in your life. How did he help you?"

"It's, ah, a long story."

"Give us every detail that runs through your mind. The more you can access, the better. That's the point of the exercise."

She takes a deep breath, but it doesn't feel like enough air, so she exaggerates an inhale and speaks like the words are happy to finally be released. "When I was sixteen, I was walking home from a volleyball practice after school. It was November, so it was already dark. The practice was boring, but I felt amazing because Todd Haskins invited me to his party third period. I liked him since freshman year, but that was the first time he said more to me than a passing greeting. I had headphones on, a Kinks song, and the music made it seem like I was in a movie. Being invited to that party made me feel unstoppable. I was two blocks from my house, adjacent to a parkette filled with toys, because it was where all the local parents took their kids, when a forearm reached around my neck and pulled me toward an alley that connected two side streets."

Richard looks at his mother with concern, so she slips a hand over his to reassure him.

"I tried to scream, but a hand covered my mouth. I remember being surprised that the hand wasn't gloved and disgusted that his skin tasted salty. I was sure I was going to die. That he would rape me and kill me just like in the movies and reports on the news that had terrified me since I was a kid. He dragged me toward the alley until a voice stopped him. I landed bum first on the ground, and a sharp pain shot up my spine. I wanted to see him but he was already gone. I was so scared that I didn't even notice it was Barrett's voice that scared the man off until he helped me to my feet. We didn't say anything for the first minute, he just hugged me.

"And I find myself, all these years later, still asking the same question that I wondered as soon as I saw Barrett that day. What if he didn't see me? What if he left the house ten minutes later? Or decided to drive or take another route? But he didn't. And I'm okay because of him. We filed a detailed report with the police, but they never found the guy. My parents, who loved me very much, arranged for me to meet with a therapist and my guidance counsellor got my teachers to cut me some slack, but that didn't work. I felt scared, hopeless, and angry. But then Barrett signed me up for a self-defence class. And not only did he drive me to every one, but he also took every one with me. He took my elbows to the chest, held the pads for sidekicks and played the dummy for every choke hold. And then he invited me on a road trip. He was halfway through university and he had planned this with three friends for more than a year, and he took me along anyway. It didn't matter that I was his younger sister or the only girl with four guys, he just brought me and treated me like I belonged. I did a lot of driving while they were drunk, slept in a lot of dirty motels, and pretended to look away while his friends went skinny dipping in every roadside lake we found. And when I came back, the fear and anger I had were gone. It was like that brief moment in my life, despite it being horrible, was just that, a brief moment in an otherwise great life. And it's because of my brother that I feel that way."

Richard squeezes his mother's hand and she slips an arm around his shoulders.

Dr. Burns smiles. "You are a courageous woman and just hearing you speak tells me that Richard will be on board with us any minute now." He stands, picks up a pink stress ball, and tosses it hand to hand. "Think of that last exercise we did as preventative. But in the case when anger has already taken over, we need another strategy. In those situations, we need to get the angries out."

Richard watches the doctor with disbelief as he walks to a cabinet and removes a red, weighted punching bag. How can the man listen to what she just said and be making this about Richard? The bag is as tall as Richard and heavy enough that it takes effort for the doctor to drag it in front of them.

"Anger is your body on an adrenaline high, so when it reaches that point it's important to have a release. Right now I want us each to hit the bag once and feel the tension leaving our bodies. Richard, you start us off."

"No, thank you."

"Really? You're looking at me like this is work, but it's a rush of its own. I'll start us off."

He rolls up his sleeves and reveals veiny arms with road maps of moles. Assuming an old-school boxing stance with his fists facing up, he slugs the bag's centre with an uppercut.

"You can feel the stress leaving your body. And I mean feel it." Burns strikes the bag again. "Are you ready to have a go?" He points at Richard, who shakes his head one more time. "You will be. How about you?" He gestures to Carol, who nods and steps in front of the bag like she's not sure what to do. "You don't have to make a fist, just slap it, chop it, whatever works for...."

Carol's war cry cuts him off as she charges the bag with a scream, knocks it to the floor, and pounces on it with her legs straddled. Hammer fists and forearms hit the bag repeatedly until her spent arms dangle by her side.

The doctor claps slowly. "Now *that* is getting the angries out." He pivots to Richard. "You're up."

Richard lifts his journal to eye level and tears off the happy face cover. He looks at his mother, now on her knees with a flush face, and back at the doctor as he rips the happy face to pieces. Watching the paper fall to the floor is gratifying until he notices that instead of being upset, Dr. Burns looks pleased.

SIXTEEN

B arrett tries to calm himself with routine. He sits in the same spot he does every day in the leather chair adjacent to the fireplace in an independent coffee shop with amazing organic butter tarts. He tries to distract himself with the newspaper, but articles about a dominatrix fighting for her charter rights, a tourist held hostage in Mexico, and a politician accused of too much travel can't compete with his personal stress. In fact, he hasn't felt this paranoid since he took three hits of acid at a ski chalet in Whistler a few years ago when he spent the evening in a staring contest with a snowman.

He finishes his coffee and is walking toward the bathroom when he notices a man in his thirties behind him. The man is well dressed, overweight, and focused on his iPhone.

Barrett looks back at the man suspiciously and continues into the bathroom as the man raises his iPhone to eye level. Barrett is sure he hears a click and spins around so fast, he tumbles.

"What are you doing?"

"I'm about to go to the bathroom."

"Did you take a picture of me?"

"Why would I want a picture of you?"

Barrett reaches for the iPhone, and the man pulls away.

"I'm texting my wife."

"Show me."

Barrett reaches again but the man pulls away too fast. The man holds the phone out to display a text on the screen and Barrett takes a step back.

"Sorry."

"You might want to remember your medication the next time you're out in public."

Barrett exits the washroom and is heading back to where he was sitting when he sees an attractive young woman in his seat. Her chocolate brown hair hangs below her shoulders and large eyes make it difficult to look at anything else. She wears a Runaways T-shirt and is highlighting a textbook when she notices him looking at her.

"I'm sorry, were you sitting here? I didn't know if the paper meant it was reserved or if someone left it."

"I was ..." Barrett gestures to the textbook. "But you look like you need it more than me."

"Third-year philosophy." She taps the book with her highlighter. "I haven't read a word in a month."

"Why read about it when you can live it?"

"I like that. I'm Pam."

She holds out her hand, and Barrett is amazed at how soft her skin feels.

"Barrett." He appraises the T-shirt. "The Runaways, huh?"

She throws up devil horns. "Sex, drugs, and rock and roll."

Barrett leans into her so only she can hear him. "Not me, I'm abstaining from the big D right now."

"Yeah?"

"I need my wits about me."

"A moment of clarity?"

"More like forced retirement."

Now she leans into him, and her lips are so close to his ear that he can feel the vibration of her words. "Me too."

"Really?"

She holds up two fingers. "Two months and counting. I've got to go to work. My car's outside. Do you want a ride anywhere?"

These are rhythms Barrett is used to, so as she gets up and leads him by the hand to the car, it feels as natural as breathing. The car smells like perfume and cigarettes.

He moves a crumpled fast-food wrapper to the back and sits in the passenger seat. Pam kisses him before he can say anything, slides onto his lap and tugs at his belt. These are the moments in Barrett's life that when he reflects on, he wonders if he is a character in someone else's fantasy.

Twenty minutes later he's sitting down to enjoy a victory coffee when his phone buzzes.

He looks to see a text from Don, the publisher: *Can you make time to talk?*

Anxiety takes over immediately and while the rest of the room slows to a blur, the text's font seems the size of a billboard. Of course he types. *What's up?*

This is a conversation that needs face time.

This is not a text he wants to see from a man whose wife he is having sex with. This is not a text he wants to see from the man who publishes the books that make him millions.

Okay.

Can you do Aideen's?

Aideen's. Don can afford to eat at any restaurant in the city, but when he wants to talk about anything serious, he chooses Aideen's. Around the corner from his office, the place hasn't had a renovation since it opened in the sixties. Black-and-white photos of pin-up girls from long ago hang on the walls and graffiti fills the worn wooden tables. This is where Don takes him to vent. Their shared love of drink led to periodical bonding sessions during nights of excess, and whenever something really riles the man up, he invites Barrett to Aideen's.

His previous tirades against ebooks, unauthorized biographies, poetry sales, and the last-minute fallout of potential acquisitions make Barrett feel like Aideen's is the natural spot to be strangled for sleeping with the man's wife.

Barrett takes a breath, reminds himself that the key to lying is composure, and types, *Sure. When are you thinking?*

I'm already here.

He types, *On my way*, and tries to stay calm, but he can't help but scan his memory for any time Don mentioned owning a gun.

He arrives at Aideen's to see that Don's face is uncharacteristically heavy. "Thanks for coming," he says as Barrett slides into the booth. "This isn't going to be a pleasant conversation."

Barrett feels his throat constrict.

"You would agree that we know each other better than most people who do business together, yeah?"

"Of course."

"I mean, we've smoked joints together."

"Many times."

"And we've been embarrassingly drunk together."

"More than once." The tension is too much so he speeds up the inevitable. "What needed face time so urgently?"

Don looks off and taps the table. "I know you've been with a lot of women in your time."

Suddenly Barrett's sip of water feels like he's swallowing an orange.

"I trust you," Don continues. "I respect your opinion and you have enough experience in this area that you're the right guy to consult."

Both Don's weakening tone and choice of words relax Barrett.

"Consult about what?" he says, seizing control of the conversation.

"I'm worried about my marriage."

"Why?" Barrett plays along. "Layla's great."

"Of course she is. She's amazing, but I'm not worried about her, I'm worried about me."

"How so?"

"We haven't had sex in two months."

Barrett thinks of the first night he had sex with Layla. Don left a movie premier afterparty early, and while drinking many tequila shots, they went from sharing complaints about how gossip magazines are destroying journalism to rolling around a hotel penthouse bedroom. He does a rough calculation of the number of days since that night, and bingo.

"That happens sometimes to people who have been married for a long time, doesn't it?"

"Not two months."

"Are you trying?"

"She's not interested. And I think it's because of the last time we had sex."

"Why?"

"I wasn't exactly a champion."

"Were you drinking?"

"Probably."

"Don't worry about it. A little flaccidity happens to all of us sometimes when booze is involved."

"It's more than a little, and now it's a mental thing. I love this woman to death, Barrett. I can't have her getting bored."

"She's crazy about you."

Don now talks out of the side of his mouth in an effort to be discreet. "I haven't had a good stiffy in months."

Barrett smiles. He can feel his heart beat slow down. "Have you taken Cialis?"

"No."

"I'll send you over a bottle."

"You use those pills?"

"Of course."

"Not me. Never will either."

"Do you want your problem to go away?"

"Those pills are like the chiropractor. Once you go, you're a customer for life."

"Do you want to run your abstinent streak to three months?"

"Do they really work?"

"It'll be the best night of her life." *Other than with me,* he thinks. "But be warned, you'll be stuck with an erection for the rest of the night."

"Yeah?"

"Oh, yeah. You could pry open windows with the thing."

Don laughs and Barrett enjoys the relief of not being caught cheating with his boss's wife.

SEVENTEEN

After writing out I WILL NOT DISRESPECT MY TEACHER a hundred times, Richard's hand feels like it belongs to a centenarian, but he'll never let Phelps know.

"A little old-school medicine is good for the soul," Phelps says. "It will help you remember if you feel the urge again to stray from the pack."

Richard steps outside the school and takes a number of deep breaths to get rid of the smell of Phelps' trench mouth. The air is cool but the sky is sunny so he heads for a bench on the other side of the playground and removes his coverless journal. He is compelled to write — but not the journals Dr. Burns wants. What he wants to do is tell a story like Russell Niles does, and that story is the day he found Wendell getting bullied by Terrence and Derrick at school. His pen touches the paper, and suddenly the eight-and-a-half by eleven surface feels the size of a football field. He wonders how he'll ever write a sentence, let alone fill the page. But then he remembers the look in the Wendell's eyes, like a snapshot where he can see every detail, and the words come to him. He's written a half page without taking his pen from the paper when an older voice stops his momentum.

"I know you," the voice says.

Richard looks up to see a kid from the junior high connected to his grade school. He's seen the kid on the sidewalk smoking many times before and a few times in front of the neighbourhood variety store, but kids from the junior high tend not to talk to kids in the other building, unless they are related or neighbours. The kid is lean, with a crooked nose that looks like it's been broken and a mop of blonde hair.

"You're the kid that beat the shit out of Terrence, right?"

The kid makes Richard nervous, so he goes with the flow and nods.

"Must be a tough little fucker to do that to him, as small as you are." He lights a cigarette, and Richard can't help but be amazed that he's brazen enough to do so with a teacher monitoring the playground only a fence and twenty yards away.

"I'm Jerry," he says, extending a fist.

Richard touches his knuckles and notices the chunky gold ring on his pinky.

"You like that, huh?" Jerry says.

"I do."

"Do you want to smoke a joint?"

"A what?"

"A joint. To get high. Have you ever smoked one?"

Richard shakes his head.

"Then you have to. It's the least I can do for someone that knocked out that little shit-talker. Follow me."

And while Richard's instincts tell him not to, follow is exactly what he does. He has no intention of smoking the joint, but he wants to be around Jerry a little longer.

Between the parking lot at the school's rear and the benches at the front, there is a twenty-foot walkway that people rarely use. Lined with trees at the top and a hill sloping to the walkway, it's the perfect spot for mischief.

Jerry sits on the grass with his feet on a wooden retaining wall littered with bad graffiti. He lights a thin joint and sucks his cheeks inward.

"You look really freaked out." He exhales on the ember so it glows. "You don't really have to smoke this. I just wanted the company."

"What does it feel like?"

"Good," he says, pausing unusually long on the oo.

"Like how?"

"Like you don't have any stress or anxiety. Like principal fucking Haskins could come out here right now and be like, 'What the fuck are you doing?' and I'd just smile and be like, 'Getting high.'" This time he drags out the iiiii.

Richard runs his tongue over the dry, peeling skin on the inside of his cheeks and considers why he's on medication. If the joint takes away his anxiety then he can stop taking the medication without his mom or Dr. Burns knowing, and he'd rather smile like Jerry is than live a lifetime with a mouth so dry it feels like he'll choke on water.

"Can I have some?" he asks.

"You sure?"

Richard nods and accepts Jerry's passing of the joint. In his hand, it's smaller than he expects. He raises it to his lips and does his best impersonation of Jerry.

"Easy," Jerry says. "You don't have to land on the moon your first time."

Richard expects to cough, but the smoke fills his lungs and absorbs into his body in what feels like one smooth motion. He takes another drag then Jerry pulls the joint from his fingers. "All right. That's enough for a first go. You heading home after this?"

"Yep," Richard says. The sound of his voice makes him smile.

"Then you'll need this to mask the smell." Jerry raises a bottle of cologne and sprays him three times. "Turn around." Richard obeys and he sprays him twice more. "All right, pie eye. You did good, now get out of here."

Richard starts off down the path with small steps when Jerry's voice stops him.

"Hey."

Richard turns around and fails to contain a smile that he knows makes him look stupid.

"Don't forget this." Jerry tosses Richard the journal.

Richard drops it clumsily. "Thanks."

He picks it up, and although it only takes ten minutes to get home, it feels like an hour.

He can feel his conscience constricting to a pin-prick before expanding again and the process repeats itself with the rhythm of a beating heart when suddenly he thinks of the term "being a vegetable" and for a moment he fears that he will literally become a radish or a carrot before a woman walking by with a triple chin makes him wonder what she looks like inside all that flesh, and he begins an incessant giggle that paces him back to his apartment.

When he steps into the apartment, he is surprised to see his mother home from work already. He wants to ask if everything is okay but his face feels funny and he doesn't want to draw attention to himself, so he stays quiet.

Carol scrapes diced strawberries from a cutting board into a bowl of fruit salad and sets down the knife. "There he is. Do I ever need a hug." She steps toward him with open arms and suddenly his heavy eyes feel the size of softballs.

"Why are you home?" he asks in an effort to keep his distance.

"We had a series of workshops on some new software off-site, so I got off early. It's good to see you. I've had the worst headache all day, and all I wanted to do is come home and give you a hug."

Richard looks at his mother and says what he's thinking without editing. "Can we go to another therapist? Dr. Burns is weird."

"He's not weird, he's innovative. And that's why I chose him. I went to a traditional therapist for a few weeks when I was a teenager, and I didn't like that style. I don't want you to have someone preaching at you, I want you to learn some techniques of your own, experience something that you can use for the rest of your life."

The answer is far too serious for Richard to process in this state. He's bending down and struggling to take off his shoes when she steps toward him.

"Now give me that hug."

She pulls his head into her stomach and buries her face in his hair, then the smell of cheap cologne forces her to clear her throat.

"Where did you get the cologne?"

"It's a friend's."

She smiles. "You know, the trick with cologne is to be subtle. You want people to want to be near you to smell more, not to step away because it's so strong."

"Okay," he says. Robots show more emotion, but he's doing everything possible to contain a smile that is sure to get him in trouble.

"It smells familiar, actually. Give me another whiff and I'll place it."

Instinct tells him to pull away, but in doing so, he exposes his front and as she leans into his chest, along with the rank smell of cheap cologne, she gets a hit of Terry's space weed. For a moment, her eyes narrow with confusion until another sniff confirms the source.

"You smell like marijuana. Did you smoke a joint?"

"No," he mutters.

"I'm going to give you another chance to be honest with me. Because I can smell it. Did you smoke a joint?"

He nods.

"Let me see your eyes." She grabs his face and forces his chin up so she can get a good look at his slitty red eyes. "You're eleven years old. Where did you get a joint?"

"From a kid in grade eight."

"What kid? I'm calling the principal."

"Don't. Do you know what will happen to me if you do that?"

"Why would you smoke marijuana? You know better than that. We've talked about drugs. You promised me you'd never take drugs."

He locks his eyes on her and the words that follow leave his mouth before he can think about their effect. "You give me drugs every day. Three times a day."

"Legal drugs, Richard. Prescribed by a doctor to help you."

"I don't see the difference. Except this one actually made me feel better."

She rubs at her face and Richard notices that her eyes look like they've aged since he entered the apartment.

"I want you to come straight home every day after school," she says. "I'm going to have Ms. Thompson across the hall check on you and if you're not back every day by 3:45 I'll call the principal. Do you understand?"

Richard nods limply.

"I want to hear it."

"Yes."

"Alright, go to your room."

The command is meant to be a punishment, but Richard is relieved. He's never felt more focused, and he can't wait to re-read one of his Mil Bennett books.

EIGHTEEN

Barrett met Sidney the night he lost his virginity at Derrick Demoe's sixteenth birthday party. Derrick's father ran an international contracting company, and Derrick had a bedroom bigger than most peoples' apartments. This was your standard rich kid high school party. Music blared, people made out in the corners, and everyone that could fit crammed into the hot tub as if it might be the last time they sat in one.

The gimmick to enter the party was a shot of 151 Jamaican rum that Derrick's father brought back from his last trip to the island. The shot didn't look like much, but Barrett spent the next hour feeling like he drank battery acid. Nausea came first, and then later he was convinced there was a hole in his stomach, and neither stage made him the life of the party, so when super-hot Angela Pixie introduced him to her even hotter, year-older cousin, Tammy Blades, Barrett barely feigned a smile.

"This is Kristy." Angela pointed to a brunette who raised her eyebrows before walking off with a senior that looked in his twenties. "And this is Tammy. They're both in from L.A. Tammy's on a TV show there."

"Cool," Barrett managed.

"She's been in all the gossip magazines this year."

"They're vultures," Tammy said with a California twang.

Barrett looked at the curls of her long, red hair, the symmetry of her facial features, and the power of her large eyes and felt completely inferior.

"Have you seen my show?"

"No." Barrett made a conscious effort not to touch his stomach. "I don't have cable."

"Your accent's cute."

"My accent? You think I have an accent?"

"Yeah. Everyone here does. But yours is sexy."

Barrett's groin tingled like it did as a kid during a roller coaster's ascent. This wasn't just stimulating, this was fear. He had no idea what to say.

"Let's go." Angela pulled Tammy's arm. "They're playing the century club upstairs and someone is about to puke."

Tammy waved her lacquered nails, and Barrett wished he was just half as cool as her.

Maybe then he could have done more than sit against the wall and hope he didn't have an ulcer.

The rest of the party, he did his best to run into them again, but he never did. He saw a guy body slam a statue into the pool, he watched a naked, muscle-bound guy on a bad acid trip hump the corner of a couch, and he watched two twins from his math class make out on a dare, but he never saw Angela or Kristy or Tammy. Of course, there were whispers of Tammy and Kristy everywhere. Rumours that Tammy's breasts were implants, talk that Kristy was a porn star.

Barrett's stomach finally settled after midnight and he was about to go home when Sidney sauntered into the living room where a few blind drunks were playing beer pong in front of the couch had Barrett sunk into. Barrett had seen Sidney around school a bit and knew he'd transferred a month back from another wealthy school in the west end, but they had never spoken.

"You're Barrett, right?"

Barrett nodded and took a good look at Sidney. With a dress shirt rolled up to his sleeves, jeans, and thick hair brushed back, he would have fit into any decade.

"I'm your driver tonight."

"I'm sorry?"

"Do you know Angela?"

"Yeah."

"I drove her and her L.A. friends back to her place and they sent me back for you."

"Really?"

"I was surprised too, but I'm on a mission for that brunette Kristy, so they get whatever they want, and apparently Tammy wants you."

He shook his car keys and Barrett followed him to a Jeep where the Red Hot Chili Peppers flowed through the speakers.

"I'm Sidney," the kid said, popping a cigarette into his mouth.

"Barrett."

They shook hands and Sidney pulled off down the street. After a few minutes, he turned to Barrett at a red light. "I need a favour."

"Okay."

"I told them all I'm a highly recruited baseball player and that the Yankees are going to sign me next year."

"The New York Yankees?"

Sidney exhaled, nodded, and accelerated on the green. Barrett waited for more but it didn't come.

"And?" Barrett asked.

"And I need you to talk me up. Tell them I'm an outfielder, I have scholarship offers all over, but they're offering me too much money not to go pro."

"Do you play baseball?"

"I haven't picked up a bat since grade school."

"And you think this is going to work?"

"Absolutely. I led in by asking how they thought the Yankees would do this year, and none of them know anything about baseball."

"What if they ask someone later that does?"

"It only has to work for tonight. But the key is you doing the talking. Hype is everything. If it comes from me, it's just another guy talking shit, but if it comes from you it'll build intrigue. Are you in?"

"Sure."

"Sure is a terrible answer. If we're going to do this I have to trust you."

He extended a hand and Barrett shook it firmly.

"Good man," Sidney said.

The Jeep pulled into the driveway and within minutes they were poolside, where the three girls sat and lay on a bright red rectangular couch that looked like it could fit a dozen people. Angela lay in the crucifix position mumbling something about a joint they smoked, Kristy sat on the couches' edge and looked at the water like she might jump in, and Tammy sat with her legs crossed so that her checkered capris hugged her knees tight. Despite two ashtrays on a glass table, she laid her cigarette on the glass so that the ember hung over the edge.

"I'm going to put my beer in the fridge," Sidney said. As soon as he disappeared Kristy tapped Barrett's leg.

"So he's a baseball player, huh?"

Barrett had never run a hustle like this before, but the formula seemed straightforward enough.

Credibility.

"Yeah. He's got a bunch of scholarship offers. Miami, Michigan, UCLA."

"The Bruins?"

Barrett had no idea what this meant, but her enthusiasm told him to nod along. Wealth.

"They're all great schools, but the pros are offering too much to resist."

"What if he gets injured?" Tammy asked.

"The signing bonus alone will keep him flush for years."

Tammy pulled back her hair into a ponytail and then released the mane. "My agent is trying to get me one of those for next season."

And a dash of celebrity.

"The Yankees even had Don Mattingly speak to him after one of their games."

Kristy perked up. "The guy that dated Cher?"

"She's old," Tammy said.

"He's hot."

And there it was. Kristy left the deck in search of Sidney and never returned.

Tammy poked Angela until she sat up. "You should go to bed, hun."

"Okay." Angela fell backwards.

"No, no, no. Bed." She helped her friend to her feet and made sure she was steady enough to head off on her own. After a few stumbles, she made it inside and left them alone on the deck.

"She's hammered," Tammy said. She lit a cigarette, took a couple of faux drags, and passed it to Barrett. "I learned quick in Hollywood to hold my booze."

She straddled Barrett's legs, causing him to fall back, and he hadn't fully sat back up before she kissed him. Barrett dropped the cigarette and let her lead.

"How old are you?" she asked.

He considered lying for a moment, but he could tell she knew. "Sixteen."

She giggled. "Are you a virgin?"

This time a lie felt like the only choice. "No."

She reached over, pulled a diaphragm from her purse and held it an inch from his face.

"So you won't mind using this?"

Sweat immediately beaded on his lip, and he scrambled for the right response until she tapped his nose with the diaphragm.

"I'm just joking. I'll take care of everything."

She flung the diaphragm like a frisbee into the pool and kissed him again.

More than two decades later Barrett reflects on that memory with amazement as he heads to his local variety store for a pack of smokes and wonders what the odds are of meeting a life-long best friend and losing his virginity in the same night. This is the same variety store he's been going to since he moved into the wealthy neighbourhood, and he likes it because it's small and packed with stuff to buy, just like any variety store in any neighbourhood.

"Hey Tina, how are you today?"

Tina is in her mid-fifties. She looks up from her gossip magazine with a smile that highlights crooked teeth and sets two packs of his brand on the counter like she's done it a million times before. He reaches for the packs as she puts an envelope labeled BARRETT FULLER down beside them. "A kid brought this in for you first thing this morning."

"A kid?"

"Couldn't have been more than twelve."

"A boy?"

"No, a girl. Dark hair."

"You're sure it was a girl?"

"Unless boys started wearing pigtails."

He grabs the packs and heads for a bench out front. There's a pattern here, and it's wearing him down. Every time he makes some progress, every time he's able to take his mind off the extortion, another letter arrives. He looks around to see if anyone noticeable is watching, then content that the extortionist isn't directly visible, he opens the letter.

OPPORTUNITY #3: ACTIONS HAVE CONSEQUENCES.
"And Mil learned that day that choices aren't just about his wants, they have consequences and those consequences affect more than him." The female you had sex with in her car the other day is a seventeen-year-old, grade eleven student. You have twenty-four hours to donate three million dollars in scholarships to the Empowering Young Women scholarship fund for disadvantaged teens and copy the Once Upon a Hypocrite site as proof, or she will go public about your intimacy, the police will visit your home, and every parent that buys your books will know you had sex with a teenager.

The pressure in Barrett's head builds until his eyes hurt and he gags. *This is someone who sees me all the time,* he thinks. *This is someone who knows my rhythms.*

He hustles home as fast as possible and storms onto the outside pool deck, where a swarthy older man with a bald crown and close-cut grey hair on the sides is skimming leaves from the pool tarp.

"Ahmose. Round up everyone and meet me in the kitchen, please."

Ahmose nods and Barrett goes to the kitchen to wait. He could have fifty employees, and he knows people who have that many. People to tend to the cars, people to do his grocery shopping, people to buy his clothes, masseuses, personal trainers, nutritionists, therapists, acupuncturists, drivers, dog walkers, dog sitters, and chefs. But he values his privacy too much for any more than the essentials. A cleaning lady, who is off today, Ahmose the pool man, and Danica and Marie, two gardeners who keep the grounds looking like a mansion should. He employs these people because they work mostly outside, during the day, and that reduces the chances of them finding him popping pills or watching pornography.

Each of them has been on the payroll more than five years, and while they don't converse more than they have to, the years they've spent on his property heightens his sense of betrayal.

Ahmose leads the way into the kitchen followed by Marie and Danica. All of them look concerned.

"Is something wrong, Mr. Fuller?" Danica asks. She is the youngest of the three by at least a decade.

"We're about to find out." He lights a cigarette and circles around them. "You all have children, right?"

After five years he should know this but they all nod anyway.

"Okay. One of you is fucking with me. At least one of you. I know what you're doing, so this is how this is going to work. One of you is going to admit you are sending me letters, or all of you are going to be fired, and I'll make sure none of you work in your industries again. Which means if you love your children and value them eating three meals a day, you'll confess."

Marie cries immediately. Loud, panicked sobbing that accentuates the flesh of her fat cheeks. Ahmose hugs her and looks at Barrett like he has rabies.

"One of you confess or all of you lose. I want you to look at each other. Do you really want two innocent people to lose their jobs because one of you is a greedy asshole?"

Danica steps forward. "Please, Mr. Fuller. We don't know what you're talking about. We like working here, right?" She looks to her colleagues, who nod in unison. "We need these jobs and we would never do anything to jeopardize them."

Barrett butts out his cigarette and rolls the tips of his fingers across the lines in his forehead. Everything about the worry in their eyes screams fear, not guilt. It occurs to him that it's possible they could all be in on it, so he inspects their eyes one more time, but there's too much shock to be hustling. The maddening part of suspicion is that in the right light anyone can look innocent or guilty, and he's never felt further from being decisive.

"Is everything okay?" Ahmose asks.

"I need you all to leave; I need my privacy right now."

Ahmose nods and leads Marie and Danica out of the kitchen. Barrett lights another cigarette and inhales like the smoke can lead him to the extortionist.

Seeing the look of fear in their eyes was unsettling, but this is a process of elimination and he just checked three more people off the list. If only the list weren't so long.

With the stress reaching stroke-like levels he heads for Sidney's place and finds him sitting at a round glass table on his penthouse deck. The sun shines, but Barrett would still be wearing sunglasses if it was pouring rain. Sidney is watering a series of brightly coloured plants with a hose and looks at him with concern.

"Tell me she at least looked older?"

"She said she was studying third-year philosophy. I won't have people talking about me like I'm Polanski. Because with the press and the parents' paranoia, it'll be a shitshow. I don't want people looking at me like I'm a dirtbag."

"Don't worry. The donations are doable. And we'll make it back long-term on the new contract I'm negotiating you. I'll set the donations up, but you should write up an announcement for the site so we can at least spin this into some positive press."

"I'm selling the place in south of France."

"Not the villa."

"The demand is for a three-million dollar donation. I've got to sell something."

"We'll catch this asshole. And when we do, I'll figure out a way to get everything you've lost back."

Barrett looks at him like he's not so sure.

NINETEEN

"I told you we're doing something different today." Barrett watches Richard's shocked expression as they follow a seal trainer with a mustache and greying hair to the feeding deck above the tank.

The man sets a large bucket of dead fish at Barrett's feet. "One good enough?"

"Perfect, thanks."

"You've got forty-five minutes." The man taps his watch and leaves the deck."

There's so much excitement surging through Richard that he bounces on the spot.

"How'd you get the zoo to open an hour early?"

"I paid them a lot of money. I need to clear my head, you need to be cheered up, and nothing's going to do that better than feeding these crazies." He tosses a fish over the circular deck, and before it hits the water a large fur seal explodes into the air and snatches it in its teeth. Richard steps back with a giggle, and Barrett picks up the bucket and tips it toward the kid. "Let's go."

After choosing the largest fish, he takes it by the tail with both hands and flings it onto the floor of their cage, where a seal so fat it's hard to believe it can move emerges from behind a pile of boulders and swallows the food as fast as possible.

Barrett gestures to the water with a fish. "You know they don't really club the seals."

"What?"

"That Greenpeace shit about seal clubbing. You know the videos with all the blood on the ice?"

"Yeah."

"It's not inhumane at all. They actually kill them with a single spike to the head, no different than they kill cows or pigs in slaughterhouses. The blood on the ice is from dragging them after they're dead. It creates a gruesome picture, but it's misleading. There's a lesson in that."

Richard throws two more into the water and wipes his hands on the back of his pants. "Do you know any gay people?"

Barrett looks at him like it was the last question he expected. "Tons. Why?"

"Just asking."

"Uh, hmm."

"I'm just curious."

"Curious like you find your friends attractive?"

"I don't find anyone attractive."

"So where is this coming from?"

"I've got a project at school, and I want to know how you feel about the subject."

"Why?"

"Because I respect you."

The words stop the conversation for a moment. The maturity of the boy's response surprises Barrett, and he feels obliged to the take the question seriously.

"Okay. Ask away."

Richard throws another fish into the water. "Do you have any gay friends?"

"Like I said, many."

"So you're not homophobic?"

"Of course not. They teach you that word in school now?"

"Why 'of course not?' Lots of people hate gays and lesbians."

"Lots of people hate different races and religions too. It doesn't mean those people are right."

Richard throws a fish onto a blue floating pad and watches as a seal dives on top and swallows the fish. He turns to Barrett, who lights a cigarette. "Why do you think people are gay or lesbian?"

"I think that's a question that has already made up its mind."

"What do you mean?"

"I mean we don't ask straight people why they like men or women. It's just accepted. So the very question about gays or lesbians implies they have to explain themselves, and they don't."

"So people just are who they are?"

Barrett exhales a thick stream of smoke. "In my experience, yeah."

"Does Mom know any gay people?"

"Sure."

"Who?"

"Does she still play cards with that heavy-set woman with the bald spot?"

"Brenda?"

"Yeah, Brenda. She's a lesbian."

"Really?"

"Hell, yeah. But you didn't hear it from me."

Richard giggles. He picks up two more fish and passes one to Barrett. "How come you and Mom don't hang out more?"

The question makes Barrett crave consecutive cigarettes. He looks up into the blue sky until the sun warms his face and enjoys the pleasure of a deep drag. "We're busy."

"She says you're not close anymore."

"That's not true."

"That's what she says when I ask why we don't see you more."

"She's just being dramatic. Listen, when people get older they don't see each other as much. They have families and careers, but that doesn't mean they aren't close. We hung out all the time growing up. Did she tell you we shared a bedroom?"

"No." A seal jumps out of the water with a yip, and Richard throws another fish into the enclosure.

"For six years. My parents boarded college students from South America, so from eight to fourteen your mom was my roommate."

"That would suck."

"Towards the end a little when I started high school, but mostly it was awesome. We'd always talk before bed, play video games, cards, wrestle."

"Wrestle?"

"Oh, yeah. Your mom is badass. Way braver than me."

Richard lifts another fish from the bucket. "Then you must not be very brave, because she's afraid of spiders."

"I'm serious. She's one of the toughest people I know. When I was in university we were on a fishing trip, I was drunk and ..."

"Drunk on a fishing trip?"

"I know. But I was. And when I cast, the hook swung back at me and stuck in my thumb. Do you know what a Repella is?"

Richard shakes his head.

"It's a hook with multiple barbs. Anyway, one of the hooks went in my thumb past the barb, right here." He holds up the thumb and points to the other side of his nail. "Which means there was no way out."

"Why?"

"Because fish hooks are designed to snag, and the nail was stopping me from pushing it through the other side."

"So what did you do?"

"Nothing. I stood there in shock, feeling sorry for myself, until your mom took me back into the cottage, gave me a bottle of vodka, and cut it out with a razor."

"She did that to you?"

"For me. And thank god she did. Because we were too far from a hospital, and I wasn't going to do anything about it."

"Did it hurt?"

"Less than the fish hook. She talked me through it, so I didn't really feel anything. She has that ability to make you believe." He drops his cigarette on the ground, steps on it, and throws another fish into the water.

Richard looks at him carefully and notices the happiness the story triggered in his uncle's eyes. "If she's wrong and you still are close, then why don't you want new memories?"

"What do you mean?"

"I mean those are cool stories and you sound like friends, but they're old stories. I love Mom too, and I would never want to only see her a few times a year."

Barrett stares over the edge of the Plexiglas and into the pool until a seal breaks the surface and splashes them as he re-enters the water. They both step back from the edge and Barrett gestures to the seals.

"Get another fish in the water. We've still got half a bucket here."

TWENTY

For the first time since the extortion, Barrett feels like writing. No psyching himself up, no doubt, just the flow of ideas that seem like they'll make his head explode if they aren't released. Thoughts connect naturally, sentences are clear, and fresh metaphors flow from his fingertips with every stroke of the keys. This is a zone he's dreamed of, and when he finishes three pages he leans back in his chair to enjoy the euphoria. In this dreamy state, a painful truth hits him. The more money he's made over the years, the less he's written. And when he does write, it's not a compulsion, it's a job. But that changed yesterday. The time with Richard and the mirth in their repartee energized him, and he's grateful for the resulting words.

He's celebrating his three pages with a cigarette when a feather duster brushing over his hand startles him. His neck twists to see his cleaning lady, Nicole, behind him in a French maid outfit.

"All done."

The timing couldn't be better. He sees this as a reward for his flurry of creativity but also appreciates the feeling of finishing three pages enough to know that if he breaks the momentum, if he changes course, it could be a long time until he feels it again.

He removes an envelope from the top drawer of the desk and passes it to her, prompting her to tickle his neck with the duster.

"Are you ready for me to clean you?"

Barrett recoils. "I've got to work."

"Yeah?"

He nods.

"Okay." She winks and leaves the room with a walk that makes him think he's an idiot for turning her down. He takes a quick breath to centre himself before turning back to the computer. His fingers are hovering over the keyboard when a chime prompts him to check his email. Reason tells him to finish another three pages and then look at the email as a reward, but compulsion leads him to click on his inbox icon immediately. The subject heading reads: OPPORTUNITY #4.

The invasion of privacy makes him recoil for a moment. This is his email, his place to flirt, post pictures or set up dates, and as he looks at the paragraph in front of him, he acknowledges just how deep this extortionist has penetrated.

OPPORTUNITY #4: TREAT ALL WOMEN AS PRECIOUS AS YOUR MOTHER. *"Mil learned that day not to judge people by their gender. And in the end he was grateful Bridgette joined the team because they couldn't have done it without her."*

This is from his fourth book. A work he knows is not his most creative, but one that sold over ten million copies worldwide. He was partying and travelling so much during that time that he can't even remember writing the passage being used to extort him, which is a shame, because a sense of pride runs through him as he reads the words. He lights a cigarette, lets the nicotine take hold, and reads on.

The way you treat women is an embarrassment to real gentlemen. You will attend a sensitivity training workshop at 500 Palson Street tonight at eight this evening and download proof of your attendance or the public will know how their beloved Russell Niles really feels about women.

All he can think of is Nicole. Nicole, made to clean in costume. Nicole, who dusts his computer and books. Nicole, who has access to his privacy and every reason to extort him. It hurts to think that she might be the one torturing him.

In fact, it stings to think that any woman he knows is behind this. He loves their company too much to hate one. Let it be a man, preferably a stranger, but don't let it be a woman.

He takes his chequebook from his desk and hustles downstairs in time to see her putting on her jacket. With the cheques held at eye level, he walks towards her like a cop with a badge.

"How much do I need to give you to end this?"

"What?"

The crazed look in his eyes startles her.

"Don't fuck with me. Sensitivity training? What is this really about? Did you want a relationship?"

"I don't know what you're talking about."

"I get a demand about sensitivity training at the same time you're cleaning my house as a French maid and I'm supposed to believe that's a coincidence?"

Nicole removes the envelope he gave her, takes out the money, and throws it at him so the bills scatter through the air.

"Keep your money. It's worth putting up with you being an asshole, but not dealing with you acting like a lunatic."

She storms out of the house, leaving him with five hundred dollars scattered at his feet. He pins the demand beside the first three on the wall beside his computer and examines the words. Sensitivity training. The words make Barrett want to tear the extortion letter to pieces, but he won't. Because no matter how frustrated he becomes, a childish temper is no match for the understanding that he is living a dream.

In a society filled with people wishing for the weekend to start again on Sunday nights and thanking god it's Friday, he is the master of his own time, and that is a privilege he will do anything to protect.

He has the money to do whatever he wants, a home designed to facilitate every desire, and work that is adored and appreciated by millions. These are facts with power he can't deny; these are the luxuries he is willing to humiliate himself for in order to keep.

That evening, after two cups of coffee, he steps out of his car and enters a yoga studio, where the smell of scented candles makes him think of a woman he dated briefly in university. Jennifer McKay. Jennifer, who knew him before his writing aspirations. Jennifer, who once asked him to go to Europe with her. He'd turned her down to take a job as a waiter to pay for tuition. If only she could see his passport now.

His first impression of the yoga studio is that this is not high-end therapy. Plastic chairs form a circle in the centre of the room. Some people are seated, others stand around chatting and drinking coffee. A sign written in marker on a flow chart reads: SENSITIVITY TRAINING. What this is, Barrett thinks, is creepy. He scans the room then a Chinese man with a faux-hawk approaches.

"Welcome, can I get you to sign in?" He gestures to a logbook on an adjacent table. "Do you live in the neighbourhood?"

Barrett shakes his head, picks up a pen, and signs in.

"So how did you hear about us?"

The question feels a little on the nose, so Barrett looks at him like he could be the one that extorted him here. "Why so many questions?"

The tone throws the man off.

"We just like to keep track of how people come to us. That's all, sir."

"Can I have a receipt?"

"I'm sorry?"

"A receipt. Proof that I was here."

"I've never had anyone ask for a receipt."

"Do you have letterhead?"

The man nods in amazement and Barrett puts a hundred-dollar bill on the counter. "Can you sign that letterhead for me proving I'm here?"

The man slides the money back to Barrett. "I'd be happy to. You can pick it up when you leave."

Barrett picks up the hundred, and as he turns from the table, a woman to his right captures his attention because she's swearing into her cell phone like she invented the words. A closer look reveals that it's Rebecca. Rebecca, who runs his fan club. Rebecca, who wowed him at their first meeting. He looks at her until they make eye contact, and he's surprised to see that she isn't embarrassed. In fact, she's just short of dismissive. A quick raise of her coffee in hello and she's off to grab a seat. Pride tells him to pretend she doesn't look good, but there's no denying her presence. With a form-fitting white track jacket, green khakis, and brown hair, he would bet the place in Vegas that she smells like flowers. Everything about her compels him to follow her, but there aren't any seats available near her, so he settles for one beside a large woman with a shaved head. Far from roses, this woman smells like a keg of beer.

A middle-aged woman in a high-end power suit steps into the circle's centre. With defined cheekbones, spiked hair, and long legs, she's not your average corporate warrior.

"For those of you joining us for the first time, I'm Angelica Mills," she says in a voice slow-roasted from years of cigarillos. "The fact that you're here means you're brazen. Some people equate that with greed and egocentricity, but I have a different theory.

"I don't see you as insensitive, I see you as desensitized. Desensitized by fractured families, sixty-hour work weeks, and nights spent under the trance of Internet porn."

The bald woman beside Barrett laughs, heightening his growing discomfort. Angelica Mills is blowing his high. She looks the part, and yes, she is sexy, but her tone is confusing. Equal parts motherly, annoying teacher, and sarcastic boss, her words make him want to erase her from his memory. But leaving isn't an option, so he looks at Rebecca and continues to listen.

"It's my job to re-sensitize you," Angelica says. "And there's no better way to start than with touch. Today, you're going to experience cuddle therapy."

A man in the front row with a pencil mustache and a thousand-dollar suit smiles in a way that attracts Angelica's attention. She steps towards him with the dogma of a dominatrix.

"Easy, Wall Street, I said cuddle therapy, not humping therapy. To begin, I'd like you all to pair up, lie down, and hug."

A panic spreads across the group. Many of them shift in their seats, giving the room the feel of a junior high dance where everyone's afraid of being the last one left against the wall. Angelica enjoys their discomfort for a moment before picking up the pace with some motivating words.

"Nothing sensual, people, just lying together in silence. Tonight, you will embrace the power of human touch."

The group is still hesitant. Some people make eye contact with potential patrons, others wait hopefully for someone to come to them. Angelica claps her hands.

"Loosen up people, this isn't AA."

Barrett doesn't see this as a chore, he sees it as an opportunity. Sweat's forming on his palms as he heads towards Rebecca, when a large man with muscles like an action figure steps in front of him.

"Need a partner?"

Barrett shakes his head and slides past the big man to see Rebecca lying on the floor with a blonde man in a tight white T-shirt. Only nicotine can calm his frustration at this point, but when he turns to leave the room, a short man with hair like a clown blocks his path. It's impossible not to stare at the curly tufts of red hair sprouting from each side of the man's head only to be betrayed by the tight and shiny skin of a bald crown.

"Looks like it's just us left," the man says with an accent Barrett places as Boston.

Barrett raises his eyebrows in acknowledgement. The nicotine will have to wait.

"I'm Drew," the short man says, extending a pudgy hand.

The hand is sweaty, and Barrett decides that nobody that short should have such a large belly. They lie down together, each of them stiff, like getting to the floor is difficult for each body, before Drew leans in and hugs him. Not a buddy hug, but a full-on hug of affection that puts them so close that Barrett can smell the hot dog Drew ate before the meeting. Pride sparks him to try and salvage the moment by flirting with Rebecca, but she won't look at him. She's only an arm's length away, but she's too busy cradling blondy to notice. This is clearly a deliberate snub. He can't remember the last time he failed to get a woman's attention, and the sting of disinterest leaves him anxious to erase this new memory.

A smirk fills Angelica's face as she walks by them. The height difference leaves them an easy target with Drew's head resting just above Barrett's stomach. They lie in silence for a moment with Barrett looking like he can't take another second and Drew looking like he's just getting comfortable before Drew raises his head to lock eyes.

"You breathe like a woman."

Barrett's still lost in Rebecca but the words grab his attention. "What?"

"From the stomach."

"Can we lose the commentary?"

Angelica rings a large brass bell three times, effectively silencing the room, and Barrett can tell from her expression that this is the part of the job she loves. Setting the pace and keeping people waiting for her next direction.

"Excellent start, everyone. This is the power of touch." She points to a woman with a bad perm. "Now, starting here, I want every other person to turn to their right and embrace the person beside you."

This is a chance to fix the snub. Only this isn't just about pride. This is about wanting Rebecca to feel the way he feels, and while he's not used to yearning from afar, he can't deny its power. But before he can do anything, he needs to get Drew to release his grip.

"Okay buddy, time to switch," he says, tapping Drew's shoulders.

Drew nods a thank-you and rolls towards a woman with a bolt through her nose.

Relief washes over Barrett. He wipes at the sweat left from Drew's cheek and prays for the smell of hot dog to dissipate.

After two deep breaths, he turns toward Rebecca, and to his surprise, she initiates the hug. It's a mechanical one, but intriguing enough for him to offer his best coy smile.

"Sensitivity training, huh?"

"I won't tell if you won't."

"I don't know, you might have more to hide."

"I doubt that."

He looks at her like she's the extortionist. Then a woman with cat glasses a couple down shushes them, prompting Rebecca to look at the woman and shake her wrist and hand in a mock jerk-off before tossing her hand forward with splayed fingers. The realization of a kindred spirit makes Barrett smile.

"Any luck with your pest?" she asks, so close to his ear his toes tingle.

"Not yet."

"I have a fan Sidney should speak with."

"Really?"

"I don't know about threatening, but he's definitely off."

Instinct tells him this is his opportunity. The tone of her voice, the conversation's rhythm. It's like he's been there before.

"Thank you. What do you think about talking more about this over dinner?"

"Dinner?"

"Yeah."

"I don't think so."

The bell chimes twice more and Rebecca breaks their embrace. Immediately, all of his nerve endings loose that magical tingle. She gets up from the floor and begins to walk away before stopping and turning back.

"Tell Sidney I'll call him."

Fuck Sidney, call me, Barrett thinks. But he's too amazed by the rejection to say anything, so he nods weakly and lies back on the floor. The reality is humbling.

This is the first time since he became a millionaire that he hasn't been able to reference his mansion or set an evening's tone with spending, which means she didn't reject his lifestyle, she rejected him. He's well aware that his habit of using money to ensure a good time is immature and vapid, but there is meaning to a life without depth, and that value is avoiding having to be rejected because the real you simply isn't interesting enough. Now he knows for certain that his childhood priest was wrong. He won't go to hell for all his debauchery, he'll go to cuddle therapy.

TWENTY-ONE

With a few glasses of Glengoyne Scotch flowing through his system, Barrett sits at his kitchen island and stares at a list of possible extortionists. Without any deep thought, the list is already at twenty-three, but the more names he writes, the more one name stands out: Todd Rempel. Todd interned with Barrett's publisher last summer. They told Todd that Barrett was in marketing, but it's possible he found out. Todd is a good enough guy, but full of ideas and ambition, two things that Barrett is only interested in when they are his own. From Barrett's point of view, Todd couldn't accept that interns work with little appreciation, and from Todd's point of view, Barrett lacked the humanity to take him seriously or talk to him with any sensitivity. Todd decided against a career in publishing after the internship and went back to school to start a Ph.D.

Barrett taps the paper with his pen and writes: *Todd feels slighted. He is bitter, jealous, and despite knowing Barrett only as a marketing executive, privy to enough of the behind-the-scenes of the Russell Niles books to organize the extortion.*

He lights a cigarette, picks up a phone, and punches in Sidney's number with aggression. It's Sidney's job to protect him, and he'll know where to find the kid.

"I can't leave work, Barrett. I've got too much to do," Sidney says.

"I called about business."

"That's not like you."

"Just listen. I want Todd Rempel in your office in an hour."

"The intern?"

"I'm on my way."

"You think he found out who you are?"

"It's possible."

"You really think he's extorting you?"

"I think he's a desperate wannabe who thinks I fucked him over."

"You did."

"Enough."

"I'm just saying that using him in a brainstorming session and then not acknowledging his contribution is fucking him over."

"Just get him in the office."

Paced by thoughts of Todd Rempel's ambitious eyes, Barrett sets down the phone, crumples up his list, and knocks it across the room with the overhead motion of a volleyball serve.

Fifty minutes later, Barrett sits across from Todd in Sidney's office. Todd wears a cheap blue dress shirt and slacks. He's not stereotypically nerdy, but he's the type whose cerebral nature has always given him an aura a decade older than he looks.

"You know why you're here, don't you?"

"Sidney said you wanted to talk about some of my ideas."

"Do you think I'm stupid?" Barrett asks.

"I think you're a megalomaniac."

Barrett circles his face with an index finger. "You're not going to do well in jail."

"Jail?"

"That's right. But you prefer other J words, don't you? Jealousy, jackal, justice."

Todd runs a hand through a thick mop of curly hair. "I'm not following you, man." He turns to Sidney. "Is he okay?"

Todd's nonchalance heightens Barrett's frustration. He's yelling more than talking now. "You think Russell Niles stole your idea."

"What idea?"

"The derivative piece of shit you begged me to pass on to him last summer."

"Henry the Hippo?"

This is too intense for Barrett not to smoke, so he draws the blinds behind Todd and lights a cigarette. Two drags allow him to lower his voice. "Do you really think he needs to get his inspiration from volunteers?"

Todd is flushed now. More so from the mention of Henry the Hippo than Barrett's accusation, and the intensity brings out a stutter that has plagued him since childhood.

"You said he called it creative."

Barrett leans forward. "I say a lot of things."

"You said he found it surprising."

"Surprisingly bad for a grad student."

Todd is past flustered. Everything about him looks underdeveloped now, more like a teenager, and as Barrett berates him he has to admit to himself that his instincts tell him that Todd isn't the extortionist, that he is nothing more than a young man struggling to get a start in life.

"You're not making any sense. What am I doing here?"

"Sidney will give you cash for a cab on your way out."

"We're done?"

Barrett nods, and Todd begins to exit the room before pausing just in front of the door and pivoting back towards him.

"Did he use my idea?"

A vein across Barrett's forehead swells like it might explode. He picks up a mini-rubber football from Sidney's desk and throws it at Todd, sending him scurrying out of the office.

He wishes Todd were the extortionist. Todd or any of the other people he's mistreated, as long as their identity becomes clear. Because a faceless extortionist means there's no one to direct his anger at and no one to blame for having to give away his yacht and money and sell his property other than himself. And that's a reality that leaves him willing to rebuke a thousand Todd Rempels.

Richard sits at his dining table and stares at his journal until his mother sets a pill and half a glass of water down beside him. She leaves the room as quickly as she entered and he sets the Ritalin on his journal, noticing that it is the same size as the three binder holes on the left hand side. Resigned, he slips the pill into his mouth, swallows it without the water, and begins writing madly in his journal. His mother re-enters the room and is so happy to see him using the journal that she tries to leave without him noticing, but he has already locked eyes with her.

"You're writing in your journal."

"Yep."

"Can I see it?"

"No."

At school, Richard says good morning to the librarian, walks to the computers, and sits at the one at the end of the aisle.

He types "Dr. Jason Burns" into Google and clicks on an article the doctor wrote about behavioural therapy. After scrolling to the bottom, he stops on the doctor's email address where people are invited to send their comments. He cuts and pastes the address into an email account with the home devilhunter9, and in the subject box he types, YOU ARE AN EVIL MAN. He then clicks back to the Internet, copies a cartoon of the devil deflating the earth with his pitchfork, and copies the picture into the message. Content with his work, he hits send and smiles for the first time since he woke up. He then pulls out his cell phone and texts Barrett. *CIGARETTES HAVE OVER A THOUSAND TOXINS IN EACH ONE...JUST A REMINDER. CAN I COME OVER IN AN HOUR?*

Barrett is back at home, standing on his second floor balcony overlooking the pool area when his phone buzzes. He glances at the text and smiles. He is about to put the Lamborghini on the market to help cover the cost of the last extortion and he is in desperate need of a moment of levity. He texts back: *Do you want to know how many toxins are in the pesticide that sprays the fruit you eat every day? See you an hour.* He hits send and feels as ready to sell the Lamborghini as he'll ever be.

He calls his accountant, Gerry, who answers immediately.

"Good to hear your voice, kid. We need to talk."

"I need you to spread the word that the Lamborghini's for sale."

"Sinatra's car?"

"Please, just get word to people who will be interested."

"What's going on?"

"I can't talk about it."

"If you're gambling ..."

"I told you I'm not gambling."

"I've got a great place you can go for a month if it's come to that."

"It's not drugs."

"You're hemorrhaging money, kid. What's with these donations I'm looking at? Four million dollars in a week? You've only got so much property before it's the mansion you're taking a second mortgage on, and don't make me remind you about the economic climate. You don't own a property that hasn't dropped in value the last quarter."

Barrett wants Gerry's guidance, he wants to take his hand and let him make things better, but right now it's about survival, and that means one step at a time. "I need to hear you say I'll get you a buyer for the Lambo."

"It won't be hard. But listen, kid. Whatever's going on, you've got a lot at stake here."

"I know. I've got to go."

Barrett hangs up and counts the seconds until he can see Richard. When the kid arrives, Barrett takes him to the screening room. Richard has never seen a screen fill a wall in a house, let alone played video games on one, so as he manipulates a soldier with his controller, he does so in bliss.

Barrett sits beside him on a half-moon of chocolate leather couches. He watches Richard lean back on one elbow, and the pose makes him envision the kid as a man. Calculations run through his mind about how old he will be when Richard is twenty-five, and a sense of remorse runs through him like he's never felt before. He lights a cigarette and inhales as deeply as possible.

Physically, he is in the room, but his mind is lost in the extortion's haze. He wonders if the extortionist is monitoring the house or if the place has been bugged. He considers which of his undignified moments he would least want shared with the public when Richard's voice breaks his trance.

"Do you have any secrets?"

The question is unnerving. "Why?"

"Because I have a big one and I don't know what to do."

"Who are you keeping it from?"

"Promise you won't tell?"

"Who am I going to tell?"

"I'm keeping it from Mom."

"That's what kids do."

"This is big one."

"At eleven years old? Who are you protecting by keeping it? You or her?"

"Her."

"Then you're doing the right thing. That's what secrets are for." Barrett leans forward so that the muscles in his legs tighten. "How big is it?"

"Life-changing."

"Life-changing?"

Richard nods intensely.

"Then you tell her."

"You just said I'm doing the right thing."

"Not if it's life-changing. Your mother deserves to know the truth. What you have to ask yourself is would you want to know if you were in her situation?"

The kid doesn't hesitate. "I would want to know. Definitely. Thank you."

"My pleasure."

Richard starts another game and speaks while he concentrates on the screen. "Do you have any secrets?"

"Of course."

"And who are you protecting by keeping them?"

Barrett looks at the kid hanging on every word, fully into the moment, and considers the last time he felt that way about anything. "Can we change the subject? Secrets make me uncomfortable."

"Okay. What was Grandpa like?"

The question gets Barrett to sit up. Grandpa. The kid's grandpa, Barrett's father. The man who died before Richard was born.

"Why are you asking about your grandfather?"

"Because I want to know how close you were to your dad."

Barrett knows this means he wants a point of comparison, but the question is tricky. His father was a provider, calm, taught him how to swim and later how to drive, but on an emotional level they weren't close at all. No doubt his father was loving, but Barrett can only remember once hearing his father tell him he loved him.

It was October of grade seven, and he was on a nature trail three blocks from his house when a friend, Derek Pines, told him about a cave beneath a fallen tree on the south side of the hill.

Barrett immediately thought this would be the perfect place to smoke cigarettes, and the two of them set off for the cave talking about how they would dress it up as a place of their own. They were so worked up that the fifteen-foot drop didn't faze either of them, and after negotiating a steep bit of hill where the tree snapped, they reached what Derek called a cave. It was actually more of a large den, a hole that had been ripped or eroded, but they could still fit in it, and it was definitely private, so they crawled inside and sat across from each other. There wasn't room to do much more but that didn't deter their enthusiasm. This was a place of their own, a place free from the eyes of adults, and that alone made them talk non-stop with excitement. They smoked four cigarettes in a row and talked about bringing a portable radio the next time before deciding to go home and spread the word to the rest of their friends. Derek was leading the way out when Barrett felt a force smash into his back, hard enough to knock him to his knees. The blow felt like someone had punched him between the shoulder blades, and before he could process the moment, another smack knocked him fully to the ground. The hole collapsed, and dirt rushed over him until he passed out.

His next conscious memory was his father's voice. Derek later told him that he ran home and told Mr. Fuller what happened. Mr. Fuller ran to the nature trail so fast that Derek was still a block away by the time Mr. Fuller dug Barrett out with a spade. And despite the dirt in his eyes, ears, and mouth, Barrett was still breathing. He'll never forget the look on his dad's face. The look of selflessness that only a parent can form. Mr. Fuller hugged Barrett tighter than he ever had and whispered "I love you." All it took was a near-death experience.

Barrett looks closely at Richard's young eyes. "Have you been thinking about your dad?"

"Yeah."

Of course he has, Barrett scolds himself. The sting of guilt for not helping his sister and Richard through the dissolving of their family heightens his discomfort, so he decides the best thing to do is answer the kid's original question with what he needs to hear.

"Your grandfather was a great guy, and I was very lucky to grow up with him as my dad."

"Do you think he would have liked me?"

Barrett takes a cigarette from his pack, lights it, and drags hard. "Are you kidding me? He would have loved you."

"How do you know?"

"Because he loved spirit, and you're full of spirit."

"What do you mean?"

"I mean you ask questions, expect answers, and then ask some more. He would have respected that about you."

Richard smiles for a moment before his face turns serious again. "How old were you when Grandpa died?"

Barrett points at him with his cigarette. "This is what I mean by spirit."

"Sorry. I understand if you don't want to talk about it."

The day Barrett heard about his father's heart attack flashes through his mind. He arrived home from a campus pub around two in the morning when Carol called to tell him that their father was dead. Nothing's been as sobering, and he often wonders if he's ever really been intoxicated since. Or maybe he's never really been sober since.

Either way, his life changed forever. He hung up after hearing the news of his dad's death, and all he could think about was how boring his visit to the house was the last time they saw each other.

"I was twenty-two, and his death was unexpected," Barrett says, reaching for another cigarette.

"What was it like to know you'd never see him again?"

"Horrible." He knows the boy's questions aren't really about his grandfather, so he steers the conversation in the right direction. "Do you think you'll ever see your dad again?"

"I don't know."

"If you don't ever see him again, don't just remember him leaving. As time goes on, you're going to be tempted to focus on that moment, but trust me when I tell you to remember all your time with him equally."

The words wash over Richard, bringing a surprising ease. Maybe it's Barrett's tone, maybe it's the care, but it definitely feels good. Richard opens a soda and the can hisses.

"You look tired."

"I'm fine," Barrett says.

"Will you read a story I wrote?"

Barrett butts out the cigarette. "I'm not really into stories."

"My therapist wants me to write my feelings in a journal, but I'd rather write stories. Like the ones Russell Niles writes."

Barrett looks at the boy for any signs that he is baiting him and decides the tone is too candid to be so calculated. "Your shrink wants you to write?"

"Every day in a journal."

"So show him."

"I want you to read it."

"This sounds like more of a mom thing. Why don't you show it to her?"

"Because she's always afraid I'm depressed, so she'll tell me it's good, even if it's not, just to keep me happy."

"You're a stoic little man, aren't you?"

"What does stoic mean?"

"It means I'll read your story. But I've got a favour I need from you."

Richard nods. He never thought Barrett would need his help, but he is excited to do anything for him.

"I need you to go into the Russell Niles fan club, ask for Rebecca, and tell her you have a Russell Niles autograph that you want to sell her."

"You have his autograph?"

"That's not the point. I do business with this woman and I want to see how she'll react. Did you hear what I need you to do?"

"Yeah."

"Say it."

"Go inside, ask for Rebecca and tell her I have a Russell Niles autograph I want to sell her."

"Good man." Barrett pulls out a mini-recorder the size of an index finger. "And I need you to put this in your pocket so I can hear everything later."

"What if she asks to see the autograph?"

"Tell her it's at home."

"Do you have the autograph?"

"What do you care?"

"I don't want to lie to her."

Barrett pops yet another smoke in his mouth and lights it in a fluid motion. "Look, think of yourself as a spy. Sometimes they have to bend the rules for the greater good."

"What's that?"

"Something uh, something that technically breaks the rules but benefits good people."

"Okay."

As Richard gets out of the car, Barrett feels a sense of relief. He has faith in the kid, and there's an ease in believing.

Richard is more excited about going into the Russell Niles fan club than carrying out the mission, but he respects Barrett and wants to impress him enough to focus on the task. He enters the fan club and approaches Rebecca, who is the only one in the room. She is busy stuffing envelopes and barely notices his presence.

"Are you Rebecca?"

"I am."

"I have a Russell Niles autograph I'd like to sell you."

"You and a thousand other dreamers, kid."

A shelf full of Mil Bennett action figures makes it a struggle to stay focused, so he takes a deep breath and makes a play for her attention.

"You don't believe me?"

She tosses the last envelope on a table and looks at him for the first time.

These aren't the loving eyes of his mother, the obligated eyes of his teachers, or the eyes of any woman he has ever seen before. This is his introduction to irreverence, and the words cute, kid, and innocent have no currency in her world.

"Are you really surprised?" she says, matching his tone.

"He signed it for me last month."

"Right." She holds up a middle finger face level. "And this means welcome."

"Why don't you believe me?"

"Because Russell Niles is too much of a conceited asshole to ever sign an autograph." She passes him a rolled-up poster. "Take a poster and have a nice day."

Richard takes the poster, but he doesn't want to leave. The shelves of Mil Bennett books, the toys, the video games, and the giant blow-up of Mil in the far corner, all fill him with excitement and curiosity. But he knows he has to get back to Barrett, so he makes a promise to himself to visit the place again and leaves.

He slides into the car and passes Barrett the mini-recorder.

"She's not very nice."

The kid's reaction makes Barrett smile. "She's feisty."

"What's that?"

"The best kind of nice."

Barrett spends the night listening to Rebecca on tape for any clues in her tone that she might be the extortionist. There's no denying the loathing is there, and she is definitely rebellious, but bitter? The type of bitterness that this extortion requires doesn't fit her personality. Or is that lust talking? The more he listens to the tape, the less he wonders if she's dangerous and the more he fantasizes about being with her.

Richard stares at his tongue in the mirror and curses Dr. Burns. He's never paid attention to his tongue before, but now it feels like it fills his mouth, and combined with the purple beneath his eyes, he is convinced that everyone who looks at him knows he is medicated. He puts a pill in his mouth and lets the bitterness dissolve until his tongue feels coated with shellac. Forget water. If he has to take these pills, he wants the taste to mirror his feelings about them.

He walks into the library and chooses his usual seat at a computer at the end of the aisle. He searches the Internet for cartoons until he finds one with a psychiatrist asleep in a chair while a patient is preparing a noose. The cartoon feels fitting, so he copies it and pastes it into an email for Dr. Burns from his devilhunter9 account. After hitting send, he feels better. It's a small measure of revenge, but it feels right to do something. He wishes he could share the moment with someone, but he knows better so he texts Barrett instead. *I just did something for the greater good.*

Barrett is in the middle of updating his website with information about the three-million-dollar donation to the woman's scholarship foundation when he gets the text. He looks to see it's from Richard and feels his blood pressure drop. The message pries a smile from his stressed lips, and he texts back: *Now you get to do something good for yourself guilt free. Talk soon.* He sets down the phone and admits he is grateful for the kid's text. The mirth puts him in the mood to write, so he finishes up with the website and is opening up a fresh page when there is a buzz from his front gates.

He turns to the video monitor and is shocked to see Martin Brouge.

Seeing him for the first time in a decade at Don's party felt odd, but now that he's being extorted, Martin's presence has him shaking with suspicion. On screen, from the camera's high angle, Martin is even better-looking than in person, and the image makes Barrett cringe. For a moment, he considers pretending that he isn't home before hustling down his winding staircase to greet him. As he watches Martin walk up the path, his mind swirls with suspicion. He's wondering if he should confront him as the extortionist when Martin's confused look makes him pause.

"Barrett? You live here?" Martin asks.

Barrett nods.

Martin cocks his head and smiles. "Really? Now that's a coincidence I'd pay for."

"What are you doing here?"

"I had no idea this is your house. I'm here to buy the Lamborghini."

"The Lamborghini?"

Martin nods slyly.

"How do you even know it's for sale?"

"My agent saw the ad and tipped me off." He gestures to the mansion. "It looks like Don wasn't exaggerating when he said you're a money-maker. What happened that you're selling Sinatra's Lambo?"

"I'm buying a new one."

Martin pats him on the shoulder. "Fair enough. So where's my new car?"

The tone makes Barrett wince. This is the type of bravado that he can't resist. Call it pride, call it insecurity, or call it a capitalist spirit, but he would rather lie than be dominated. "I'm sorry," he says. "But I got an offer this morning."

"I'll give you fifty thousand more."

"I already accepted the offer."

"A hundred."

This is exactly what Barrett would do if he wanted someone's car, and the ease that Martin is pulling this off with leaves him seething.

"I'm sorry. But I've already accepted the offer."

"I see. Well, if you change your mind, call me. And remember, I've got a launch tomorrow night. I'd love to see you there."

Everything about his tone heightens Barrett's suspicion. With the frustration of a child flowing through him, Barrett marches upstairs, grabs the life-size doll of Mil Bennett from the corner of his office and rips it apart. First the right arm, then the left leg, and then he pulls so hard on the head that he falls awkwardly onto the floor with the doll's torso on top of him. He is about to put the doll in a headlock when the phone rings. He sees Sidney's name and hits speaker.

"You sound out of breath," Sidney says. "Did I catch you in the middle of something?"

Barrett pushes the doll off his chest. "Nothing fun."

"I have some good news for you. Rebecca's having that fanatic she mentioned come to her office under the guise of winning a contest."

"Good." It's difficult to focus on being extorted when he hears her name. "Did she mention anything about running into me?"

"Just that she did. Is there more to mention?"

Barrett shakes his head casually but internally screams in frustration that she would reduce him to an afterthought. If she's bringing this fanatic by the office, he wants to be there.

"I'll go," he says.

"You sure?"

"I don't want to miss this."

"You like her, don't you?"

"Of course I like her."

"So?"

"I'm working on it."

Sidney smacks his lips. "You think if it works out you can pass me on some of your regulars?'

"I'll think about it."

By the time Barrett reaches the fan club, it's clear to him that he would give Sidney the phone number of every woman he's ever met in return for it working out with Rebecca, and this is a reality that makes his palms sweat. Maybe it's because she's rejecting him, but he can't stop thinking about her. The mischief in her voice, the fact that she was at sensitivity training, and the way she gave the finger to the woman that shushed her, all left deep impressions in his mind. This isn't just desire, these are feelings. He taps himself on the temples as a reminder that his career is at stake and greets Rebecca with a smile. She is all business though and talks fast while leading him to a back office.

"I'll give you a minute to get ready before I bring him in," she says in a voice just raspy enough that he imagines her saying more erotic things.

The office is even smaller than the room in which he first met Rebecca, but sliding doors lead to a back patio that lets in enough light to avoid claustrophobia.

Now that the surroundings have his attention, a sigh slips out of his mouth. Russell Niles memorabilia is piled everywhere, making it look more like a toy store inventory room.

He considers going out onto the patio for a smoke but Rebecca returns with a dishevelled man with long dirty blond hair pulled into a ponytail.

"This is Phillip Nawe," she says, escorting him to a seat across from Barrett.

Barrett wants her to stay, but she's gone before he finds a way to ask her.

This Phillip smells like a pawnshop, as if he has slept with mothballs for the last decade. A quick appraisal provides a strong outline. Late teens with fingernails chewed until the corners are bloody and glasses so thick his eyes look like a cartoon character. Everything about him is anxious, and it is clear being here has him stressed. The writer in Barrett can't resist the setup, so he leans back in his chair and offers his best detective face.

"I understand you wrote Mr. Niles some rather nasty letters."

"Not nasty, disappointed."

Phillip's voice is surprisingly confident, yet over-pronunciation suggests he used to have a speech impediment of some sort.

"Disappointed?"

"Yes. He was on his way to being a legend."

"On his way?"

"His stories aren't evolving, okay? Any writer with his impact evolves. There's a responsibility to the reader. Take Spider Man, for example.

"With the introduction of the Spectacular Spider Man came an edgy character living in a society that had moved beyond the morals of the sixties and the Amazing Spider Man. And the readers were forced to evolve with the character.

"And then the Web of Spider Man evolved to fit the dark side brought out by materialism. It reflected the eighties, it mirrored the time. The Niles books don't evolve, okay? They don't live up to their responsibility."

Barrett is amazed that anyone takes his books this seriously, and while his ego is effectively stroked, it always surprises him to see an adult so passionate about children's books. But as he watches Phillip wipe at his chapped lips, there is no denying that this man qualifies as a fanatic. The real question is whether or not he's dangerous.

"Is it fair to say you're angry at Mr. Niles?"

"Oh, I couldn't be angry at Mr. Niles?"

"And why's that?"

"Because I learned to read with his books. I knew how to scan symbols before them, but I learned to read because of their intrigue." He taps his glasses. "And when you have a situation like mine, you're a little more connected to the experience than the average person. Hell, if Russell Niles walked into the room, I'd bow."

Barrett gives an "if you only knew" look before turning away. As much as he wants Phillip to be the extortionist, he knows he isn't. This is a man too wrapped up in the magic of his own thoughts to observe anyone for long. And as much as Barrett wants Phillip to be evil, as much as he longs for this to be over, he has to admit that the man is gentle in a way he envies.

Rebecca steps into the room, walks past him, and gestures to the outside patio. Aloof has never felt so good. He takes a few breaths to make sure not to appear too eager and joins her at a set of cheap, green plastic furniture. She sips from an extra large mug of coffee that makes him wonder how much liquor she can drink.

"Any luck?"

"I don't know. He's definitely over the top, but not vicious like the letters. That's part of the problem, anything's possible."

"I hope that wasn't a waste of your time."

"No lead's a waste at this point."

"Mr. Niles is still getting the letters?"

Barrett nods, and if she knew him better, she would recognize it as the most truthful thing he's done yet.

"You work with Russell Niles directly, right?"

Instinct cuts through his lust, leaving him painfully aware that the question feels too convenient. A part of him wants to take a defensive stand, but the survivor in him knows it's better to take her lead and see where they end up.

"I do."

"What's he like?"

"I, uh, I'm not supposed to talk about him."

"Pretend I'm someone you can trust."

"Okay. He's a good guy, funny, charming, generous."

She puts her giant mug of coffee on the table with a bang. "I heard he was gay."

Barrett's eyes widen. "Gay?"

"Yep."

"He's not gay."

"Really?"

"I know he has gay friends, but I get the impression that he wouldn't keep it a secret if he was gay."

"How do you know?"

The statement leaves him flushed and while his composure unravels, her grin widens. "Because I've seen him with a lot of women."

"Could be friends."

"They weren't friends."

She takes a pack of gum from her pocket and snaps four pieces from their plastic tombs into her hand. "What about money? Is he as cheap as everyone says?" She pops the gum into her mouth and chews like she's avoiding smoking or biting her nails.

"Who says he's cheap?"

"It would be faster to say who doesn't."

"Name, names."

"Bill Lecker. Bill Lecker said he heard he doesn't tip more than five percent no matter how big a bill."

"Well, Bill Lecker's a jealous fuck."

"What are you so defensive about? Does Russell give you bonus money for being his guard dog?"

"No, but he's a good guy, and I don't like hearing him run down. I'm not a fan of gossip."

Rebecca blows a small bubble and sucks it back with a jarring pop. "Can you keep a secret?"

Barrett's so worked up that he wants to let her know how ironic the question is, to let her know that if she's toying with him that he's on to her, but he settles for, "Go on."

She leans into the table, and the smell of vanilla makes Barrett imagine massaging the back of her neck. "I don't even like his books."

Barrett is equal parts offended and impressed. "Really?" He smiles. It's as if the woman can read his mind, as if he wrote her dialogue for her. "And yet you manage the fan club?"

"I needed a job, the pay is reasonable, and the work is straightforward. And years later, I'm too comfortable to do anything else. Pretty bad, huh?"

"No, pretty great. I'm a fan of his early work, but the latest stuff is terrible. Disappointing really."

"Really?"

"Totally. The last few are uninspired dog shit, and I'm amazed so many people buy them."

"Do you want to have dinner sometime?"

It's not often Barrett finds himself surprised, but the question freezes time. "I thought you weren't interested."

"That was before I knew we had something in common."

"Then I'd love to, but only if I can pay."

TWENTY-TWO

The stress of being extorted makes Barrett crave distractions, so he transforms the putting green at the northern tip of his compound into a makeshift shooting range. Two mannequins, both dressed as soldiers, sit in the sand trap, and Barrett and Richard stand fifteen yards away with their guns pointed straight at them.

Richard is excited but nervous. "I've never fired one of these before."

"Me neither, but it's just a paintball gun. Point the barrel and squeeze the trigger." Barrett lights a cigarette and takes a moment to enjoy the sun's warmth as a cloud passes it by. "All right. Who is your mannequin?"

"What do you mean?"

"I mean who are you shooting at? It's more fun when you're releasing frustration."

"Who is yours?"

"Someone who has been sending me some nasty letters."

"Like complaints?"

"Sort of. Now, who is yours?"

"My psychiatrist."

"Then say goodbye to your shrink."

Barrett shoots a paintball that splatters red against the mannequin's camouflaged chest.

The boy lowers his gun. "Did you read my story?"

Barrett fires again, this time hitting his own target in the face. "I did."

"And?"

Barrett squeezes the trigger twice more before answering without taking his eyes off the mannequin. "And it's better than I expected. You're a creative kid."

"Really?"

Barrett stops shooting and flicks his butt into the sand trap. "Yeah, most adults can't write as honestly as you do, but you need to activate the honesty in your writing and use some of it in your real life."

"Why?"

"Because it's not good to hold in stress." He points to his forehead. "It's why your brow's furrowed all the time."

"How do I activate honesty?"

Barrett gestures to the mannequin. "With your shrink, to start. You obviously don't like going to him, but have you ever told him?"

Richard soaks in Barrett's words. Everything about the tone empowers him, and he watches with admiration as Barrett raises the paintball gun and unloads on the mannequin until it is covered in red paint.

In the afternoon, Richard carries his uncle's words to his therapy session. Dr. Burns sits on his stool and rolls his shoulders. A v-neck sweater is pulled halfway up his forearms, exposing his overly hairy arms. Richard sits beside his mother, who can't hide the worry on her face.

Dr. Burns drops Richard's coverless journal on the table between them. "Lots of writing, lots of make-believe, but still no journals, I see. Can you tell me why you won't give this a try?"

"I remind him all the time," Carol interjects. "But he's taken to writing short stories."

"I love your support, Carol, but this works better if Richard answers for himself. Are you writing short stories, Richard?"

Richard doesn't respond.

"Because that's excellent. It means you can easily write journals. Self-reflection is an important tool for you to help yourself. If you start writing journals you'll see ..."

Richard interrupts with a primal, ear-piercing scream. This is loud, this is shocking, this is a year of frustration hoping to break the sound barrier. "Shut up! Shut up! Shut up!" Richard gets up, picks up the dish of candies on the table and throws it across the room, where the bowl hits the wall and scatters red and white mints through the air. "Shut up! Shut up! Shut up!" He looks like he might charge Burns until his mother restrains him, and when all the adrenaline is gone, he collapses into her arms, and she hugs him so tight it hurts.

Barrett paces in the first floor of his house while on his cell phone. He looks at the giant cylinder fish tank in the centre of the room that is large enough to snorkel in and fears he won't be able to afford such extravagances much longer.

"I am willing to come down, but seventy-five under asking is crazy. Remember, this was Sinatra's Lamborghini."

He stops talking when he sees Carol on the video monitor standing at the front gates. He buzzes her in and returns some of his attention to the phone. "You can have the car for seventy-five less. You're an asshole and Sinatra will haunt you, but you can

197

have the car. But I've got to go, I'll call you back." He closes the phone and walks outside to greet her.

Panic that Richard has been in an accident leaves him tingly, and when he sees that she is upset, his throat tightens.

"Is everything okay?"

It's a stupid question, but he prays for a positive answer until he notices that she is upset with rage and not sadness. He feels relieved for a moment until she speaks.

"I can't believe you'd tell Richard to tell off his therapist."

"What?"

"How do you tell a child to trash his therapist's office?"

"Whoa. I told him to be honest."

She is so worked up, her eyes flutter and the words leave her mouth in rapid fire. "You should know he's susceptible to male influence right now. What kind of a role model are you? What kind of a man are you that you give a kid advice like that?"

"I know you're upset but ..."

"You're an asshole. You wanted to spend time with him and I knew better, but I hoped the man I know you can be would show up for him. And then ..." Her voice trails off into a whisper. She swipes at the air with a backhand and leaves Barrett alone. He has spent a lot of time alone over the years, but this time he feels his insignificance.

A feeling of overwhelming emptiness brings him to the beach. If he's going to be extorted, lose his possessions, and disappoint his sister then he needs to put those emotions into a story. Only he can't write a word, so he heads to the beach for inspiration. He believes this is where all his best ideas come from, but more realistically, this is a place that relaxes him enough to do the emotional mining that writers do.

Perched below the city, looking at water that seems to go on forever, it is easy to imagine that he is somewhere else, and once his imagination gets going, the ideas flow like thousand-dollar champagne.

But the ideas aren't flowing today. The sun shines strong and the water moves rhythmically, but his mind is too backed up with stress to be creative. He squeezes a mini-recorder in one hand, and an empty notepad and tennis ball sit beside him. It has been a while since he's moved, and his free hand begins to drum on the bench.

"Think like a kid."

He grabs the tennis ball and walks to the adjacent brick wall of a boat club. Three storeys of red brick with the sun illuminating every detail.

"Think like a kid. Think like a kid. Booger."

He fires the ball at the wall and catches the rebound.

"Fart."

This throw is even harder, forcing him to backpedal to catch the rebound. He cocks back to throw again but notices someone staring at him. A black kid about Richard's age watches him from his dirt bike about ten yards back on the boardwalk. They look at each other for a moment, and Barrett notes that the kid has wise eyes before pivoting back to the wall and throwing the ball again. What he doesn't see is the kid get off his bike, set it on the ground, and walk over to him. Another catch, and Barrett turns to see the kid beside him with his arm holding out an envelope. A ripple of unease runs through Barrett's body. He looks to see if anyone is watching them before taking the envelope from the kid. While he examines its generic style, the kid hustles back to his bike.

"Wait a minute."

Despite Barrett's plea, the kid begins to bike down the boardwalk.

"Who gave you this?" Barrett holds the envelope up high before jogging after the kid. "Stop."

For a moment it looks like he might catch up until the bike gains speed and Barrett's tar-filled lungs begin to tire, leaving him to watch as the kid slowly disappears into the distance.

Winded and sweaty, Barrett looks down at the envelope then opens it to see another letter. OPPORTUNITY #5: HONESTY. *"And only when Mil told the truth did he realize that there had been a veil over his thoughts."*

Barrett knows this is from his second book, and he remembers writing the sentence on a bench about twenty yards down the beach from where he now stands. Having his writing used against him is infuriating, but he reads on.

You have twenty-four hours to record yourself admitting to your publisher that you've been having an affair with his wife and then upload your admission to me or I will expose you to the world.

Barrett's eyes fill with panic. This is the worst-case scenario. He imagines the lake rising up on him like a tsunami before heading for Sidney's office and tries to figure out who knows he has had sex with Don's wife, when he remembers that Martin Brouge saw him leaving the pool shed the night of Don's disco party. Rage runs through him so strongly, he struggles to hold the wheel steady. He enters Sidney's office to find him in the downward dog position during a private yoga session with a stunning Japanese woman in her forties.

"I need a minute."

Sidney nods to the instructor, who huffs and flashes Barrett a dirty look on her way out.

Barrett holds up the latest extortion. "Martin Brouge is the one putting me through this hell."

"And why would a man that prestigious want to extort you?"

"Because he's jealous."

"He's one of the most popular authors of his generation."

"Of my sales, my money. That prick found out who I am, and he can't take that I'm making more money than him."

Sidney wipes his face down with a towel. "It's a stretch. What's got you so worked up?"

"You think he just happened to be at Don's house asking if I still write? And then today, he showed up looking to buy the Lamborghini."

"Please tell me you didn't sell it to him."

"Of course I didn't, but the point is, how did he even know it was for sale?"

"What an asshole."

"And now he's going after my publisher."

"You need to relax, regain your focus."

Barrett hands Sidney the extortion letter. Sidney reads the next demand and looks up from the paper.

"You need to panic. I'm talking five-alarm blaze."

"I am."

Sidney passes him back the demand. "You understand you can't do this?"

"I don't have a choice."

"Don can out you as fast as this extortionist."

"Only he makes too much money off me to ever do that." Barrett tries to offer a look of confidence, but seeing the worry on Sidney's face confirms that the worst has indeed arrived.

TWENTY-THREE

All this stress makes Barrett want to smoke a joint. Anything to forget for a moment that he's being extorted, anything to introduce a moment of levity into the muck of his reality. Of course it is his incessant need for levity that led to having sex with his editor's wife. Don, who took a chance on him when he had nothing; Don, who helped guide every bestseller; Don, who never asks for credit he deserves; Don who made him a multi-millionaire.

Barrett knows that sleeping with Don's wife makes him horribly ungrateful. Hell, he knows it makes him a horrible colleague, but it happened, it happened often, and now he has to admit his gluttony. He is resigned to the reality; he just wishes it didn't feel so bad. Smoking a joint might dull his guilt for a bit, but he figures it's how the extortionist expects him to react, and he is determined not to let his tormentor win. As he sits cross-legged on his blue felt pool table, he feels the weight of consequences for the first time in years.

Less than an hour later, Barrett walks into Don's office, like it is just another afternoon. Another chance to argue about deadlines, push the story further than he is interested, and simplify it for the largest audience possible. He puts a hand into his jacket pocket and touches a mini-recorder. The smile on Don's face makes it clear that he has no idea what's coming.

"Morning Barrett, coffee?"

Barrett shakes his head. Don is always happy in the morning. Not happy in a jovial way, more happy with himself. And why not? He is two months past his fifty-second birthday and he looks a decade younger thanks to five days a week at the gym, a nightly application of skin cream, and, of course, a little help from the hair dye that leaves his hair the stained brown that only colouring can achieve.

"Look at this." He drops a document in front of Barrett. "Another idiot starting a company that charges people to download books. I've been in this business thirty years, and it's never been more difficult. Do you know why I don't retire?"

"Because you love books."

"I haven't read a book cover to cover in five years. I do this because of the teamwork."

Barrett removes the mini-recorder from his jacket pocket and places it on his thigh beneath the desk. "The teamwork?"

"I love it. You've got all these personalities working together, and you know we don't always agree."

"Rarely agree."

Barrett presses the recorder's button and watches as Don waves an index finger like a conductor.

"Yet we make it work. And we, in particular, make it work on a multi-million-dollar level."

"There's something I have to tell you, and you're not going to like it."

Don looks at him for a moment and smiles. "Ah-ah-ah. Don't start talking negotiations with me. That's what agents are for. I know your contract needs to be renewed, but you're not just an author to me. I started your career, and you know I'll take care of you."

The irony makes Barrett want to wince, but he knows the time for guilt is long gone. This is about self-preservation now, and there is no point in dragging it out. "I've been having sex with your wife for the past three months."

Don looks at Barrett for a moment, but more the way he would look at a hyperactive child than with a look of anger. He reaches for his cup of coffee with a snarl.

"That's crude, even for you, Barrett. You know I've been having problems with Layla in that department. If you feel I'm rambling on, just ask me to stop."

"I'm serious."

The words leave Don appropriately stunned. Barrett watches as the man looks at him for signs that this is a cruel joke and quickly finds eyes that promise the claim is all too real. Barrett waits for him to respond, but instead he glances at the clichéd framed photo of his wife on a shelf before pacing the length of his desk. When his eyes return to Barrett, they burn with intensity.

"Why are you telling me?"

Because I have to, Barrett thinks. But he knows better and says, "It was never in your bed."

As the reality sinks in, Don's face contorts somewhere between anguish and rage.

"You need to know," Barrett says, the words more an attempt to convince himself than Don. But Don isn't listening anymore. He is seething and Barrett is the sole focus of the rage.

"I started your career."

"I know."

"I published you when I could have published anybody."

"I know."

"People have affairs every day without being discovered. Why would you make it so I have to look in her eyes and know?"

The truth seems appropriate now, so he manages a barely audible, "I have to."

"You have to humiliate me on top of betraying me? You let me sit there and confess I'm having problems in bed, and you were having sex with her?"

"Do you want to hit me?"

The muscles above Don's eyes are twitching now. A large vein snaking up his neck bulges, and his face is red. Everything about his posture suggests he does want to hit Barrett and hit him hard, but he settles for slapping the desk with a palm loud enough that Barrett takes a step backward.

"What I want to do is make sure you never have another word published, but you're not the only one who would be hurt by that, so I'm going to treat you like you treated me. You will sign a contract for half of your old percentage points and deliver your next book in one week, or I refuse to renew your contract and I'll spread the word that we did so because there were rumours of inappropriate behaviour with kids on tour."

"We just released a book."

"And I want the next one in store by summer. I'm scheduling a press conference for Friday, which you will attend under the guise of a marketing executive and announce Niles new book, or I'll replace you."

"Replace me?"

Don nods.

"And who could replace me?"

"Martin Brouge. He has been asking me about getting into children's lit, and this is the perfect transition point."

The name tightens Barrett's throat like poison. If he is being sent to hell for all of his deeds, now he knows who is Satan. The sun shines as Barrett steps out of Don's building, but he wishes for rain.

If Martin Brouge is set to take over his empire, then he doesn't want a sunny sky or people to pass him with smiles; he wants cracks of thunder, grey that robs everything of detail, and deserted streets.

He moves with purpose until he sees a plywood wall that guards a construction site plastered with posters. Between a row for a boy band and some for an action movie are ones for Martin's latest book, *Cold Showers Make Me Sleepy*. Blown up to this size, the cover looks particularly impressive. A woman with dark hair is drawn so that if you hold the cover straight up she is laughing, and if you turn it upside down, what were her feet on the cover form a vision of her with tears falling down her cheeks. The cover is brilliant and the perfection makes Barrett scream.

He tilts his head back into the sun. The posters prick at his insecurities, and they make him wonder if this journey of children's writing involves more luck than talent. The street is quiet now as he stares at the posters, hating every detail until the urge to destroy them takes over, so he charges the plywood and jumps to reach the highest one, ripping it in half. The next moments are a blur and soon his hands are filled with paper, but his rage leaves him clumsy and his motion is so awkward that he almost falls over when a boy about twelve with shoulder-length hair and a skateboard under his arm startles him.

"What are you doing?"

Hate burns in Barrett's eyes as he turns to the boy. Hate for Martin Brouge, hate for the extortionist, and hate for what his own writing has become.

"Fuck off."

"Bite me, old man."

The boy glides off on his skateboard while Barrett stands with remnants of posters in each hand. What he needs to do now is smoke. Deep and rhythmic, until that boy looks like a boy again. He takes another drag and remembers that he is meeting Rebecca for dinner. A dinner he is almost late for.

Forty minutes later, he sits across from her at a private table in a posh restaurant thinking that it should be heaven, but he can't settle his nerves. He has freshened up enough that his exterior looks fine, but internally, he is a dishevelled mess struggling to stay composed. What he wants to do is go out for a smoke, but he just got back from one so he has to settle for ordering a double vodka tonic. He wishes he could focus on wanting to have sex with her, but he can't take his mind off Don and Martin Brouge, and all he really wants is for her to like him. *Be charming*, he tells himself. But he can't reach for his drink with a steady hand. It's amazing how easy this usually is when he doesn't care.

Rebecca forks a piece of double chocolate cake into her mouth and looks up at him. "What?"

"I think you just revolutionized the idea of an appetizer."

"I like to eat what tastes best first."

"Fair enough."

She forks another piece of cake like she can't eat it fast enough, and Barrett can't help but be in awe of how cool she is. Nothing about her feels rehearsed, and her ease relaxes him enough to say what comes naturally.

"You've got to tell me how you ended up in a sensitivity class."

"Why?"

"Because there was a room full of assholes and you. There's got to be a good story there."

Rebecca finishes the last of her cake. "I'll tell you what, tell me something most people don't know about you, and I'll tell you how I ended up in a sensitivity class."

"Okay, like what?"

"Something that will make you memorable."

"That's pressure."

"You can handle it."

Barrett takes another sip of his drink to buy a moment. *Stop thinking,* he scolds himself. *Just react.* He stets the drink down with a smile. "All right, I like to smoke pot and watch kung fu movies."

"You can do better than that."

"Better than pot and kung fu movies?"

"Absolutely. Something more personal."

"More personal?"

"Something real."

"Okay. I'd like to see my name on a book."

"Really?"

"Something good, something people will associate with my name for years. Long after I'm dead."

"Yet you're in marketing?"

"Sadly."

"There you go. That's something I'll remember." She picks up Barrett's vodka, toasts him, and takes a drink. This is a gesture he finds both shocking and erotic.

"So I've fulfilled my end?"

"You have. But you should know, you're about to be the first person to ever hear this story."

"I'm ready."

She straightens herself. "I stun-gunned Sindu the Starfish."

"*The* Sindu the Starfish?"

She nods and contains a laugh. "I was at a convention, and the idiot dressed as Sindu kept coming over and bothering me. He was swearing and messing with the displays. So I reminded him he was being paid to be in the suit to entertain people, not drive them away. Not rude, but stern. Only he didn't listen and instead he patted me on the ass, so …"

"So you electrocuted him."

"And in order to keep my job, I ended up in sensitivity class."

"You stun-gunned Sindu the starfish."

Rebecca gets up from the table and bows, prompting Barrett to raise his glass to her.

"You have no idea how cool I think that story is."

"Order me a vodka tonic and you might hear another."

Barrett signals for the waiter as a woman with short, dark hair and heavy eye make-up approaches the table. She looks through Barrett to address Rebecca.

"You don't want to spend another second with this man."

"Really?" Rebecca responds, matching her aggression.

The woman looks remotely familiar to Barrett, but he remembers her with longer hair and less swollen lips. She's either an art dealer or an artist. Or the wife of an artist.

"He's the biggest asshole on the planet."

"Let me guess, he never called you again?"

Rebecca's irreverence makes him want to marry her, but the lack of sisterhood only cranks the woman's volume.

"No, he fucked my daughter."

Rebecca scans the woman to do the math. Late thirties means her daughter can't be more than twenty. She looks at Barrett with raised eyebrows.

"We're having some drinks," he intervenes, grabbing the woman's closest arm. But she shrugs him off.

"Don't trust him for a second."

Barrett wipes at his brow as she storms away and then clasps his hands together. "I'm so sorry. I …"

"Don't be. You're not the only one with a past."

"Really?"

"Really."

"You're not upset?"

"It takes more than a plastic surgery casualty to freak me out."

"You're amazing."

"I know."

The waiter puts two drinks on the table, Barrett tips him a twenty, and turns to see a camera in Rebecca's hands.

"Smile," she says playfully.

But his lips don't move. All he can think about is the extortion and someone following him everywhere he goes. He points at the camera.

"What are you doing?"

"Waiting for you to smile."

"I don't like my picture taken."

"Come on."

Both hands form a shield in front of his face. "I'm serious."

"Too late," she says, turning the camera around to show a shot of his concerned face filling up the screen. The potential irony of her words strikes hard. Too late to start a relationship; too late to save his career; too late to recognize he may have fallen for his extortionist.

TWENTY-FOUR

Thoughts of the extortion worm their way into Barrett's mind so that it's all he can think about. The vision of Martin signing autographs for a room full of excited kids loops until his body hums with stress. And when he tries to distract himself with sexual fantasies, his default method for dealing with things that make him uncomfortable, the naked image of Rebecca saunters toward him before stopping and raising a camera to his face. She smiles like he's a fool for not knowing she is his tormentor, and he snaps into the moment. The anxiety is intense enough to panic his breath, so he tears through his kitchen until he finds a Ziploc bag with pills in a drawer filled with bottle stoppers, barbecue accoutrements, and wine openers. Chalky Percocet, green Oxycontin, and eggshell Vicodin with the letters printed across the pill in block capitals seem the size of basketballs as he holds them at eye level. He built up this collection over the years due to stiff backs, a strained knee from a fall skiing, and gifts from a variety of dealers looking to keep a wealthy man numb and happy. And the extortion leaves him craving numb and happy like never before.

He sets the bag on the table and looks at it for a moment before sliding open the Ziploc and fishing out a Vicodin. The pill is almost in his mouth when the front gates buzz. A look at the monitor shows Richard looking particularly young in front of the massive gates. He buzzes the kid in, puts the pill back in the bag, and stuffs the bag in the back of his pants, where it is hidden by his shirt.

Just seeing the pills has his face flush, so he runs some water and splashes it on his cheeks to get rid of both the heat and guilt. When he opens the door, Richard is halfway up the steps.

"Hey," Barrett says, doing his best to appear normal. "What are you doing here?"

"I'm on lunch."

"How did you get here?"

"A cab."

Barrett waves the kid in. "A cab, huh? I'll give you some money when you leave."

Richard nods but Barrett can't help but notice the kid's solemn look. He follows Richard to the kitchen and leans against the counter while Richard sits at a stool.

Barrett opens a bottle of root beer and slides it toward Richard like he would a beer. "I'm sorry I got you into trouble with your therapist."

"He's increasing my medication."

Barrett wants to apologize more but he knows the word doesn't do the situation justice.

"I already have a dry mouth and a rash. What's going to happen to me when I take stronger pills?"

"I don't know. I'll talk to your mom and we'll see about getting you out of therapy."

"Really?"

"I'll try. That's what friends do for each other."

"Forever?"

Barrett looks at Richard and nods. He would swear to him that Santa Claus exists if that could take the look of defeat out of the kid's eyes. "Forever. Now tell me what you want for lunch so you're not late getting back."

"Can you do hamburgers?"

"Of course. I'll grab the patties, you turn on the barbecue."

The kid exits outside. Barrett makes sure he is out of eyesight, pulls the Ziploc bag from the back of his pants and tosses it into the garbage.

Richard is sprawled on a lounge chair when Barrett meets him outside with the burgers.

"Do you want cheese?"

Richard nods.

"Have you written any new stories?"

Richard nods again but his eyes stare into the distance.

"What's that look for?"

"I got detention for being rude to my teacher, so now he makes me read my writing to the class every day."

"Good, show him how talented you are."

"The reading isn't a big deal, I just don't like the way he talks to me."

"How does he talk to you?"

"Like he's better than me."

Barrett scoops a patty off the grill and drops it onto a bun. "Your burger's ready. You better eat up so you're not late."

Back at school, Richard sits with his eyes locked on his desk. Mr. Phelps hands out grammar sheets to the class and stops at Richard's desk.

"I can't wait to hear what you have to share with us today."

The man's teeth are overly white and too large for his mouth. Just the sound of his voice makes Richard drop his head lower. Phelps takes his position at the front of the class, shoots a chubby kid doodling a harsh glare, and holds up a sheet of paper.

"Precision is the art of communication, yet we are rarely precise when we speak. I listen to this class every day and I hear you ask how much people were at the game and say between us all. The following is a list of commonly misused words." The chubby kid is still doodling, so Phelps steps toward him and stops when he sees Barrett standing in the doorway.

Richard's eyes bug with curiosity.

"Can I help you?" Phelps asks.

Barrett motions Phelps over to the doorway and keeps his voice down so the class can't hear. "I'm Richard's uncle, Barrett."

"And?"

"I'm not sure if Richard's mentioned it to you, but his father left the family last year and he's been having a tough time dealing with it."

"This is not the time for discussion. If you call and make an appointment, we can discuss this at a later date."

"This doesn't need to be long. Richard mentioned you two have had some conflict, and I'm hoping you can take it easy on him."

Phelps curls his upper lip in disgust. "My father left my family when I was nine."

"Then you know how it feels."

"And I know that it is no excuse to disrespect authority. Now, if you'll excuse me, I have a class to teach."

Phelps steps back in front of the class. He is long of limb and he picks up a piece of chalk with a motion that makes Barrett think of a praying mantis.

"Alright, people. Let's copy down the word pairings on the board and I'll make sure everyone takes one up. Because as President Roosevelt said, 'When you cease to make a contribution, you begin to die.'"

Barrett steps into the classroom, and every student's head turns in his direction.

"President Roosevelt didn't say that."

Phelps pivots toward Barrett. He is holding the chalk like a cigarette, and his head his cocked in aggression.

"His wife did. Eleanor Roosevelt, columnist and humanitarian, not President Roosevelt."

"We're in the middle of a class."

Barrett points to the notes on the board. "And by the way, affect means influence, not result. That's effect."

The class starts clapping and oohing.

Phelps sets down the chalk. "Do I need to get a hall monitor?"

The man's face is beet red, so Barrett leans in close to heighten his frustration. "Cut him some slack or I'll be happy to share your lack of competence with the principal."

Phelps looks appropriately frazzled. The class is beginning to ripple out of control with noise, but he is too stunned to do anything.

Barrett winks at Richard, who can't stop smiling, and leaves the classroom.

What Barrett should do is go home and write so he can meet Don's deadline and preserve what's left of his career, but Martin Brouge is having a launch tonight, and he needs to look into his eyes to see how serious Don's threat is. Plus, Brouge wants him there for a reason, and he needs to find out why.

He arrives at the lounge in a ten-thousand-dollar suit with a watch on his wrist worth more than most peoples' cars. He knows this is immature, petty, even shameful, but he also knows that despite that, these accoutrements have the power to shield him from the glares every other Brouge wannabe will get.

The lounge is low-lit, with high-end art on the walls. Leather seats dress up four-person booths and drapes block off VIP areas. This is a long way from the average book reading, but then again, how many others have a mix of CEOs, professors, and actors at their launches?

Barrett steps up to a wall display of Brouge books with a deep drink in his rock glass. This is a wall that commands respect, a body of work that makes people nervous to meet the man. A projection of *Cold Showers Make Me Sleepy* centres Brouge's previous work. The place is packed, and people buzz around the display like it's a shrine. Beautiful people, intelligent people, the type of people that Barrett worries only read his books to children.

Barrett takes a deep drink and winces at the display until he turns to see the man himself, Martin Brouge, walking towards him.

"Hey, I'm glad you came. Any chance the Lambo buyer fell through?"

"No, that worked out."

"You have a great home. Let me know if you're ever thinking of selling. We'll do a private sale."

Instinct tells Barrett to tackle him and punch him until he admits to being the extortionist, but he refuses to be intellectually bullied.

"I had lunch with Don the other day, and he said you were thinking of getting into children's books. Any chance the next launch I attend has a bunch of people in costumes?"

"You never know. I'm not one to turn down easy money."

Barrett's fingernails press into his palms, but he knows this isn't time for emotion. Match a poker face with a poker face. He raises what's left of his drink, then a woman with cat glasses approaches Martin in a hush.

"One minute."

Martin turns to Barrett. "I've got to go. Let's have dinner soon."

"Sounds good."

The woman with cat glasses clicks up to the microphone in stilettos and the room goes quiet.

"Good evening. It's our pleasure tonight here at the Vatic to welcome one of the most celebrated writers of this century, Martin Brouge."

The words echo in Barrett's ears, and the room erupts into applause as Martin steps in front of the microphone. Sitting still is impossible, so Barrett shifts his weight and glares at Martin enviously as he begins his preamble, and suddenly the moment hits Barrett with a clarity that strips him of his pretense, leaving him more insecure and unsure about life than he has ever felt. Martin Brouge isn't just an adroit speaker; he isn't just a man able to enjoy his fans' admiration; he isn't just a man able to feel the pride of representing his work — he is a man fully capable of taking over the Mil Bennett empire, replacing it with his own genius and leaving the Russell Niles-authored books as an afterthought.

TWENTY-FIVE

Barrett sits across from Sidney in their favourite pub, but he's too distraught to drink. He picks at a Guinness stew while Sidney sips his second pint.

"All the women in the world and you pick your publisher's wife?"

"That's what made it fun."

"It was stupid. You had to know it was going to come back to hurt you." Sidney sets a contract in front of Barrett. "Don sent this over with a demand that it returns to him signed within the hour or he goes to the press."

Barrett looks at the contract, winces at his new seven per-cent return and signs beside the yellow flags. He sets down the pen and pushes the contract back to Sidney.

"Shouldn't you be protecting me? Isn't it your job to antici-pate things?"

He might as well have spat in Sidney's face.

"Like I protected you at the mayor's party?"

The mayor's party. There's no retort for that night. After tak-ing four Percocet for a disk he slipped the night before while wrestling with two escorts and skipping dinner in favour of a night of martinis, he'd decided to flirt with the mayor's wife. Yes, she had an amazing body for a fifty-three-year-old, and her speech about poverty earlier in the evening was oddly sexy, but this was the mayor's wife, so when he sauntered up to her with glossy eyes and unsteady legs, she was thoroughly unimpressed.

"I love poor people," he said, unable to contain a smile that didn't fit his words.

Her eyes told him to fuck off while she offered him her best political nod and move-on.

"Whoa," he said, grabbing her closest wrist. "Be nice."

She leaned into him so only he could hear her. "Be sober."

"Do you know who I am?"

This snapped Sidney's attention towards them from his seat at the bar where he was watching a football game.

"Do you know what I donated to your husband's campaign? I can buy this place," Barrett said, his volume growing.

The mayor's wife pointed him out to security at this point, but that wasn't what worried Sidney. What concerned him was what he knew Barrett would say next.

"Have a look at your husband's funding, find my name at the top, and then come back to me and talk to me like this. I'm a writer. I'm ..."

Sidney's hand slipped over his mouth before the words "Russell Niles" could escape. He raised a finger to stop the security guards' progress and steered Barrett towards a side door. Forget saving face, this was about saving a career.

Now Barrett finishes his beer feeling sure that the mayor's party is better left in the abyss of hazy memories. He rubs at his eyes, choosing silence as his defense against guilt and shame, as if by refusing to engage the challenge, he can make it go away.

"Don told me about the press conference," Sidney says, wiping at the sweat on his pint glass.

"Did he tell you he threatened to replace me with Martin Brouge?"

Sidney nods. "It's a faster turnaround than we planned on, but you should be alright."

"I haven't been doing a lot of writing."

"What happened to you asking me if I can get you a bonus for submitting two manuscripts at a time?"

"I've written three or four pages since I finished the last book."

"Jesus, Barrett. I thought you had a draft of something or at the very least an outline if you were exaggerating, but nothing? You have a hundred-page manuscript due in a week. I don't care if it's for kids, that's a lot of writing."

"I can't let Brogue replace me."

"Listen, I'm saying what I'm about to say because I'm your friend and I care. Forget your pride. This is about your lifestyle. You just lost eight percent a book. You tell me how much you need to bring in a month to keep your house running. Because if Don cuts you off, publicly smears you like he threatened, and replaces you with Brouge, then everything ends. The video games, the pencil cases, the cartoons. Every stream of income will dry up and no one on the planet will publish you."

Barrett stabs a piece of beef with his fork then puts it back into the bowl. "Do you think if he does replace me with Martin that he'll actually sell books?"

"It's children's publishing with a big publisher behind him, so yeah, he'd sell."

"Do you think he'd sell as many books as me?"

"Of course not."

The words are what he wants to hear, but nothing about Sidney's tone reassures him. He had never thought about being replaceable, and the reality is dark.

"I think we should hire a detective," Sidney says. He finishes his pint and motions to the bartender for another. "There's a guy I used to follow that model I was dating. He's good and I think we need a professional on this."

"No way. We'd have to tell a detective too much, and I don't want anybody else with leverage."

"We're running out of time, Barrett."

Richard sits adjacent to Dr. Burns and watches as the man loosens his tie and sets it on the table. The tie smells of cologne, and Richard wonders why the man would use so much of something designed to attract women at his place of work.

"Was your father prone to outbursts?"

Richard glares at him and wishes he could transport him to another place.

Carol unclenches her hands to answer the question. "No, he doesn't have a temper."

"Then perhaps it's atavistic."

"I'm sorry?"

"Perhaps it's a trait passed down to you from many generations ago."

Richard looks at Carol and is eager to hear her response as the doctor picks up his laptop.

"My father was a quiet man. And I never met my husband's father, but he always talked about him positively."

Burns clicks away on his laptop before setting it on the table. He moves his stool back a few feet and steps forward. "Today, I want to introduce you to a relaxation technique. Breathing is the key to relieving stress, so we inhale deep and pick our stress up as high as we can ..." Slowly, he raises his arms above his head until his dress shirt strains against his girth.

"And then we exhale and push our stress beneath us." He lowers his hands as he exhales and pushes the air beneath him palms up.

Richard gives his mom a look like it's not going to happen and she returns a look that warns him to cooperate.

"Up ..." Burns says again. He raises his arms, and Carol follows. "And down."

Richard raises his arms and breathes in deep. He wishes he could take in enough air to blow Burns through the wall with his exhale like a superhero from a comic book he'd read, but the doctor's voice is too distracting to inhale any deeper.

"Good, Richard. Good. Now push that stress beneath you."

As much as he hates the man, he wishes it were that easy. Do a few breathing exercises and push the secret he keeps from his mother out of memory, push how much he misses his father beneath him, push how much he hates his father for leaving the family away forever. But it's just air beneath his palms.

"Excellent." Burns claps. "Now, to grow as people we need to accept responsibility, and that takes practice." He takes a bent cactus the length of an index finger from a windowsill with other potted plants with green leaves and passes it to Richard. "Your task is to take care of it for a month. Respect it, nurture it, and return it to me in the same condition it is today or better."

"I don't like plants."

"That's irrelevant. The point is it will give you practice caring for something else. I'll be depending on you, and I know you'll do a great job."

"I'll make sure he does," Carol says, taking the plant into her lap.

Dr. Burns walks to a mini-fridge and removes a small bottle with GINSENG printed on the label. "Would you like anything to drink?" Both Richard and Carol shake their heads.

He shakes the bottle intensely before opening the cap and taking a sip that from the look on his face does not seem satisfying. He gestures at Richard with the bottle. "Why are you here?"

"Because my mom makes me come."

"I haven't known you long, Richard, but I've known you long enough to know you are smarter than that. Perhaps it will help if I rephrase the question. Why does any person go to therapy?"

"To get better."

"To be the best person that he or she can be. Say it with me. To be the best person that he or she can be."

Carol says it on cue while Richard more moves his lips than makes noise.

"Part of being the best person is selflessness. Giving to other people as much as you receive. I'd like you to give a possession or possessions that you have enjoyed to someone else. For example, I love my tennis racket. I won first place in last year's over fifty doctor's league with that racket, and in an effort to be the best person I can be I gave that racket to a foundation that teaches kids from disadvantaged neighbourhoods to play tennis."

Richard looks at him like he's crazy.

"Can you think of anything you could give?"

Richard wants to say no but he knows that will lead to trouble, so he considers an answer that will make everyone happy. "I have thirty dollars I could donate."

"That's nice of you," Carol says.

"It is nice of you, but I was thinking of something that can bring more happiness than money." Burns finishes the ginseng in a long drink and wipes at his lips.

"Your mother mentioned that you're fond of the Mil Bennett books. I'm thinking that donating your collection would make someone very happy."

"I can't do that."

"Why not? You've read the books, haven't you?"

"Lots of times."

"And you enjoyed them?"

"I love them."

"Then there's no reason not to share that love with someone else. What do you say, Mom? Can this be arranged?"

"Of course."

Richard grits his teeth so hard that his cheekbones bulge. "I don't want to give away my books."

"We can always get you new ones, dear. It's in the spirit of giving."

"The spirit of being the best we can be," Burns adds.

Forget being angry — crying feels appropriate, but Richard's eyes are so dry he can't will a single tear, and he wonders if it's all the medication he's taking that's robbed him of the ability to weep.

At school, Richard counts down the minutes to lunch, rushes to the library and logs into his usual computer. He types in his devilhunter9 address and clicks on new mail.

This time, he doesn't just want to send Burns a message, he wants it to sting.

Just the thought of giving away all his Russell Niles books makes him fret, and he wants Burns to feel the same kind of stress. He's typed Burns' address into the send box when a heavy hand touches his shoulder. He turns to see principal Haskins.

"Log out and come with me."

Richard knows exactly what will happen next.

Nothing principal Haskins says will be as bad as facing his mother, so he just absorbs the man's scolding then his obligatory guidance and waits for the inevitable.

At home, he sits on his bed while his mother hovers in front of him so intensely it looks like she might strike the closest object.

"I know you're upset about your father, but Dr. Burns is trying to help you, and lashing out at him isn't going to change our situation. What you did is unacceptable, and I know you're a better person than that. No video games for a month." She gestures to his bookshelf. "And I want every one of these Mil Bennett books packed and ready to donate to a charity before dinner. Are we clear?"

Richard nods and watches as she sets his medication on the bedstand. He stares at the pills for half an hour before taking them. The only thing worse than taking the pills is being alone, and Barrett is the only person he wants to communicate with, so he picks up his cell phone and sends him a text. *I'm grounded. Call me.*

Barrett is sitting on a bench and looks up at a billboard promoting his latest book when he receives the text. He's seen billboards promoting his work many times before, but this is the first time he appreciates just how huge they are. One ad campaign in New York had the cover of his third book filling one side of a thirty-storey building.

The cost was over one hundred grand a week. He considers how many thousands of people have looked at the billboard as he calls Richard and stands to get better reception.

"Hi," Richard answers, his voice setting the tone of his mood.

"Grounded, huh?"

"Yeah."

"What did you do, get caught with one of those animes with naked women?"

"I got caught sending my therapist mean emails from a computer at school."

"Really?"

"My mom is out shopping. Can you come over for a quick visit? I'm not allowed to leave the apartment for a week."

"Of course."

Barrett ends the call and puts his phone in his pocket. Then he notices an attractive young woman staring at him. Before the extortion, this was an invite for debauchery, but now it only stokes his paranoia. He watches her until she fades into the distance, and he wonders first why she stared at him and then if she'd even stared at him at all.

When he knocks on Richard's door, he is surprised that the kid answers immediately.

"You're sure your mom's not going to be back for a bit?"

Richard nods.

"Because I haven't snuck into anyone's house when they were grounded since I was a teenager, and I don't know if you're worth the risk Sherry Hayes was."

The boy drops his weight into a chair. "My mom is making me give my Mil Bennett books to charity."

"Why?"

"Because my therapist says sharing something I've enjoyed will help me be the best I can be."

"Weird."

"See. It's horrible. I can't believe I'm grounded."

"Everyone gets grounded a few times."

"But you think my mom's wrong for grounding me, right?"

"No, I think she loves you and is trying to do what's best for you."

"You wouldn't ground me though, would you?"

"For sending prank emails? Grounding's not my thing and I admire your spunk, but making your therapist angry isn't the way to go. You have more to lose than him."

Richard takes a moment to absorb Barrett's words.

"How did you get caught, anyway?"

"I sent them from the same computer in the library every time. If I had sent them from different places, they would have never found out, but I sent it from the school library every time and always at lunch, so they tracked me down."

The words fill Barrett with an insight that makes his face glow. "Thank you."

"For what?"

"I've got to go, but thank you." He kisses Richard on the head, and the boy pulls away. "Call me tomorrow." Barrett rushes out of the apartment and texts Sidney as fast as possible. *Who is the most computer-savvy person you know?*

Fifteen minutes later, Barrett walks into an angular building at the end of an alley. The front of the building is a pastel purple that makes him think of South America. Inside, it is spare.

A stainless steel drafting table, a wooden table full of computers, and a few high-back rolling chairs are the only items in the place. There is no art on the walls, no couches, and no kitchen. This is a space dedicated to work.

Barrett walks toward Crance, who sits in front of ten computer monitors of various sizes.

Crance is somewhere in his thirties and looks like he eats once a day and sleeps no more than he has to. Tight cornrows draw attention to a half-moon scar centring his forehead.

"Can I help you?" His voice sounds like someone is sitting on his chest.

"I'm Barrett Fuller. Sidney Taylor says you're the problem solver."

"He's a good man."

"I need you to track a website address and check every Internet cafe and library in the city to see if the webmaster is logging in from any of their computers and whether or not there is a pattern in the times or days they are sent."

Crance picks at a frayed cornrow but keeps one eye on a computer screen with an image of an intersection somewhere downtown. "Is tomorrow reasonable?"

"Tomorrow's great."

"And Sidney told you my fee?"

"This is so important, I'm paying you double." He passes the guy a slip of paper with the Once Upon a Hypocrite website and an envelope that struggles to contain its contents.

TWENTY-SIX

Crance gives Barrett enough hope that he can face Don's threat and write. With all the extortion demands taped to the wall behind his computer screen, he sits down and begins to type. The words don't come easy, but he has something to say and it's a start. Each stroke of the key is more rhythmic, until he finally writes a sentence he is happy with. And then the phone rings. He looks to see Don on the call display and hits speakerphone.

"How's the writing coming?" Everything about Don's tone makes it clear he is enjoying Barrett's angst.

"Great."

"I'm about to have lunch with Martin, and I thought you might want to be there for our discussion."

"Where are you?"

Of course he wants to be there. Even though he knows Don is baiting him, he can't resist.

Twenty minutes later, a waiter with heavy eyes and a slouch leads Barrett to a booth where Martin and Don are drinking wine. As soon as he sees Barrett, Martin raises his glass.

"Hey, Barrett. I'm glad you could join us."

"I wouldn't miss this."

Don offers Barrett a smug smile. "Barrett."

"Don."

"You really have to talk to me about the market," Martin says. He swirls his wine around in the glass. "Because my advisors are killing me."

Barrett ignores the question. He needs to determine how much Martin knows. "What brings you two together?"

"We're talking about collaborating."

"Children's books?"

Martin nods, but his face is hard to read. Is he being coy or is he being cautious?

"Martin has some brilliant ideas," Don says.

"Thank you, but it's really more a case of how stale the genre's become."

"Stale?" The muscles in Barrett's back tighten.

"Absolutely. The Niles books feel like they're written in his sleep, like he's on auto-pilot."

Don fills his glass and locks eyes on Barrett. "He is getting a little comfortable."

As if working in tandem, Martin leans back in his chair and gestures at Barrett with his glass. "Have you ever read any of Niles books?"

"Sure."

"And?"

"They're solid."

Martin scoffs. "If cookie-cutter moral lessons count as pillars."

"What about the emotional appeal?"

"The first few years, I'll give you. But the last couple books are soulless. He's selling on his name, and once the readers see a better product, they'll realize that."

Barrett looks at Martin for a moment without saying anything. Then he rises from his seat. "I've got to go."

"You just got here," Don says.

Barrett holds up his phone. "It's a work thing."

"A work thing?"

Barrett nods intently.

"Good to see you, Barrett." Martin raises his wine glass and Don flashes Barrett the content smile of revenge. It's difficult to tell who's playing him more.

Craving a cigarette, Barrett steps outside and takes out his pack just as his phone buzzes. He looks at his screen to see a text from Sidney: *Meet me at my office immediately.*

When Barrett reaches Sidney's building, he is surprised to find him waiting outside. Sidney steps forward and extends an envelope with BARRETT FULLER in the centre.

"This was under my windshield wiper when I got back from lunch."

Barrett looks at the envelope for a moment before opening it and removing a letter.

> OPPORTUNITY #6: LOVE YOURSELF. *"Only when Mil admitted his secret did he feel the weight lifted from his chest." I see that you have a new woman in your life. One that lasted more than a night. Admit to her who you really are or she'll find out with the rest of the public. You have twenty-four hours to upload your taped confession.*

Barrett looks at Sidney with the same combination of rage and disappointment that he would if he caught him stealing from his wallet. "You found this under your wiper?"

"Don't bother."

Barrett holds the letter at eye level. "This is someone with access to every detail of my life, and you're telling me you found it under your wiper?"

"You know I have nothing to do with this."

"Maybe fifteen percent isn't enough."

"Really, stop before you offend me."

"Who else on the planet knows enough about me to do this? Who else knows my rhythms enough to arrange all this? And now I'm supposed to believe a demand was stuck on your windshield?"

"This is sad, Barrett. Do you think I like that some wacko knows where I work? I'll check the security cameras to see if there's anything that can help, but you need to get it together, or this is going to break you. What I want is this to end so we can get back to long lunches and making ridiculous amounts of money. What I don't want is you looking at me like I'm not your best friend."

Barrett watches Sidney walk away and immediately feels guilty about the accusation. He folds the letter, puts it in his pocket with dismay, and craves the company of someone innocent. What he needs is to be around the kid, to clear his head for a bit, and then to face this latest demand fresh.

When he arrives at the apartment, Carol answers the door and regards him spitefully.

"This isn't a good time, Barrett."

"What's wrong?"

"Richard's grounded."

"He told me. I was hoping I could visit him here."

She arches her neck slightly so that she is as tall as possible and looks at him like her stare can burn through him. "I don't want you to see Richard anymore."

"What?"

"His teacher called and said you threatened him."

"Did he tell you why?"

She turns to enter the building and Barrett puts a hand on the door.

"He likes it at my place."

"You're out of control. You smell like cigarettes and beer and he comes home smelling the same. Your advice got him in trouble at therapy, and now his teacher called and said you interrupted class and threatened him."

"Has Richard told you how he treats him?"

"He's a kid, Barrett. Kids complain about their teachers. That doesn't give them the right to swear at them or have their uncles threaten them."

"Listen ..."

She pulls the door open despite his arm. "You're a bad influence, he's at a crucial point in his development right now, and I can't have you around him."

"What?"

"I don't want him to see you anymore."

"Wait. Shouldn't you give him a say in this?"

"I'm his mother."

The seriousness of her words sinks in and Barrett feels sick. "I don't do anything around him other than smoke, and I can start going outside if you want. He doesn't like therapy. I was just trying to help him express himself. And with the teacher, I just wanted to make sure he wasn't getting bullied."

"A couple visits with him and you're an expert now?"

"He's a great kid, I'd never ..."

"Goodbye, Barrett."

"Can he at least call me?"

She walks inside without answering, and he feels like he might float into the grey sky and drift into the nothingness. The extortion leaves his thoughts tainted with insecurity and fear, but even in the confusion he is sure that he has to see the kid again, he simply has to.

Barrett wants to make it up to Carol and Richard, but to do that, he needs to end this extortion and to do that he needs to write a manuscript by the end of the week. One brick at a time, he tells himself. That little phrase saved him many times as a writer. Whenever he feels overwhelmed or wordless, he tells himself, one brick at a time. And he needs that crutch more than ever. He reads the latest extortion letter again, but for the first time, he hears a woman's voice. He had hoped it was a man, and a part of him was sure it was Brouge, but now he hears Rebecca in every extortion. Their random meeting at sensitivity class, her probes about writing, her position as head of the fan club, and now a demand to tell her who he really is. A chill runs through his body, quickly followed by rage. Fuck her for captivating his attention, and fuck her for making him care. He hales a cab and gets in with more purpose than he's felt in months. It's not enough to confront her — he needs to know why she's extorting him. The challenge is to get his anger to override how disappointed he is that they don't have a future.

He enters fan club headquarters with taut shoulders and approaches a mousy-looking woman in her early twenties stuffing Mil Bennett stickers into envelopes.

"Is Rebecca in?"

"She's in her office."

The woman points down the hall, but he's already on his way. The door to her office is open and Rebecca sits behind a desk. When he knocks on the door, she looks up with surprise.

"What are you doing here?"

He tosses an envelope on her desk. "I brought you this."

She opens it and looks inside. "An empty envelope?"

"It's what everything you've arranged is worth."

"What?" His aggression provokes a reciprocal response.

"All this drama."

"Don't be weird."

"Don't fuck with me anymore. You just happened to be at sensitivity class?"

"Where is this coming from?"

"And now I get a demand that just happens to want me to tell you who I am?"

"What are you talking about?"

"Here you go. You want me to admit who I am? Fine. You want to hear me say it? Done. To put an end to this fucking nightmare, I'm happy to. I'm Russell Niles. At least that's my pseudonym."

Rebecca looks at him closely for a moment before bursting into laughter. This isn't a laugh-with-somebody laugh, this is a full-blown laugh-at-him laugh. "*You're* Russell Niles?"

The implication of her laughter triggers a defensive response. Who is she to think it's impossible for him to be that skilled? He gestures around the room to the various Russell Niles paraphernalia. The dolls, posters, bed sheets, video games. For a moment, he feels good about himself again. "All this is me."

Rebecca still chuckles. "You don't have to do this. I'm sorry I was condescending about you being in marketing before, but you don't have to lie to me. I already like you."

Barrett's face is passed flushed. A vein in his neck bulges, and a nerve in his left eye twitches incessantly. "Russell Niles is my pseudonym. This is the truth. For the first time since we met, this is the truth."

"Are you high? Because this is pathetic."

The realization sets in with an acidic quality. She has no idea. No matter how good it would feel to discover the extortionist, despite the implications, it's clear from the purity of her disappointment with him that she isn't the culprit. Drowning in humiliation, honesty never felt more appropriate. He leans against the wall like he'll drop to the ground without the help.

"Someone's been extorting me."

"Extorting you?"

"Making me do things or they'll reveal who I am to the public. That's the only reason I was at sensitivity class."

"Are you serious?" She inspects him for signs that he is drunk, high, or crazed.

Barrett offers an exhausted nod.

"You're saying you're a world-famous children's author? You?"

Barrett nods again, and suddenly her smile is gone. She steps towards him with a tongue ready to spit flames.

"I don't know why you're doing this. I don't know what's a lie and what's the truth. All I know for sure right now is that you're an asshole."

She picks up the empty envelope from the desk, tosses it in the garbage, and leaves him alone in the office with the irony of being surrounded in Mil Bennett products.

TWENTY-SEVEN

Richard is stretched out on his bed rereading the first Mil Bennett book for the tenth time when his mother enters the room.

"You're supposed to be packing that up."

"The side effects are getting worse," he says without taking his eyes from the page.

"What do you mean?"

"My tongue is filling my mouth."

"Let me see." She gets closer, and he opens his mouth so she can get a good look at his scaly tongue. Her fingers trace his jawline, hoping to bring him the relief of touch. "Nothing's changed since you first started with the medication."

"It looks bigger to me."

"I promise you, it's not." She gestures to the shelf, which is full of books that she's bought him over the years. "Will this be easier for you if I pack them up?"

His eyes return to the page and he reads the same sentence again and again while she picks up a single packing box and begins taking the Mil Bennett books from the shelf. *Mil sat on the bench in despair, but something about the way the tree's branches swayed in the wind made him hopeful.*

"You're getting a little old for these books anyway."

The first book drops into the box with a thud that Richard feels in his bones.

"I mean, you're a pretty advanced reader for your age, and these books are only a hundred pages or so."

Another thud.

Richard's tongue feels like he has an entire pack of gum in his mouth. He presses it against his palate, and it feels so full that he expects the pressure to push fluid out of his ears when there's another thud. This time, he decides to read the sentence aloud.

"Mil sat on the bench in despair, but something about the way the tree's branches swayed in the wind made him hopeful."

The thuds stop. Carol pivots from the shelf and looks at him. "I want to talk to you about something."

The tone warns him that he's not going to hear good news, but he looks up from the page anyway.

"You're not going to see your uncle for a while."

"Why?"

"Because I want you around positive people right now, and he's not in a positive place."

"What does that mean?"

"It means he's not a good guy." She tosses another book into the box and the thud returns.

The news brings Richard to his feet. "He's a great guy."

"People aren't always what they seem."

"He's not just my uncle, he's my friend."

"There are things about him you don't know."

"There are things you don't know about life too."

A surprisingly aggressive tone leaves him shaking, and it's clear he's too worked up to remain composed.

"There are many things I don't know about life, my dear, but it doesn't change my opinion about your uncle."

The need to tell his secret flows through him with an unstoppable urgency. This is the time he's been waiting for, this is something he has to do, and his frustration allows the words to flow naturally.

"I know why Dad left."

"Richard ..."

"I know why Dad left."

"What?" The change of topics to something so upsetting shocks her.

"I came home early from school the day before he left and saw him kissing a man on the bathroom floor."

He isn't sure what to expect, but her response definitely confuses him. With her eyes closed, she sits on the edge of the bed and rubs at her face. "Listen to me. You shouldn't lash out, okay? Trying to hurt me by making up a story like that is mean, it's upsetting, and it's not going to change my decision about you seeing your uncle."

"I'm not making up anything. It was a blond man he was kissing, and they had their shirts off."

The liquid in his eyes and strain in his voice makes her realize this is more than rebellion. "You swear to me you saw that?"

Richard nods.

"You swear? Because this isn't something to lie about. This is our lives." He nods again, and an explosion of panicked anger surges through her so strong that her hands shake. "Why didn't you tell me when he left?"

"Because you were so sad and I was scared it would just make it worse."

"Because he cheated on me?"

"Because it was a man."

"It doesn't matter that it was a man."

"I know that now, but I was confused."

"What matters is that he broke our bond. What matters is that he left our family. You should have told me."

"I'm sorry."

She is yelling now, and everything about the contortion of her face and anger in her voice startles him. "That was my marriage." She leans into his face and he turns his head. "*My* marriage."

"He's my father," he says, deadpan.

"And him betraying me is something I should find out, not you."

She leaves the room, and Richard has never wanted to cry more in his life. His eyes sting and his nose is stuffed, but the medication leaves his eyes dry.

He walks to the bookshelf and hooks the remaining Mil Bennett books into the box with his arm. The next target is the cactus Burns gave him to take care of. He tosses it in the box upside down and drops the thickest Mil Bennett book on it so that its plastic holder shatters. The box is heavy, but he shuffles his way to the bathroom and locks the door. His tongue feels like sandpaper, so he sticks it out as far as possible until his distorted reflection in the faucet looks like a cartoon character, but nothing about it is funny. What he should see is the well-rested face he's grown fond of over the years, but instead he looks at purple bags under his eyes and feels like he might choke on his tongue. Hatred fills him.

Hatred for his father for leaving, hatred for his mother for making him go to a therapist, and hatred for Dr. Burns for drugging him. He hustles to the kitchen and flips through the counter drawer until he finds a box of matches. The next stop is the hall closet, where he reaches behind a container of bleach to the back of the shelf for a small bottle of lighter fluid. And with the matches in one hand and the lighter fluid in the other, he walks back to the bathroom like it's the most natural thing he's ever done.

He picks up the box of Mil Bennett books and the broken cactus and dumps them awkwardly into the bathtub. The sight of the books with bent covers, open spines, and pinned pages makes his lips curl. He moves to the spot on the floor where he found his father kissing the bearded man that life-altering day and looks down at a series of smudges on the tile. What he wants to do is beg anyone that will listen for his father to come back, but what he can't stop himself from doing is worrying that he will swallow his massive tongue. A quick twist of the lighter fluid cap and he's hovering over the white porcelain. Without hesitation, he squeezes the bottle until the fluid covers the tub and drips down every cover. This is an all-hands operation now. Put down the bottle, pick up the matches, remove one, and strike it against the box's flint. He holds it for a moment, appreciating the flame's power, and makes a wish that it was as easy to erase history. To burn the last year, brush off the ashes, and start fresh with his father back at home. But that's fantasy, so he focuses on what he can do and drops the match into the bathtub.

Flames burst upwards, the tallest ones stretching for the ceiling. Immediately, it is hot enough that he needs to take a step back, but he's not worried about the heat.

The flames are efficient and definitive in their ability to destroy anything in front of them, but they aren't content in their home. They flow over the tub's side and he watches as they move towards the floor in search of a new connection.

The door shakes when his mother tugs on the other end, but Richard is too entranced to notice.

"Open the door, Richard," she screams. But he doesn't. He hears her kick the door three times, he hears her scurry down the hall, and he hears her strike the wood again and again until she enters with a hammer in her hand. The flames are at their peak as she steps into the room, which prompts a scream that spills out of her mouth the whole time she runs back to the kitchen for the fire extinguisher. Thick smoke fills the room, and Richard can hear the panic in her voice, but he still stares at the tub, and only when she nudges him in the chest with an elbow and sprays the extinguisher at the flames does he move.

The hiss of the extinguisher breaks his trance. White foam and the smell of chemicals make up his focus now, and while he's sad to see the flames gone, there is a moment of relief that they've done their job until his mother shakes him by the shoulders.

"What were you thinking? You could have burned the place down. Why would you do that? Why?"

The words are appropriately irrational, and her questions only make him want to question her back. *Why didn't you stop Dad from leaving? If Dad didn't want a family, why was I born? If you love me so much, how come you send me to a man that medicates me?*

He stares at the burned pages of his favourite books and breathes in the smell of their ashes, then he feels his mother grab his shoulders and steer him out of the bathroom and into the hall. He watches with envy the tears streaking down her face.

There is no sobbing, only liquid eyes that say everything for her. She hugs him tight and whispers that she is happy he is not burned, and he knows that she prays that his actions have a sane explanation.

TWENTY-EIGHT

It's not easy to admit his faults, but Barrett knows it is time to stop hoping someone finds the extortionist and to start searching more for himself. The real problem all this time, it occurs to him, was his emotional reaction to each letter. Fear, anger, self-pity. All of those feelings have blurred his reason. What he needs to do is get the letters to a fresh space, and as he moves the demands from the wall above his computer and tapes each one to the white wall across from his bed, he feels confident that if he looks long enough he'll see a clue, commonalities, or a mistake. He stares determined when the phone's buzzing rhythm cuts through the silence.

"Hello?"

"I need you to come over right away." It's Carol and she speaks so fast it almost comes out of her mouth as one word.

Her tone tells him to say yes without asking any questions. This clearly isn't about yelling at him, or venting — this is urgent. Maybe Richard ran away, maybe he was in an accident, or maybe it's financial trouble. Whatever the case, he knows to get there as fast as possible.

The smell of smoke makes him flex his nostrils as soon as he enters the apartment. Carol points him to the patio from the far end of the room and retreats into her bedroom. There's only enough time to see her tired eyes and stressed brow before she's gone. This is not Barrett's scene. A month ago, he couldn't have made up such a setting, and here he is standing in the reality. He moves through the apartment and steps onto the patio, where Richard sits on a deck chair with rusty legs. The air is cool, yet the boy wears only a T-shirt, exposing the smudged ash on his forearm.

Barrett takes a box of fries and a big-dog burger from a paper bag and sets them on a plastic stool beside Richard. He leans with his back on the railing and watches as the boy begins to pick at the fries.

"You almost burned down your bathroom," he says, passing Richard a package of ketchup.

"It's your fault."

"My fault?"

"I told her my secret like you said, and she got upset. I told her my father left because I found him kissing another man in our apartment."

Barrett looks at the kid and the pain in his eyes makes sense. "Jesus, I'm sorry you have to deal with that. I didn't know that was your secret." He arches his neck to the chipped paint on the overhang above them. "You did the right thing, though. Your mom deserves to know the truth."

"No, I didn't. I made her mad and I upset her. Mom's right, you're not a good guy."

"Hey. Go easy. You know how much I like you."

"You said we'd be friends forever, and you said you'd get me off this medication and now I'm not allowed to see you and I'll be taking these drugs for the rest of my life."

"Listen ..."

"Mom doesn't want you here."

"Your mother called me and asked me to come."

"I don't want you here."

The boy's words thicken the room's air. Now that he knows Richard, now that he's not in the haze of euphoric nights and hung-over mornings, he can't lie to himself anymore. He can't pretend that his last book is loosely based on Richard dealing with his father leaving the family, and he can't rationalize that he was too busy to be there for the kid during the family's time of need. This is a reality best framed in formal terms, and the reality is that he found out his sister's husband left her, he needed a story for an upcoming deadline, and he used the stories of his nephew's angst as fodder for his next bestseller without ever caring enough to even call the kid and feign interest in his pain. And now he's worried enough about Richard that he would give his fortune to the extortionist if it could fix whatever made the kid light his bathtub on fire. The irony makes his eyes burn.

Barrett leaves the room to see Carol leaning against the living room wall. Her eyes look sore and her lips are chapped.

"Where are you going?" she says.

"He doesn't want me here."

"I was hoping he would talk with you."

"We'll give him some time. See how he feels tomorrow."

He hugs her, and while she resists at first, her body needs the embrace.

"Call me if you need anything. And I mean anything."

She nods, wipes at her eyes, and raises a hand in goodbye.

The kid's rejection pricks at him as he leaves their apartment, heads for the street, and leans against a cement retaining wall. He wants to believe what he told his sister and that all Richard needs is some time, but the look of disappointment in the boy's eyes warns otherwise. That was the look of someone who has been disappointed before, someone learning to expect to be let down, someone who will soon decide not to trust people.

He lights a cigarette with thoughts of his burned books in the tub and is wondering if he deserves to have every copy in print destroyed when the buzz of his cell demands his attention. He looks at the screen to see Crance's number and a text that reads: *I found what you want. Come see me.*

When Barrett arrives at Crance's place, the man is shirtless. He is professional athlete ripped with a single tattoo of a nail running the length of his right forearm. They shake hands and Crance pours a shot of green liquid into a shot glass with an open eye decorating the outside. He extends the drink.

"Wheatgrass?"

"No, thanks."

Crance shoots the wheatgrass, winces, and slides his tongue across overly white teeth. "Sorry for the heat in here. My AC broke yesterday, and I'm still waiting on the repair man."

Barrett looks at the half-dozen fans toggling around the room. His eyes drift to the series of computer monitors where Crance holds court. The closest shows surveillance footage of an abortion clinic, another has surveillance footage of a massage parlour, and the largest screen frames a software company.

"What's going on here?" Barrett asks.

"You don't want to know." Crance downs another wheatgrass and spins his swivel chair toward Barrett. "Okay." He rubs his eyes then raises his hands like a conductor. "The website you gave me is only ever accessed at one location. A library a few blocks from here. And there's a pattern." A man enters the software company on the centre screen, and Crance clicks away on the keyboard until the man's image is larger and framed in red. Crance drags the image to a folder and returns his attention to Barrett.

"Every Tuesday between one and one fifteen, someone accesses the Once Upon a Hypocrite site from the west-branch library. You go there tomorrow and you'll find who you're looking for."

Barrett counts nine hundred dollars as he removes the bills from his wallet, wishes he had a thousand, and sets it beside Crance.

"What's this?" Crance asks.

"Gratitude."

Crance waves him off. "You're a friend of Sidney's. You already paid too much."

"I appreciate that. But for the problem you're solving for me, you deserve more, and if it works out tomorrow, I'll make sure you get it."

Flashes of the extortion fill Barrett's thoughts. The kids delivering the demands, the guilty faces of everyone he looks at these days, and the millions of dollars he's lost. A library. He thinks of an impish, jealous reader, and then he imagines the kids delivering the demands again and isn't sure what to think. Brouge is diabolical enough to use kids. Whatever the case, by one tomorrow he hopes to discover the extortionist's identity.

He steps out of Crance's place feeling hopeful for the first time since Don threatened him with Brouge, so he takes out his phone and keys in Rebecca's number. She didn't deserve to be the target of his paranoia, and he wants to make it up to her. The ease he felt during their conversation over dinner was rare. He's used to having to be the entertainment, but she carried the conversation, and he wants to hear her voice so he can thank her for being so interesting. But she doesn't answer. Voicemail responds on the fifth ring and the rare tone of her voice makes him anxious as he scrambles to think of something to say. He is about to speak when she answers.

247

"This better not be the window company. I asked you very nicely not to call again two days ago and not so nicely yesterday, so ..."

Her irreverence makes him wish he could take back the day he accused her of being the extortionist. He decides he needs to say something really charming but all he can manage is, "It's Barrett."

"Barrett?"

"Yeah, I ..."

The dial tone hurts more than anything she could have said. He hasn't been rejected since the money started coming in. In fact, he hasn't cared about being rejected since the money started coming in, and the sobriety of this side of the coin is startling.

He steps into his mansion, walks up the spiral staircase and sits gingerly on a couch in his office. Then it occurs to him that of all the things he enjoys about being rich, he likes the control the best. Control came with the first million, and since then everything's come to him. Meetings, people, time, women, travel, peoples' respect. He rises from the couch, moves to the computer and decides to control what he still can. And the words have never flowed so fluently. Ideas play out in his head like a movie, and the perfect adjective or simile seems to pour out of his fingertips as they glide over the keyboard, creating page after page. All of his angst, rage, and insecurity crystallize into the clearest communication he has ever produced. This is artistic euphoria, these are the moments writers daydream about, this is what gets a book published.

TWENTY-NINE

Barrett wakes hungry for closure. If Crance is right and the extortionist will be at the library at one, then this nightmare could be over in a few hours, and the excitement of that possibility leaves him unable to focus on anything else. He showers, cooks some eggs and bacon that he can't eat more than a few mouthfuls of, and flips through two newspapers, but it's all just passing time until he can confront the extortionist. A part of him wants to tackle and beat this person for torturing him; to release the compounding frustration and prove that he is really the dominant one. But another part of him needs answers. How did he, she, or they find out he is Russell Niles? How did the extortionist find out that he isn't being truthful about the charitable donations he claims on the website? In a world full of morally corrupt CEOs, actors, athletes, and politicians abusing their riches and power, why go to all this trouble to punish him?

He leaves his mansion at twelve fifteen so there is no chance he'll be late, but a marathon for breast cancer makes driving in the downtown core impossible, so he parks the Audi six blocks from the library. He walks through the runners with a feeling of remorse. There they are sweating with pink ribbons pinned proud over their hearts, doing what they can to help people in need, and here he is with enough money to help fund a good run at any disease on the planet and he's about to pop a cigarette in his mouth.

The first thing he notices about the West Branch library when he steps inside is that the computer section is full of users. Rows of people sit hunched over keyboards with their eyes locked on the screens. These computers draw a cross-section of society.

Men, women, Chinese, black, white, Indian, teenagers, and even one guy who must be eighty doing his best to shield people from watching him look at pictures of scantily clad women. A quick scan of the first row reveals only the usual surfers. News sites, sports sites, YouTube, video games. The second row is a bust too. A few people check their email and a few others peck away at school reports and resumes. He starts down the third aisle when he stops at a boy around twelve looking at the Once Upon a Hypocrite site. The boy has long hair and is dressed in oversized clothes. Barrett's fingers tingle. He puts a hand over the boy's, which is on the mouse.

"You like this site, huh?"

The boy looks back with startled eyes. "What?"

"I'll give you clever points for the title but I can't approve of the content."

"I don't know what you're talking about."

"Who put you up to this?"

"What?"

"The site."

"I just saw some lady looking at it a couple of minutes ago and it looked cool."

"What lady?"

"Her."

The boy points down the aisle at Carol, who's walking toward them when she notices Barrett and the boy pointing and turns.

Her image magnifies until from Barrett's perspective, his sister's eyes fill the room.

"Carol?"

She hustles to exit the library but Barrett runs after her, and just as she reaches the lobby, he grabs her arm.

"What the fuck is going on?"

She shrugs off his grasp and looks straight at him. Her eyes are tired and her face is drained, but he can't fully read her. All he can manage is to look at her with disbelief.

"You did this?"

She nods, expressionless. No smirk, no sadness. And that lack of response intensifies his fury.

"How did you find out?"

There is no guilt in her eyes, and her tone makes it clear she is as angry at him as he is at her. "I didn't intend to."

"What do you mean you didn't intend to? You extorted me."

"I was planning an intervention and started following you to figure out where best to have it."

"An intervention?"

"That's right. I wasn't going to go bed another night wondering if you were driving drunk or overdosing. And the few times I year I do see you, I hoped to do so without you hung-over or coming down."

"I don't need an intervention."

"You got one of sorts, didn't you?"

He shakes his head and clenches his teeth so hard, it feels like they might crumble.

"I followed you to the beach one day and I saw you writing. It's certainly not what I expected.

"And then you tore a page out of a journal, ripped it in half, threw one crumpled piece into the garbage and punted the other balled up one onto the sand. I waited until you left, took the two

251

pieces and taped them together, and when I saw it was a story about Mil Bennett I was in shock. I mean, I didn't know for sure you were Russell Niles, but it was possible, and I freaked because Richard is obsessed with the books and the thought that you wrote them all fucked up was just so wrong, and then it hit me that that the latest book was about a kid being abandoned by his father, and I wanted to strangle you. I mean how fucking dare you do that to any child, let alone your nephew?"

"How dare I? You're extorting your brother?" An elderly woman walks past, and Barrett pauses for a moment until she's gone and leans in closer. "All this from a piece of writing you found on the beach?"

"That just made me curious, but then I remembered that you said Sidney is an agent, and it was as easy as going on Google to find out he's Russell Niles's agent. So I followed you two and saw you go into your publishers. That pretty much solidified you were Russell Niles. But to be sure, I came up with the extortion plan, knowing that if you never responded then maybe this was all a coincidence, but if you did respond, then there would be no doubt that you are Russell Niles."

The details stun him. He listens to her talk and can't stop thinking that she was once a little kid he had to help feed.

"I wasn't sure what to threaten you with," she says. "The debauchery was obvious, and it wasn't hard to catch you in the act, but I needed something that tied you to the books, so I examined every detail of your life I could find until I discovered your connection to Blast energy drink.

"Their allegations of child labour gave me leverage, but I still needed enough proof to scare you into action. Tracing your taxes would show payments from Greystone that only the author of the Russell Niles books could receive, but taxes aren't public record. The payments would also be visible on your bank records, but I couldn't get a teller to risk their job for the grand I could offer. But then I went to the Library of Congress and searched the copyright. I wasn't surprised that your name wasn't on the document, because I figured your publisher would warn you that it's a public record, but what I saw was your mistake. That's when I saw that the copyright was under Sanford Corbett."

"Was Richard involved in this?"

"Of course not. I wanted you to spend some time with him, to be his uncle. I didn't expect him to get so close to you."

"What about all the kids delivering the demands?"

"They were random kids I paid. I was hoping they would have an emotional impact, make you think about your responsibilities as an author."

Barrett paces and runs through the extortion's demands. "You paid an underage woman to sleep with me?"

"She's not underage, you just had to be paranoid enough to believe she was. She's a third-year university student. I only paid her to kiss you — she did the rest on her own."

Every cell in Barrett's body needs nicotine. He gestures to the door with his pack. "Let's go outside."

Carol sits on a bench in front of a garden box of green bushes, but Barrett needs to stay on his feet. A few deep inhales give him renewed energy.

"I'm your brother. How could you do this to me?"

"Because I love you. And because I spent my youth idolizing you and my adulthood respecting you more than anyone on the planet, and you have strayed so far away from the man you should be that it's terrifying. I was planning an intervention before I found out you write the Niles books. This just gave me the leverage you needed to feel to inspire you."

"Inspire me? You think this inspired me?"

"It forced you to do things that were your nature before you drank and drugged yourself into an egocentric haze."

"Fuck you."

"Fuck *you*. You have the resources to do anything you want, to help people, to make real change in their lives, and instead you're living some frat-boy fantasy. You're better than that. You mean more than that."

Barrett exhales a cloud that looks particularly thick. "And where was this going to end? With me bankrupt and out of publishing?"

"If that got you back to being you."

But Barrett doesn't hear past his own retort. All he listens to is her admission of extorting him, of betraying him, of dismantling her brother. He steps within an inch of her face.

"If you'd spent as much time digging into the details of your son's life as you did mine, he wouldn't need to be in therapy."

And with that his back is turned and he's on his way across the street. There's nothing else to say from his perspective. She betrayed him and put him through hell, and right now that means she's dead to him.

THIRTY

Richard sits in Dr. Burns' office and notices that his mother looks like she belongs in therapy more than he does. Her eyes look like she hasn't slept in days, her face has adopted a perpetually worried look, and her eyelids are the type of red that make Richard wonder if she's on medication too.

Dr. Burns wears a tight brown turtleneck with the cuffs rolled halfway up his forearms. The intensity in his eyes makes it clear that he is all business today. No pleasantries, no offer of juice or tea, no acknowledgement that Carol is in the room.

"Have the recent events inspired you to write in your journal?"

Richard watches his mother drop her head in defeat and leans forward on the couch.

"I'd rather tell you how I feel. Both of you."

"Okay."

"I don't want to be on pills."

"You're on medication because ..."

"I'm not finished. I feel bad about myself when I'm taking pills, not when I don't. And I don't want what you call minor side effects anymore. You spend a day feeling like your tongue might suffocate you and then you can call them minor. And I don't need to be in therapy either."

"Your mother disagrees."

Richard turns to his mother. "I don't need to be in therapy." He absorbs the shock on her face as she starts to respond.

"Richard, listen ..."

But he stands now so that he can cut her off both physically and verbally.

"You listen. You want to do what you think is best for me, and I love you for that, but you're wrong. I don't need a stranger or pills to help me deal with Dad leaving, I need time with you. And not time when you look at me like you might cry, or when you're protecting me, or when you're scared that I'm sad, but just time together." Richard turns to Burns and points at him aggressively. "Dad leaving is our problem, not his. We're the ones that have to keep living."

Burns appears unfazed. Everything about his training and experience tells him to stay on track, to remain the leader, and he does so with unwavering dogma. "It's these outbursts that have us so concerned, Richard. Your constant disregard for authority is a classic example of oppositional defiant disorder." He reaches over to a stack of papers on an adjacent stool, picks up a brochure, and passes it to Carol. Richard looks at the large school on the cover, which is surrounded in trees and green grass.

"That is Grove Academy. It's a new school that is opening this September. It's located a half hour outside of the city, and it specializes in students with behavioural issues. Because I'm on the board, they have agreed to give full scholarships to a few of my patients, and I recommend that you're one of them."

Carol looks up from the brochure. "You want him to go to school away from home?"

"I want what's best for Richard."

"You want him to live outside of the city?"

Burns points to the brochure. "The increasingly alarming events of the past few weeks speak for themselves. Grove Academy is the best place for him, and you are lucky to have the opportunity to go there."

The muscles in her calves twitch and a surge of energy fills her upper body until she is on her feet. "Stop talking to my son like he isn't an eleven-year-old kid."

"Ms. Fuller?"

"You talk to us every week like you have all the answers, and then he goes home and gets further and further away from who he is."

"May I remind you that you came to me because I don't use traditional methods."

"This will be our last visit, doctor."

Richard takes her hand and follows her out of the office and down the hall to the elevator.

"I'm sorry, baby." She hugs him as tight as possible without hurting him.

"It's okay. Did you see the look on his face?"

Carol nods and they both begin to giggle.

"I'm also sorry about the way I acted after you told me why your father left. That was a huge burden for you to carry, and I appreciate that you were trying to protect me. I'm proud of you."

"Why? I kept the truth from you."

"Yeah, but it says a lot about your character that you were willing to suffer in order to protect me. All mothers should be so lucky."

Richard smiles.

"And you're absolutely right with what you said to Dr. Burns. Your father leaving is our reality, and it's you and me that will discuss him when we need to. Sound good?"

Richard nods, and for the first time since taking the medication his tongue feels lubricated.

Barrett sits across from Sidney in their favourite lunch spot, a Japanese restaurant with regal booths, the best apple martinis in the city, and flash-fried black cod that makes them wish all food tastes so heavenly. Sidney takes a mouthful of his martini while Barrett sips at an Asahi. Two trays of ginger scallion sauce sit between them. After his first eight straight hours of sleep since the extortion, Barrett looks refreshed.

Sidney isn't as comfortable. His job as an agent is to look forward, and Barrett can tell by how fast he's drinking his martini that while the man is grateful the extortion is over, he knows the aftermath is far from clean, and he knows they still have to deal with a press conference.

"I had all traces of the Once Upon a Hypocrite site erased," Sidney says. "But I can't get Don to budge with this press conference."

"I finished the book."

Sidney straightens. "What?"

"I finished the book."

"You wrote a hundred pages in a week?"

"A hundred and three."

"Wow. Can you feel my blood pressure dropping?"

Barrett smiles.

The news prompts Sidney to raise his martini. "To being back in business." He finishes his drink and looks at Barrett, whose beer still sits on the table. "I'm sorry it was Carol."

"We don't need to discuss it."

"I know, but I'm just saying. That's a lot to deal with, and I'm sorry I didn't resolve it for you."

Barrett nods enough to be polite.

"Enough serious talk," Sidney says with a smile. "We've done enough of that the last few weeks to last us a lifetime. What we need to do is talk about property, and I wouldn't be a good friend or a good agent if I didn't come with a gift." He puts pictures of a beach house in front of him with white sand and water so blue it looks fake. "I got word this place goes on the market tomorrow for two hundred less than it's worth. The owner ran a software company that just went bankrupt, and he's under the gun to unload the place."

Barrett looks at the photos but he can care less about property. What he wants to do is see Rebecca, so he plays along with Sidney's enthusiasm, pays for lunch, and heads to the Russell Niles fan club determined to right his wrong.

When he enters, the fan club is packed with people buying merchandise. He approaches the receptionist and forces a smile. "I'm here to see Rebecca."

The woman stuffs Mil Bennett stickers into envelopes. "Down the hall," she says with glazed eyes.

Barrett approaches Rebecca's office and stands in the doorway until she notices, pivots from a bookshelf, and slams the door in his face.

"Rebecca?" The door's grey paint makes him think of prison cells. "Open the door, please."

Her silence says more than any response could. He imagines her holding a middle finger to the door.

Even in this vulnerable state, he's too egotistical to anticipate such a response to his visit, so he rubs a hand across both eyebrows as a stress reflex before reaching into his jacket to remove a large envelope. Bent down, he slides the envelope under the door confident that the contents will grab Rebecca's attention. He knows that a part of her wants to throw it in the garbage, but he believes a stronger part of her is curious and that she'll pick it up and tear it open as fast as possible. His first instinct was to buy her a gift capable of making her forgive anything, but he knows she would find an attempt to buy her more insulting than enticing, and he wants to do justice to her effect on him, so he embraced the way she puts him at ease and placed a picture of himself dressed as Sindu the Starfish from the day he read at the bookstore in the envelope. A message running across the bottom's white border reads NOW YOU SEE WHY I LOVE YOUR SINDU STORY. YOUR BIGGEST FAN, BARRETT. The picture is ridiculous. His stubbly face is surrounded by the fluffy white starfish headpiece, and the white tights make his skinny legs look even more cartoonish. The picture is the epitome of humility.

The envelope slides back under the door toward Barrett, and he bends down with a smile. The idea of her playing along with his romance is fitting, and he's eager to see what she put back in the envelope until he notices GO AWAY written in black marker where a mailing address would be. *Go away.* This type of rejection is beyond humbling, it's painful. Because ultimately, she's not rejecting his approach, she's rejecting him. He turns from her door, walks down the hall, and tosses the envelope in the first garbage he sees.

A black man with pronounced cheekbones plays the steel drums a block down the street. Barrett stares at the man and watches his hands move effortlessly across the instrument. He walks across the street, and a sports car blaring rap music honks at him. One of the teenagers sticks his head out the window and swears at him, but he doesn't notice.

He heads for a bench in front of a bookstore, tosses an abandoned carton of half-eaten French fries into the adjacent garbage and takes a seat.

Seeing the kids through the window makes him miss Richard. He pulls out his phone, thinks for a moment then texts: *Your next driving lesson is Saturday. I'll pick you up at one.* He sends the text and leaves his phone out, eager for the kid's response. A pyramid display of his latest book fills the store's display case, and he watches as kids point at the books with excitement. Some parents sit in the chairs lining the far wall and read the book with their daughter or son, others take their child by hand to the cashier. He considers how many bookstores there are in the world and how many places there are that sell books. The variety stores, drug marts, subway huts, airports, hospitals, gift shops. And then he thinks of kids in all those stores and how many of them have bought his books with their parents or guardians or grandparents, and how many hours of family time he's responsible for. He looks at his phone to make sure he didn't miss Richard's response then sets it down again. He waits another hour while he looks at the display case but the text never comes.

THIRTY-ONE

Sidney wanted Barrett to arrive at the press conference an hour early so they could get a feel for the room and prepare some responses, but Barrett arrives fifteen minutes before the start. Sidney gives him a hug and appraises his wardrobe. Jeans and a blue dress shirt open enough at the top to reveal a hint of his white singlet.

"A little casual, no?"

"No."

"It's your moment. Wait until you see the look on Don's face. The old crust doesn't think you finished. You might give him a heart attack today."

Sidney escorts him down the hall and into a private lounge with a large TV on the wall playing a talk show and a bowl of fruit and assorted treats on a platter in the centre of a coffee table.

"Relax here for a bit, and I'll get you when they're ready to start."

Barrett nods and takes a bottle of water. He takes out his phone and sends Richard another text.

In fifteen minutes, turn on channel 22. He puts away the phone when he sees Rebecca walk by the room. He hustles into the hall and sees her looking at a seating chart.

"Hey," he says. "It's good to see you."

A press pass dangles from her neck, designating her as the fan club representative. She holds up the pass with a sigh. "Only because I have to."

She continues down the hall so Barrett walks beside her.

"I want to apologize for the other day. I ..."

"This is a really bad time."

"Listen ..."

"A really bad time and a really inappropriate time."

She walks away and turns the corner so fast, he wonders if she was ever there. Maybe he's just daydreaming or hoping, but then the aftermath of the vanilla smell that trails her everywhere confirms that she has just dismissed him again.

A hand on his shoulder startles him into the moment.

"Showtime. You ready?" Sidney says.

Barrett nods.

"You sure? You look stunned."

"I'm fine."

"Because you should be happy. Make this announcement to the crowd and it'll be like the extortion never happened."

Sidney leads the way to the end of the hall and opens a door to a packed room of hungry journalists, bloggers, and gossip-mongers. The air smells of coffee and the heat is turned up so high that people roll up their sleeves and wipe at sweaty upper lips. Barrett makes his way to Don, who stands in front of a microphone set up in the main space behind a podium that makes him think of debate contests. Don greets him with a nod and begins.

"Thank you all for being here today. We are very excited

today at Greystone Publishing to make a major announcement, and it is our pleasure to have our head of marketing, Barrett Fuller, here to do the honours."

Cameras flash incessantly as Barrett takes the podium. Everyone stares at him but he is the one doing the watching. He watches as Don sits beside Martin and absorbs how pleased he is with himself.

He watches as Martin looks at him with confusion then turns to Don and whispers in his ear; he watches Sidney fuss with his watch, the way he does when he's anxious, and he watches Rebecca look everywhere but at him.

Public speaking has never bothered Barrett before, but the weight of the moment leaves him tingling. He thinks of the cliché advice that public speakers should relax by picturing their audience naked and grins when he realizes that it feels like he is the one naked with everyone staring at his frightened penis. He takes a deep breath that is unable to steady his stomach and speaks anyway.

"I'm here today to announce ... I'm here today to announce that my name is Barrett Fuller and I write the Russell Niles books."

Journalists "ooh" and Sidney mouths "Fuck me" as every camera in the room clicks.

"I've hidden my identity for a long time, but some people came into my life recently that made me rethink things. A boy that reminded me why I love to write and a woman that made me want her to know who I am. So starting today, not only do I want to be truthful with my fans, but I also want to interact with the readers as much as possible. I will read at every launch, I'll be available to sign autographs whenever anybody asks, and I'll be the one giving out free books at literacy centres. I'd love to answer any questions you have, but if I don't have a Scotch, I might pass out."

Laughter fills the room and he sees Rebecca smile. He steps away from the podium and is immediately swarmed by journalists sticking digital recorders in his face.

"One moment," he says, doing his best to be polite while wading through the room, but when he gets to Rebecca's seat, she is gone.

He stands there blankly, unable to hear the details of every question being asked until Sidney leads him by the elbow out of the room, down the hall, and back into the lounge where Don and Martin wait for him. Barrett looks at them for a moment before turning to Sidney.

"I'll catch up with you in a minute."

"I'll be down the hall."

Barrett waits for Sidney to exit and addresses Don. "So I guess this is a new beginning for us."

Don's lips curl as his head shakes aggressively. "No, this is an ending."

Barrett absorbs the disdain in his eyes. "Yeah?"

"The public loves redemption so there's no doubt your backlist will see an increase in sales as a result of your dramatics, but you still had sex with my wife, so as far as branding a new series, you're on your own. And I can't say I won't make a phone call or two letting people know you're not the most trustworthy man to deal with."

Barrett raises his brow, resigned, and while it's unpleasant to be the object of such anger and the rejection stings, he has to admit he would do the same thing if their roles were reversed. He turns to see Martin looking at him with disbelief.

"You're Russell Niles?"

Barrett nods.

"You've ..."

"Published more books than you, sold more copies than you, and made more money than you."

A vein that runs up the side of Martin's nose and between his eyebrows bulges as his face reddens.

"By the way," Barrett says, tapping him on the arm. "I'm calling your publisher tomorrow. I have an idea for a mainstream fiction book she's going to love."

Martin's eyes look like they might pop from their sockets.

With an eyebrow raise in farewell, Barrett exits the room, and Sidney waits in the hall.

"I've got a limo waiting out back," Sidney says.

"I sent a present to your office."

"Something better than what you did in there?"

"It's the first of a new line of children books under my real name."

"So you're a changed man?"

"A little bit."

"Lovely."

"I need you to find me a new publisher."

"Real work, huh?"

"Are you going to be okay with this?"

"On two conditions."

"Anything."

"I'm upped to twenty percent."

"Done."

"And from now on I get to introduce myself as Russell Niles to any woman that doesn't know better."

Barrett nods with a grin when his phone buzzes. He looks at it to see a text from Richard. *I watched. Thank you.* He slips his phone back in his pocket and smiles as they go out a side door and are greeted by a sun that illuminates every grain in all the concrete that surrounds them. He walks ahead and sees that Rebecca is standing in front of the limo. Barrett hustles toward her with excitement and Sidney hangs back.

She steps toward him slowly. "I've never been more excited by a man than after listening to your speech."

"I'm glad you were able to be there."

"And I've never been more disappointed by a man when you accused me of extorting you and completely disrespected me."

"You have no idea how much I don't want to be that guy."

"I'm curious, I'll give you that."

"When can I start redeeming myself?"

"Wait for me to call you, and if I do, never have a false moment with me again."

"Done."

She smiles and turns away. The vapors of her panache leave him staring until it occurs to him that if her smile was the only smile he ever saw again, he would consider himself blessed.

THIRTY-TWO

What Barrett wants to tell Carol can't wait, so he walks into her office and up to her cubicle with a folder in hand to find her with her back to the door and earphones dangling from her ears. She is the only one in the office, and she is completely engrossed in the design on her monitor. He knocks on the cubicle, but she doesn't respond, so he taps her on the shoulder. Startled, she turns from the screen and double-takes when she sees him. She pulls the earphones from her ears and sets them on the desk.

"Do you have a minute?" Barrett asks.

She nods.

"I'm sorry I've been such an asshole. You're my sister, I love you, and I want to spend more time with you."

"I saw your press conference."

"How did I look?"

"Good. A little haggard, but good. The spotlight suits you. So you're a recovered man?"

"I'm quitting smoking."

"Really?"

"I'm going to try."

"And drugs?"

"Never again. No trying there."

"What about drinking?"

"Let's not be crazy."

She laughs and Barrett sets the folder in front of her.

"What's this?" she asks.

"It's a contract."

"For what?"

"It's a job offer. I've got to re-brand myself, and I need a good publicist."

She opens the folder and picks up the contract to see a salary offer of two hundred thousand dollars a year. "I don't understand."

"You're my sister, you opened my eyes, and now we're here. What do you say?"

"I have no idea what a publicist does."

Barrett grins. "After what you pulled off with me, I have a feeling you'll be just fine."

Richard is next on his list. He sits across from the boy at a picnic table in the schoolyard. Richard eats the burger Barrett brought him and has an enormous drink container in front of him.

"I can't believe my uncle is Russell Niles."

"Me neither." Barrett smiles, lifts a box out of a bag, and sets it on the table. "I brought you something."

"A present?"

"More like a thank-you. I'm starting a new line of books, and the main character is based on you."

"Me?"

"Yeah. I thanked you in the prologue. With any luck, a lot of people will read about how cool you are. Have a look."

Barrett takes the manuscript from the box and hands it to Richard.

"What do you think?"

Richard looks at the title page for a bit and narrows his eyes into a harsh squint.

"The title sucks."

Barrett can't hide his shock. This is not how he imagined the moment, and he's not sure what to say but he manages, "Really?"

They lock eyes and Richard holds the squint until he can't contain his mischievous smile any longer. "Gotcha."

He raps his knuckles on the table and laughs along, but on the inside he's relieved that Richard is joking. In all his years of writing children's books, he's never actually witnessed a kid's reaction to his words, and while it feels good to see Richard's response, it feels even better to care.

ACKNOWLEDGEMENTS

Thank you to Matthew Stone for your innovation and for making every phase of this creative journey enjoyable. To Benjamin Gilbert, Mark Adriaans, and Christopher Sandy for your friendship, passion, and creative insights. To the following wonderful people whose creative spirits have influenced this novel: Paul Hamilton, Sean Morong, Steve Dalrymple, Ben Mathai, Shelley Ring, Skye Thietten, Sean Carter, Jen Bush, John and Kate Bush, Matt Bush, Holly Nichols, Elora and Alan Gregg, Matthew Deslippe, Chris, Amy, Evelyn and Hugo Haworth, Mariana, Scott, and Eloise MacIntosh, Debbie, Eddie and Simon Gilbert, Zoe Coop Stone, the TSAA Family, where much of this novel was written, and Albert and Amy at the Combine, where every chapter of this novel was celebrated. To Allister Thompson, for being great at what he does, to Jesse Hooper for designing such a stunning, fitting cover for the novel, and to Sylvia McConnell and the Dundurn team for your support and guidance.

BY THE SAME AUTHOR

Blind Luck
978-1926607009
$18.95

In Scott Carter's acclaimed debut novel, Dave Bolden's life feels like it's on repeat. He works his eight hours at an accounting firm, goes home, gets drunk, and wakes up the next day to go back to work with a hangover. But his life changes when an eighteen-wheeler crashes through the windows of his workplace, killing everyone except him. Shortly after the accident, he is approached by an eccentric businessman, Mr. Thorrin, who interprets Dave's survival as luck and sets out to exploit what he perceives as a gift. Thorrin wants Dave to participate in gambling, stock manipulation, and extreme betting, all based on this belief. What transpires is a series of extreme tests of luck, orchestrated by Thorrin. The more Dave denies that he is lucky, the more he finds himself in situations that make it appear that he is. As the stakes rise both financially and personally, he is left to decide whether his run of good fortune is a gift or a curse.

DUNDURN

Visit us at
Dundurn.com | @dundurnpress | Facebook.com/dundurnpress
Pinterest.com/dundurnpress